He found his voice…
She lost her heart.

DON'T MISS THE NEXT
MAIDEN LANE NOVEL!

Dearest Rogue

available in Spring 2015
Please turn to the back of this book for a preview.

AND LOOK FOR THE REST OF THE SERIES

Available at a special low price!

He was there—the monster.

He was in the pond, his back to her.

And he was quite nude.

Lily blinked, frozen in place. His massive shoulders were bunched, his head lowered. She ought to speak, ought to make her presence known...

All thought left her head as the giant plunged beneath the water. Lily's mouth half opened.

The setting sun broke through the cloud cover and bathed the pond in golden light. He burst from the water. He was facing her now. The muscles bunched on his arms as he slicked his wet, shoulder-length hair back from from his face. Her pity evaporated, burned away by the sudden realization that she had it all wrong.

He was...

She swallowed.

Good Lord. He was *magnificent.*

PRAISE FOR
ELIZABETH HOYT'S
MAIDEN LANE SERIES

Duke of Midnight

"Top Pick! A sensual tale of forbidden love...Plenty of action and intriguing mystery make this a page-turner."
—***BookPage***

"Richly drawn characters fill the pages of this emotionally charged mix of mystery and romance."
—***Publishers Weekly***

"4½ stars! Top Pick! There is enchantment in the Maiden Lane series, not just the fairy tales Hoyt infuses into the memorable romances, but the wonder of love combined with passion, unique plotlines, and unforgettable characters."
—***RT Book Reviews***

"I *loved* it. I loved Artemis. I loved Max, and I loved their story. I have enjoyed every Elizabeth Hoyt book I have read (and I have read most of them)."
—**All About Romance (LikesBooks.com)**

Lord of Darkness

"*Lord of Darkness* illuminates Hoyt's boundless imagination...Readers will adore this story."
—***RT Book Reviews***

"Hoyt's writing is imbued with great depth of emotion...
heartbreaking... an edgy tension-filled plot."
—*Publishers Weekly*

"*Lord of Darkness* is classic Elizabeth Hoyt, meaning
it's unique, engaging, and leaves readers on the edge
of their seats... an incredible addition to the fantastic
Maiden Lane series. I Joyfully Recommend Godric and
Megs's tale, for it's an amazing, well-crafted story with an
intriguing plot and a lovely, touching romance... simply
enchanting!"

—JoyfullyReviewed.com

"I adore the Maiden Lane series, and this fifth book is
a very welcome addition to the series... [It's] sexy and
sweet all at the same time... This can be read as a stand-
alone, but I adore each book in this series and encourage
you to start from the beginning."
—*USA Today*'s **Happy Ever After blog**

"Beautifully written... a truly fine piece of storytelling
and a novel that deserves to be read and enjoyed."
—TheBookBinge.com

Thief of Shadows

"An expert blend of scintillating romance and mystery...
The romance between the beautiful and quick-witted Isa-
bel and the masked champion of the downtrodden propels
this novel to the top of its genre."
—*Publishers Weekly* (**starred review**)

"Amazing sex scenes...a very intriguing hero...This one did not disappoint."

—*USA Today*

"Innovative, emotional, sensual...Hoyt's beautiful blending of the essential elements of a fairy tale into a stunning love story enhances this delicious 'keeper.'"

—*RT Book Reviews*

"All of Hoyt's signature literary ingredients—wickedly clever dialogue, superbly nuanced characters, danger, and scorching sexual chemistry—click neatly into place to create a breathtakingly romantic love story."

—*Booklist*

"When [they] finally come together, desire and long-denied sensuality explode upon the page."

—*Library Journal*

"With heart and heat rolled into one, *Thief of Shadows* is a definite must-read for historical romance fans! Hoyt really has outdone herself...yet again."

—UndertheCoversBookblog.blogspot.com

"A balanced mixture of action, adventure, and mystery and a beautifully crafted romance...The perfect historical romance."

—HeroesandHeartbreakers.com

Scandalous Desires

"Historical romance at its best...Series fans will be enthralled, while new readers will find this emotionally charged installment stands very well alone."
—*Publishers Weekly* (starred review)

"4½ stars! This is the Maiden Lane story readers have been waiting for. Hoyt delivers her hallmark fairy tale within a romance and takes readers into the depths of the heart and soul of her characters. Pure magic flows from her pen, lifting readers' spirits with joy."
—*RT Book Reviews*

"With its lush sensuality, lusciously wrought prose, and luxuriously dark plot, *Scandalous Desires*, the latest exquisitely crafted addition to Hoyt's Georgian-set Maiden Lane series, is a romance to treasure."
—*Booklist* (starred review)

"Ms. Hoyt writes some of the best love scenes out there. They are passionate, sexy, and blazing hot...I simply adore Ms. Hoyt's books for her sensuous prose, multifaceted characters, and intense, well-developed story lines. And she delivers every single time. It's no wonder all of her books are on my keeper shelves. Do yourself a favor and pick up *Scandalous Desires*."
—TheRomanceDish.com

"*Scandalous Desires* is the best book Elizabeth Hoyt has written so far, with endearing characters and an all-encompassing romance you'll want to hold close and never let go. If there's one must-read book, especially for historical romance fans, it's *Scandalous Desires*."
—**FallenAngelReviews.com**

Notorious Pleasures

"Emotionally stunning…The sinfully sensual chemistry Hoyt creates between her shrewd, acid-tongued heroine and her scandalous, sexy hero is pure romance."
—***Booklist***

Wicked Intentions

"4½ stars! Top Pick! A magnificently rendered story that not only enchants but enthralls."
—***RT Book Reviews***

DARLING BEAST

ELIZABETH HOYT

DARLING BEAST

GRAND CENTRAL
PUBLISHING

NEW YORK   BOSTON

Grand Central Publishing
Hachette Book Group
1290 Avenue of the Americas
New York, NY 10104

HachetteBookGroup.com

Printed in the United States of America

OPM

First Edition: October 2014
10 9 8 7 6 5 4 3 2 1

Grand Central Publishing is a division of Hachette Book Group, Inc.
The Grand Central Publishing name and logo is a trademark of Hachette Book Group, Inc.

The Hachette Speakers Bureau provides a wide range of authors for speaking events. To find out more, go to www.hachettespeakersbureau.com or call (866) 376-6591.

The publisher is not responsible for websites (or their content) that are not owned by the publisher.

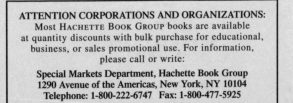

For my lovely agent, Robin Rue, who got me the contract so I could write Darling Beast.

Acknowledgments

Thank you:

To Susannah Taylor, who took time out of an around-the-world, once-in-a-lifetime cruise to read the first draft of *Darling Beast*.

To Cindy Dees, who helped untangle the end of a rather convoluted plot and found a motivation for Valentine to boot.

To Jennifer Green, who came up with Daffodil's fabulous name.

To Grand Champion Gioia Mia's Femme Fatale, affectionately called Sienna by her owner, Elissa Dominici, for being the inspiration for Daffodil.

To S. B. Kleinman, who did a wonderfully thorough job of copyediting this book.

And to Leah Hultenschmidt and all the fabulous people at Grand Central for once again producing such a gorgeous book.

Chapter One

Now once there was a king who lived to wage war. His clothes were chain mail and boiled leather, his thoughts were strategy and conflict, and at night he dreamed of the screams of his enemies and in his sleep he smiled…
—From *The Minotaur*

APRIL 1741
LONDON, ENGLAND

As the mother of a seven-year-old boy, Lily Stump was used to odd topics of conversation. There was the debate on whether fish wore clothes. The deep and insightful discussion over where sugared plums came from and the subsequent lecture on why little boys were not allowed to break their fast with them every day. And, of course, the infamous controversy of Why Dogs Bark But Cats Do Not.

So truly it wasn't Lily's fault that she did not pay heed to her son's announcement at luncheon that there was a monster in the garden.

"Indio," Lily said with only a tiny bit of exasperation, "must you wipe your jammy fingers on Daffodil? I can't think she likes it."

Sadly, this was a blatant lie. Daffodil, a very young and very silly red Italian greyhound with a white blaze on her chest, was already happily twisting her slim body in a circle in order to lick the sticky patch on her back.

"Mama," Indio said with great patience as he put down his bread and jam, "didn't you hear me? There's a *monster* in the *garden*." He was kneeling on his chair and now he leaned forward over the table to emphasize his words, a lock of his dark, curly hair falling into his right, blue, eye. Indio's other eye was green, which some found disconcerting, although Lily had long ago grown used to the disparity.

"Did he have horns?" the third member of their little family asked very seriously.

"Maude!" Lily hissed.

Maude Ellis plonked a plate of cheese down on their only-slightly-singed table and set her hands on her skinny hips. Maude had seen five decades and despite her tiny stature—she only just came to Lily's shoulder—she never shied away from speaking her mind. "Well, and mightn't it be the Devil he saw?"

Lily narrowed her eyes in warning—Indio was prone to rather alarming nightmares and this conversation didn't seem the best idea. "Indio did not see the Devil—or a monster, for that matter."

"I *did*," Indio said. "But he hasn't horns. He has shoulders as big as *this*." And he demonstrated by throwing his arms as far apart as he could, nearly knocking his bowl of carrot soup to the floor in the process.

Lily caught the bowl deftly—much to the disappointment of Daffodil. "Do eat your soup, please, Indio, before it ends on the floor."

"'Tisn't a dunnie, then," Maude said decisively as she took her own chair. "Quite small they are, 'cepting when they turn to a horse. Did it turn to a horse, deary?"

"No, Maude." Indio shoved a big spoonful of soup into his mouth and then regrettably continued talking. "He looks like a man, but bigger and scarier. His hands are as big as...as..." Indio's little brows drew together as he tried to think of an appropriate simile.

"Your head," Lily supplied helpfully. "A tricorn hat. A leg of lamb. Daffodil."

Daffodil barked at her name and spun in a happy circle.

"Was he dripping wet or all over green?" Maude demanded.

Lily sighed and watched as Indio attempted to describe his monster and Maude attempted to identify it from her long list of fairies, hobgoblins, and imaginary beasts. Maude had grown up in the north of England and apparently spent her formative years memorizing the most ghastly folktales. Lily herself had heard these stories from Maude when she was young—resulting in quite a few torturous nights. She was endeavoring—mostly without success—to keep Maude from imparting the same stories to Indio.

Her gaze drifted around the rather decrepit room they'd moved into just yesterday afternoon. A small fireplace was on one charred wall. Maude's bed and her chest were pushed against another. Their table and four chairs were in the middle of the room. A tiny writing table and a rickety dark-plum settee were near the hearth. To the side, a door led into a small room—a former dressing room— where Lily had her own bed and Indio his cot. These two rooms were all that remained of the backstage in what had

once been a grand theater at Harte's Folly. The theater—
and indeed the entire pleasure garden—had burned down
the autumn before. The stink of smoke still lingered about
the place like a ghost, though the majority of the wreckage had been hauled away.

Lily shivered. Perhaps the gloominess of the place was
making Indio imagine monsters.

Indio swallowed a big bite of his bread and jam. "He
has shaggy hair and he lives in the garden. Daff's seen
him, too."

Both Lily and Maude glanced at the little greyhound.
Daffodil was sitting by Indio's chair, chewing on a back
paw. As they watched she overbalanced and rolled onto
her back.

"Perhaps Daffodil ate something that disagreed with
her tummy," Lily said diplomatically, "and the tummy
ache made her *think* she'd seen a monster. I haven't seen a
monster in the garden and neither has Maude."

"Well, there were that wherryman with the big nose,
hanging about the dock suspicious-like yesterday," Maude
muttered. Lily shot her a look and Maude hastily added,
"Er, but no, never seen a real monster. Just wherrymen
with big noses."

Indio considered that bit of information. "*My* monster has a big nose." His mismatched eyes widened as he
looked up excitedly. "And a *hook*. Per'aps he cuts children
into little bits with his hook and *eats* them!"

"Indio!" Lily exclaimed. "That's quite enough."

"But Mama—"

"No. Now why don't we discuss fish clothing or...or
how to teach Daffodil to sit up and beg?"

Indio sighed gustily. "Yes, Mama." He slumped, the

very picture of dejection, and Lily couldn't help but think that he'd someday make a fine dramatic actor. She darted a pleading glance at Maude.

But Maude only shook her head and bent to her own soup.

Lily cleared her throat. "I'm sure Daffodil would benefit from training," she said a little desperately.

"I suppose." Indio swallowed the last spoonful of his soup and clutched his bread in his hand. He looked at Lily with big eyes. "May I leave the table, please, Mama?"

"Oh, very well."

In a flurry he tumbled from his chair and ran toward the door. Daffodil scampered behind him, barking.

"Don't go near the pond!" Lily called.

The door to the garden banged shut.

Lily winced and looked at the older woman. "That didn't go well, did it?"

Maude shrugged. "Mayhap could've been better, but the lad is a sensitive one, he is. So were you at that age."

"Was I?"

Maude had been her nursemaid—and rather more, truth be told. She might be superstitious, but Lily trusted Maude implicitly when it came to the rearing of children. And a good thing, too, since she'd been left to raise Indio alone. "Should I go after him, do you think?"

"Aye, in a bit. No point now. Give him a fair while to calm himself." Maude jerked her pointed chin at Lily's bowl. "Best get that inside you, hinney."

The corner of Lily's mouth curled at the old endearment. "I wish I could've found us somewhere else to stay. Somewhere not so..." She hesitated, loath to give the ruined pleasure garden's atmosphere a name.

"Uncanny," Maude said promptly, having no such trouble herself. "All them burnt trees and falling-down buildings and not a soul about for miles in the nights. I place a wee bag of garlic and sage under my pillow every evening, I do, and you ought as well."

"Mmm," Lily murmured noncommittally. She wasn't sure she wanted to wake up to the reek of garlic and sage. "At least the workmen are about during the day."

"And a right scruffy bunch, the lot of them," Maude said stoutly. "Don't know where Mr. Harte got these so-called gardeners, but I wouldn't be surprised if he found them in the street. Or worse"—she leaned forward to whisper hoarsely—"got them off a ship from Ireland."

"Oh, Maude," Lily chided gently. "I don't know why you have this dislike of the Irish—they're just looking for work like anyone else."

Maude snorted as she vigorously buttered a slice of bread.

"Besides," Lily said hastily, "we're only here until Mr. Harte produces a new play with a part for me."

"And where would he be doing that?" Maude asked, glancing at the charred beams over their heads. "He'll need a new theater first, and a garden to put it in afore that. It'll be at least a year—more, most like."

Lily winced and opened her mouth, but Maude had gotten the bit between her teeth. She shook her piece of bread at Lily, showering crumbs on the table. "Never trusted that man, not me. Too charming and chatty by half. Mr. Harte could sweet-talk a bird down from a tree, into the palm of his hand, and right into the oven, he could. Or"—she slapped a last daub of butter on the bread—"talk an actress with all of London at her feet to come play in his theater—and *only* his theater."

"Well, to be fair, Mr. Harte wasn't to know his pleasure garden and the theater would burn to the ground at the time."

"Nay, but he *did* know it'd put Mr. Sherwood's back up." Maude bit into her bread for emphasis.

Lily wrinkled her nose at the memory. Mr. Sherwood, the proprietor of the King's Theatre and her former employer, was a rather vindictive man. He'd promised Lily that he'd make sure she'd not find work anywhere else in London if she went with Mr. Harte and his offer of twice the salary Mr. Sherwood had been paying her.

That hadn't been a problem until Harte's Folly had burned, at which point Lily had found that Mr. Sherwood had made good on his promise: all the other theaters in London refused to let her play for them.

Now, after being out of work for over six months, she'd gone through what few savings she'd had, forcing her little family to vacate their stylish rented rooms.

"At least Mr. Harte let us stay here free of charge?" Lily offered rather feebly.

Fortunately, Maude's reply was nonverbal since she'd just taken a bite of the soup.

"Yes, well, I really ought to go after Indio," Lily said, rising.

"And what of your luncheon, then?" Maude demanded, nodding at Lily's half-finished soup.

"I'll have it later." Lily bit her lip. "I hate it when he's upset."

"You coddle the boy," Maude sniffed, but Lily noticed the older woman didn't make any further protest.

Lily hid a smile. If anyone coddled Indio it was Maude herself. "I'll be back in a bit."

Maude waved a hand as Lily turned to the door to the outside. The door screeched horribly as she pulled it open. One of the hinges was cracked from the heat of the fire and it hung askew. Outside, the day was overcast. Deep-gray clouds promised more rain and the wind whipped across the blackened ground. Lily shivered and wrapped her arms around herself. She should've brought her shawl.

"Indio!" Her shout was thinned by the wind.

Helplessly she looked around. What had once been an elegant pleasure garden had been reduced to sooty mud by the fire and the spring rains. The hedges that had outlined graveled walks were burnt and mostly dead, meandering away into the distance. To the left were the remains of the stone courtyard and boxes where musicians had played for guests: a line of broken pillars, supporting nothing but sky. To the right a copse of straggling trees stood with a bit of mirrored water peeking out from behind—what was left of an ornamental pond, now clogged with silt. Here and there green poked out among the gray and black, but she had to admit that, especially on an overcast day like this one, with wisps of fog slinking along the ground, the garden was ominous and rather frightening.

Lily grimaced. She should've never let Indio out to play by himself, but it was hard to keep an active young boy inside. She started down one of the paths, slipping a bit in the mud, wishing she'd stopped to put on her pattens before coming outside. If she didn't see her son soon, she'd ruin the frivolous embroidered slippers on her feet.

"Indio!"

She rounded what once had been a small thicket of

trimmed trees. Now the blackened branches rattled in the wind. "Indio!"

A grunt came from the thicket.

Lily stopped dead.

There it was again—almost an explosive snort. The noise was too loud, too deep for Indio. It almost sounded like . . . a big *animal*.

She glanced quickly around, but she was completely alone. Should she return to the ruined theater for Maude? But Indio was out here!

Another grunt, this one louder. A rustle.

Something was breathing heavily in the bushes.

Good Lord. Lily bunched her skirts in her fists in case she had to leg it, and crept forward.

A groan and a low, rumbling sound.

Like *growling*.

She gulped and peeked around a burned trunk.

At first what she saw looked like an enormous, moving, mud-covered *mound*, and then it straightened, revealing an endlessly broad back, huge shoulders, and a shaggy head.

Lily couldn't help it. She made a noise that was perilously close to a squeak.

The thing whirled—much faster than anything that big had a right to move—and a horrible, soot-stained face glared at her, one paw raised as if to strike her.

In it was a wickedly sharp, hooked knife.

Lily gulped. If she lived through the day she was going to have to apologize to Indio.

For there *was* a monster in the garden.

THE DAY HADN'T been going well to begin with, reflected Apollo Greaves, Viscount Kilbourne.

At a rough estimate, fully half the woody plantings in the pleasure garden were dead—and another quarter might as well be. The ornamental pond's freshwater source had been blocked by the fire's debris and now it sat stagnant. The gardeners Asa had hired for him were an unskilled lot. To top it off, the spring rains had turned what remained of Harte's Folly into a muddy morass, making planting and earth moving impossible until the ground dried out.

And now there was a strange female in his garden.

Apollo stared into huge lichen-green eyes lined with lashes so dark and thick that they looked like smudged soot. The woman—girl? She wasn't that tall, but a swift glance at her bodice assured him she was *quite* mature, thank you—was only a slim bit of a thing, dressed foolishly in a green velvet gown, richly over-embroidered in red and gold. She hadn't even a bonnet on. Her dark hair slipped from a messy knot at the back of her neck, waving strands blowing against her pinkened cheeks. Actually, she was rather pretty in a gamine sort of way.

But that was beside the point.

Where in hell had she come from? As far as he knew, the only other people in the ruined pleasure garden were the brace of so-called gardeners presently working on the hedges behind the pond. He'd been taking out his frustration alone on the dead tree stump, trying to uproot the thing by hand since their only dray horse was at work with the other men, when he'd heard a feminine voice calling and she'd suddenly appeared.

The woman blinked and her gaze darted to his upraised arm.

Apollo's own eyes followed and he winced. He'd

instinctively raised his hand as he turned to her, and the pruning knife he held might be construed as threatening.

Hastily he lowered his arm. Which left him standing in his mud-stained shirt and waistcoat, sweaty and stinking, and feeling like a dumb ox next to her delicate femininity.

But apparently his action reassured her. She drew herself up—not that it made much difference to her height. "Who are you?"

Well, he'd like to ask the same of her but, alas, he really couldn't, thanks to that last beating in Bedlam.

Belatedly he remembered that he was supposed to be a simple laborer. He tugged at a forelock and dropped his gaze—to elegantly embroidered slippers caked in mud.

Who *was* this woman?

"Tell me now," she said rather imperiously, considering she was standing in three inches of mud. "Who are you and what are you doing here?"

He glanced at her face—eyebrows arched, a plush rose lower lip caught between her teeth—and cast his eyes down again. He tapped his throat and shook his head. If she didn't get *that* message she was a lot stupider than she looked.

"Oh," he heard as he stared at her shoes. "Oh, I didn't realize." She had a husky voice, which gentled when he lowered his gaze. "Well, it doesn't matter. You can't stay here, you must understand."

Unseen, he rolled his eyes. What was she on about? He worked in the garden—surely she could see that. Who was she to order him out?

"*You.*" She drew the word out, enunciating it clearly, as if she thought him hard of hearing. Some thought that since he couldn't speak he couldn't hear, either. He caught himself beginning to scowl and smoothed out his features. "Cannot. Stay. *Here*." A pause, and then, muttered, "Oh, for goodness' sakes. I can't even tell if he understands. I cannot believe Mr. Harte allowed..."

And it dawned on Apollo with a feeling of amused horror that his frustrating day had descended into the frankly ludicrous. This ridiculously clad woman thought *him* a lackwit.

One embroidered toe tapped in the mud. "Look at me, please."

He raised his gaze slowly, careful to keep his face blank.

Her brows had drawn together over those big eyes, in an expression that no doubt she thought stern, but that was, in reality, rather adorable. Like a small girl chiding a kitten. A streak of anger surged through him. She shouldn't be out by herself in the ruined garden. If he'd been another type of man—a brutal man, like the ones who'd run Bedlam—her dignity, perhaps even her *life*, might've been in danger. Didn't she have a husband, a brother, a father to keep her safe? Who was letting this slip of a woman wander into danger by herself?

He realized that her expression had gentled at his continued silence.

"You can't tell me, can you?" she asked softly.

He'd met pity in others since the loss of his voice. Usually it made him burn hot with rage and a sort of terrible despair—after nine months he wasn't sure he'd ever regain the use of his voice. But her inquiry didn't provoke his usual anger. Maybe it was her feminine charm—it'd been a while since any woman besides his sister had attempted to talk to him—or maybe it was simply *her*.

This woman spoke with compassion, not contempt, and that made all the difference.

He shook his head, watching her, keeping his face dull and unresponsive.

She sighed and hugged herself, looking around. "What am I to do?" she muttered. "I can't leave Indio out here by himself."

Apollo struggled not to let surprise show on his face. Who or what was Indio?

"Go!" she said forcefully, suddenly enough that he blinked. She pointed a commanding finger behind him.

Apollo fought back a grin. She wasn't giving up, was she? He slowly turned, looking in the direction she indicated, and then swiveled back even more slowly, letting his mouth hang half open.

"Oh!" Her little hands balled into fists as she cast her eyes heavenward. "This is maddening."

She took two swift steps forward and placed her palms against his chest, pushing.

He allowed himself to sway an inch backward with her thrust before righting himself. She stilled, staring up at him. The top of her head barely came to his mid-chest. He could feel the brush of her breath on his lips. The warmth of her hands seemed to burn through the rough fabric of his waistcoat. This close her green eyes were enormous, and he could see shards of gold surrounding her pupils.

Her lips parted and his gaze dropped to her mouth.

"Mama!"

The hissed word made them both start.

Apollo swung around. A small boy was poised on the muddy path just outside the thicket. He had shoulder-length curly dark hair and wore a red coat and a fierce expression. Beside him was the silliest-looking dog Apollo had ever seen: a delicate little red greyhound, both ears flopped to the left, head erect on a narrow neck, pink tongue peeping from one side of its mouth. The dog's entire demeanor could be labeled *startled*.

The dog froze at Apollo's movement, then spun and raced off down the path.

The boy's face crumpled at the desertion before he squared his little shoulders and glared at Apollo. "You get away from her!"

At last: her defender—although Apollo *had* been hoping for someone a bit more imposing.

"Indio." The woman stepped away from Apollo hastily, brushing her skirts. "There you are. I've been calling for you."

"I'm sorry, Mama." Apollo noticed the child didn't take his eyes from him—an attitude he approved of. "Daff an' me were 'sploring."

"Well, explore nearer the theater next time. I don't want you meeting anyone who might be…" She trailed away, glancing nervously at Apollo. "Erm. Dangerous."

Apollo widened his eyes, trying to look harmless— sadly, nearly impossible. He'd hit six feet at age fifteen and topped that by several inches in the fourteen years since. Add to that the width of his shoulders, his massive hands, and a face that his sister had once affectionately compared to a gargoyle's, and trying to appear harmless became something of a lost cause.

His apprehension was borne out when the woman backed farther away from him and caught her young son's hand. "Come. Let's go find where Daffodil has run off to."

"But, Mama," the boy whispered loudly. "What about the monster?"

It didn't take a genius to understand that the child was referring to him. Apollo nearly sighed.

"Don't you worry," the woman said firmly. "I'm going to talk to Mr. Harte as soon as I can about your monster. He'll be gone by tomorrow."

With a last nervous glance at him, she turned and led the boy away.

Apollo narrowed his eyes on her retreating back, slim and confident. Green Eyes was going to be in for a shock when she found out *which* of the two of them was tossed from the garden.

Chapter Two

The king had a great army and with it he marched across field and mountain, subjugating all the peoples he met until at last he came to an island that lay in an azure sea like a pearl in an oyster shell. This he conquered at once and, seeing how beautiful the island was, sent for his queen, and caused a golden castle to be built there for their home. But on the first night he slept in that place a black bull came to him in a dream...
—From *The Minotaur*

For a man who owned a pleasure garden, Asa Makepeace certainly didn't live in luxury—if anything, he sailed perilously close to squalor.

Apollo finished climbing the three flights of rickety stairs to Makepeace's rented rooms the next morning. Makepeace lived in Southwark, which was on the south bank of the River Thames, not terribly far from Harte's Folly itself. The landing held two doors, one to the right, one to the left.

Apollo pounded on the right-hand door, then paused and placed his ear to it. He heard a faint rustling and then a groan. He reared back and thumped the wood again.

"D'you mind?" The left door popped open to reveal a

shriveled elderly man, a soft red velvet cap on his head. "Some like to sleep of a morning!"

Apollo turned his shoulder, shielding his face behind his broad-brimmed hat, and waved an apologetic hand at the man.

The old man slammed his door shut just as Makepeace opened his own.

"What?" Makepeace stood in his doorway, swaying slightly as if in a breeze. "What?" His tawny hair stood out all around his head like a lion's mane—assuming the lion had been in a recent cyclone—and his shirt was unbuttoned, baring a heavily furred barrel chest.

At least he was wearing breeches.

Apollo pushed past his friend into the room—although not far. There simply wasn't much space to move. The room was swarming, teeming, *breeding* with things: towers of stacked books stood on the floor, a table, and even the big four-poster bed in the corner, a life-size portrait of a bearded man leaned against one wall, next to a stuffed raven, which stood next to a teetering pile of chipped, dirty dishes, and next to *that* was a four-foot-tall model of a ship, rigging and all. Colorful costumes were piled haphazardly in one corner and papers were scattered messily on top of nearly everything.

Makepeace shut his door and a few sheets fluttered to the floor. "What time is it?"

Apollo pointed to a large pink china clock sitting on top of a stack of books on the table before looking closer and realizing the timepiece had stopped. Oh, for God's sake. He chose a more direct way to show the time by dodging around the table, crossing to the only window, and yanking the heavy velvet curtains open.

A cloud of dust burst from the fabric, dancing prettily in the early morning sunlight streaming into the room.

"Ahhh!" Makepeace reacted as if skewered. He staggered and flung himself back on the bed. "Have you no mercy? It can't be noon yet."

Apollo sighed and crossed to his friend. He pushed one leg over ungently and perched on the side of the bed. Then he took out his ever-present notebook and a pencil stub.

He wrote, *Who is the woman in the garden?* and shoved the notebook in front of Makepeace's eyes.

Makepeace went cross-eyed for a second before focusing on the writing. "What woman? You're mad, man, there isn't any woman in any garden unless you're talking about Eve and *that* garden, which would make you Adam and that I'd *pay* to see, especially if you wore a girdle of oak leaves—"

During this ramble Apollo had taken back the notebook and written more. Now he showed it to the other man, cutting him off mid-rant: *Green eyes, overdressed, pretty. Has a little boy named Indio.*

"Oh, *that* woman," Makepeace said without any show of embarrassment. "Lily Stump. Best comic actress in this generation—perhaps any generation, come to think of it. She's impossibly good—it's almost as if she casts a spell over the audience, well certainly the *male* members. Uses the name Robin Goodfellow on the stage. Wonderful thing, made-up names. Quite useful."

Apollo gave him a jaundiced look at that. Asa Makepeace was more commonly known as Mr. Harte—though very few knew both of the man's names. Makepeace had taken the false name when he'd first opened Harte's Folly nearly ten years ago. Something to do with his family being a religious lot and disapproving of the stage and pleasure gardens in general. Makepeace had been vague about it the one time Apollo had quizzed him on the subject.

Apollo scribbled in the notebook again. *Get her out of my garden.*

Makepeace's eyebrows shot up when he read the note. "You know, it's actually *my* garden—"

Apollo glared.

Makepeace hastily held up his hands. "Although, of course, you have a significant investment in it."

Apollo snorted at that. Damned right a *significant investment*—to wit: all the capital he'd been able to scrape together four and a half years ago. And since he'd spent most of the intervening time ensconced in Bedlam, he hadn't been able to acquire any other capital or income. His investment in Harte's Folly was it—his only nest egg and the reason he couldn't simply flee London. Until Harte's Folly was once again on its feet and earning, Apollo had no way of getting his money back.

Hence his decision to help by overseeing the landscaping of the ruined garden.

Makepeace let his hands drop and sighed. "But I can't make Miss Stump leave the garden."

Apollo didn't bother writing this time. He just arched an incredulous eyebrow and cocked his head.

"She hasn't anywhere else to stay." Makepeace rolled off the bed, suddenly alert.

Apollo waited patiently. One good thing about being mute: silence had a tendency to make others talk.

Makepeace sniffed his underarm, grimaced, and then pulled off his shirt before he broke. "I might've stolen her away from Sherwood at the King's Theatre, which for some reason Sherwood took personally, the ass. He's made it impossible for her to get work anywhere in London. So when she came to me last week unable to pay the rent on her rooms..."

He shrugged and tossed the dirty shirt in a corner.

Apollo's eyebrows snapped together and he wrote furiously. *I can't keep in hiding with strangers running about the garden.*

Makepeace scoffed. "What about the gardeners we've hired? You haven't made a fuss about them."

Can't help them—we need the gardeners. Besides. None of them are as intelligent as Mrs. Stump.

"*Miss* Stump—there's no Mr. Stump, as far as I know."

Apollo blinked, sidetracked, and cocked his head. *The boy?*

"Her son." Makepeace reached for a miraculously full jug of water, which he poured into a chipped basin. "You know how theater folk are sometimes. Don't be such a Puritan."

So she wasn't taken by another man. *Not* that it mattered—she thought him a literal idiot and he was in hiding from the King's men after escaping Bedlam.

Apollo sighed and wrote, *You need to find her other lodging.*

Makepeace cocked his head to read the outthrust note, and dropped his mouth open like a gaffed carp. "Good God, what a wonderful idea, Kilbourne! I'll just send her to my ancient family castle in Wales, shall I? It's a bit run-down, but the seventy or so servants and acres and acres of land should more than make up for any inconvenience. Or maybe the château in the south of France would be more to her liking? I don't know why I didn't think of that myself, what with my many, *many*—"

Apollo cut short this diatribe by shoving his friend's head in the basin of water.

Makepeace came up roaring, shaking his head so vigorously that Apollo might as well have taken the dip himself.

"Ahem."

Both men whirled at the gentle cough.

The aristocrat who stood just inside the door to Makepeace's rooms wasn't particularly tall—Asa had several inches on him and Apollo topped him by more than a head. The man was posed, one hip cocked gracefully, his hand languidly holding a gold-and-ebony cane. He was attired in a pink suit lavishly embroidered in bright blues, greens, gold, and black. Instead of the common white wig, he wore his golden hair unpowdered—though curled and carefully tied back with a black bow. Apollo had mentally named Valentine Napier, 7th Duke of Montgomery, a fop the first time he'd met him—the night Harte's Folly had burned—and he'd had no cause to change that impression in the intervening months. He had, however, added an adjective: Montgomery was a *dangerous* fop.

"Gentlemen." Montgomery's upper lip twitched as if in amusement. "I hope I'm not interrupting anything?"

He looked slyly between them, making Apollo stiffen.

"Only my morning toilet," Makepeace said, ignoring the insinuation. He grabbed a cloth and vigorously rubbed his hair. "Feel free to go away and come back at a more convenient time, *Your Grace.*"

"Oh, but you're such a busy man," Montgomery murmured, poking with his gold-topped cane at a stack of papers piled on a chair. The papers slid off, landing with a dusty crash on the floor. A tiny smile flickered across Montgomery's face and Apollo was reminded of a gray cat his mother had once kept when he was a boy. The creature had loved to stroll along the mantelpiece in his mother's sitting room, delicately batting the ornaments off the shelf. The cat had watched each ornament smash on the hearth with detached interest before moving on to the next.

"Do have a seat," Makepeace drawled. He pulled open a drawer in a chest and took out a shirt.

"Thank you," Montgomery replied without any sign of embarrassment. He sat, crossed his legs, and flicked a minuscule piece of lint off the silk of his breeches. "I've come to see about my investment."

Apollo frowned. He'd been against taking money from Montgomery from the start, but Makepeace had somehow talked him into it with his usual glib tongue. Apollo couldn't shake the feeling that they'd made a pact with the Devil. Montgomery had been abroad for over ten years before his abrupt return to London and society. No one seemed to know much about the man—or what he'd been doing for those ten years—even if his title and family name were well known.

Such mystery gave Apollo an itch between the shoulder blades.

"Good," Makepeace said loudly. "Everything's going just dandy. Smith here has the landscaping well in hand."

"Sssm-i-th," Montgomery drew out the ridiculous name Makepeace had given Apollo, making the sound into a sibilant hiss. He turned to Apollo and smiled quite sweetly. "And I believe that Mr. Makepeace said that your first name is Samuel, is it not?"

"He prefers Sam," Makepeace growled, tacking on a hasty "Your Grace."

"Indeed." Montgomery was still smiling, almost to himself. "Mr. Sam Smith. Any relation to the Horace Smiths of Oxfordshire?"

Apollo shook his head once.

"No? A pity. I have some interests there. But it *is* a very common name," Montgomery murmured. "And what plans do you have for the garden, may I ask?"

Apollo flipped to the back of his notebook and showed it to the duke.

Montgomery leaned forward, examining with pursed lips the sketches Apollo had made.

"Very nice," he said at last, and sat back. "I'll drop by the garden later today to take a look, shall I?"

Apollo and Makepeace exchanged glances.

"No need for that, Your Grace," Makepeace began for the both of them.

"I know there's no need. Call it a whim. In any case, I shan't be denied. Expect me, Mr. *Smith.*"

Apollo nodded grimly. He couldn't put his finger on why it bothered him, but he didn't like the idea of the duke sniffing about his garden.

Montgomery twirled his walking stick, watching the glint of light off the gold top. "I collect that we'll soon be in need of an architect to design and rebuild the various buildings in the pleasure garden."

"Sam's just started work on the garden," Makepeace said. "He's got quite a lot to do—you've seen the state the place is in. There's plenty of time to find an architect."

"No," Montgomery replied firmly, "there isn't. Not if we're to reopen the garden within the next year."

"Within a year?" Makepeace squawked.

"Indeed." Montgomery stood and ambled to the door. "Haven't I told you? I'm afraid I'm quite an impatient man. If the garden isn't ready for visitors—and the money they'll spend—by April of next year, I'm afraid I shall need my capital repaid." He pivoted at the door and shot them another of his cherubic smiles. "With interest."

He closed the door gently behind him.

"Well, bollocks," Makepeace said blankly.

Apollo couldn't help but agree.

"Is *WANTONISH* a real word?" Lily asked Maude several days later.

She sat at the kitchen-cum-dining-room table while Maude hung their washing next to the fireplace.

"*Wantonish*," Maude said, rolling the word around her mouth. She shook her head decisively as she twitched one of Indio's shirts into place over the drying rack. "No, never heard of it."

Damn! Lily pouted down at the play she was writing, *A Wastrel Reform'd*. *Wantonish* was such a wonderful W word—and she really needed more of those. "Well, does it *matter* if 'tisn't a real word? William Shakespeare devised all sorts of new words, didn't he?"

Maude gave her a look. "You're right clever, hinney, but you're no Shakespeare."

"Hmm." Lily bent back to her play. *Wantonish* sounded like a perfectly lovely word to her—quite sly and suggestive, rather like the heroine of her play. Just because no one had thought of the word before now didn't seem like a good enough reason *not* to use it.

She dipped her quill in the inkpot and wrote another

line: "A Wastrel might indeed be wantonish but he'd surely not be wastefulish as well."

Lily cocked her head, eyeing the drying ink. Hmmm. Two imaginary words in one line. Best not tell Maude.

Someone knocked on the theater door.

Both Lily and Maude paused and stared at the door, because *that* had never happened before. Granted, they'd lived at the theater for less than a sennight, but still. It wasn't the sort of place most people happened by.

Lily frowned. "Where's Indio?"

Maude shrugged. "Went out to play right after luncheon."

"I told him to stay close," Lily muttered, feeling a faint twinge of apprehension. She'd walked around to Mr. Harte's rooms the day after she'd met Indio's "monster," but the man had been ridiculously adamant that the hulking brute couldn't be moved from the garden. None of Lily's well-reasoned arguments had persuaded the stubborn man and in the end she'd been forced to come away again, quite unsatisfied. Fortunately the mute hadn't ventured near the ruined theater since. *Un*fortunately Indio had acquired a strange fascination with him. Several times the boy had disappeared with Daffodil into the garden, despite Lily's dire threats regarding pudding and little boys who didn't mind their mothers.

She sighed as she rose to get the door. She was going to have to speak to Indio again about his "monster"—always assuming her son emerged from the garden.

Lily pulled open the door to find a man dressed in a violet suit standing without, his back to her as he surveyed the garden.

He turned and she was dazzled by his alarming prettiness. He had bright-blue eyes, long chocolate lashes, cheekbones sharp enough to cut glass, and a soft, curving mouth that she really *wasn't* envious of. And to top it all off—as if to prove Providence really, *truly* wasn't fair— he had guinea-gold hair, smooth and curling perfectly.

When Lily had been a very small girl she'd prayed every night for golden hair.

She blinked now. "Erm...yes?"

He smiled. Lethally. "Have I the pleasure to address the illustrious Robin Goodfellow?"

Lily straightened and raised her chin, employing her *own* smile—which, she had on good authority, could be *quite* devastating. Lily Stump might occasionally have bad posture, might have hair that wasn't gold and some- times wasn't perfectly arranged, might in the dark of night have fears and self-doubts, but *Robin Goodfellow* had none of those things. Robin Goodfellow was a *very* popular actress who was beloved by all of London.

And she knew it.

So Robin Goodfellow smiled with just the right amount of impishness at the very pretty man—and by God made *him* blink.

"You do indeed," she said throatily.

A spark of admiration lit within his gorgeous blue eyes. "Ah. Then may I introduce myself? I am Valentine Napier, Duke of Montgomery. I was informed by Mr. Harte that you resided here and I thought to make your acquaintance."

He swept the lace-trimmed black tricorn from his head and bowed low, holding his stick in the other hand.

Behind her, something clattered.

Lily didn't turn to see what Maude had dropped. Instead she inclined her head coquettishly and dipped into a curtsy. "I'm most pleased to meet you, Your Grace. Won't you take a dish of tea with me?"

"I'd be honored, ma'am."

Lily pivoted and exchanged a significant look with Maude. They hadn't planned for such a contingency, but Maude was an old hand in the theater and knew well the art of a false facade. "It's such a lovely day. We'll take our tea in the garden, Maude."

"Yes, ma'am," Maude said, immediately assuming the mask of a perfect servant.

When Lily looked back, the duke was eyeing her speculatively. "Isn't it a bit cold for tea outside?"

She didn't so much as narrow her eyes. He knew damned well why she wouldn't let him in the wretched theater—she wasn't about to parade her lowered state of affairs before him.

"La, Your Grace, but I like the fresh air. Of course should *you* prefer a stuffy indoor setting—"

"No, no," he demurred, a gleam in his eye.

She'd scored that point and well he knew it. But he seemed to take the setback in good humor. He stepped aside as Maude hurried out with two chairs—mismatched, of course, but Lily knew better than to apologize. To show any sort of weakness to a man like the duke was as ill-advised as a mouse's bolting in front of a waiting cat.

He gestured gallantly to a seat and she settled herself gracefully, watching as he took his own chair. The duke moved with a sort of lazy elegance that, she thought, belied how dangerous he might be.

He glanced around at the devastated garden. "It's a rather macabre spot, don't you find?"

"Not at all, Your Grace," Lily lied. Surely he didn't

think he'd catch her out with such a mundane snare? "The atmosphere of the garden is terribly *mysterious.* I find it altogether charming—and a wonderful influence for my stagecraft. An actress must always find inspiration for herself and her art."

"I'm gratified to hear you say so," the duke replied smoothly, "for as you know, I am now part owner of Harte's Folly." She must've given herself away somehow—a slight, involuntary movement or a widening of the eyes—for he leaned forward. "Ah, you *didn't* know."

Wretched creature. She made herself relax. "La, I'm not apprised of every little business dealing with the garden, Your Grace."

"Of course not," he murmured as Maude came out with a small footstool. She set it between them and disappeared back into the theater. The duke cocked an eyebrow at the plain wooden footstool and addressed it. "But this 'little business dealing' does put me in the position of your"—he cleared his throat delicately and looked up at her—"*employer.*"

Maude returned with a tray of tea at that moment, saving Lily from an ill-conceived reply.

Lily smiled as Maude set down the tray and poured tea for them both. Maude handed her the dish of tea with a question in her eyes. Lily held her gaze and murmured her thanks, signaling that she wasn't in need of help.

The maidservant gave a quiet huff and left.

"She's very loyal, isn't she?" the duke observed.

Lily took a sip of the tea. It was weak—Maude must've used the last of the good tea leaves—but hot. "Aren't all good servants loyal, Your Grace?"

He cocked his head as if seriously considering her

comment, before replying decisively. "Not necessarily. A servant can serve quite adequately—even superbly—without any loyalty to his master at all." He smiled, quick and mercurial. "As long, of course, as the master has fitted the servant with a proper bit between his teeth."

Lily repressed a shiver. What a very loathsome image. But then aristocrats weren't like other people. They played with the lives of ordinary folk as easily as Indio poked a stick into an ant's nest, never considering the destruction they caused.

"I find I don't much like the thought of bits," Lily murmured.

"No?" he asked. "Would you allow horses to run free?"

"*People* aren't horses."

"No, but *servants* are quite close," he retorted. "Both servants and horses live to serve their master—or at least they should do. Otherwise they're quite useless and need to be put down."

She stared at him, watching for the twinkle of the eye, the twitch of the lip, to indicate he jested.

His countenance was pleasant but grave.

Was he jesting?

He took a sip of tea, watching her. "Don't you think so, Miss Goodfellow?"

"No, Your Grace," she said sweetly, "I do not."

At that his wide lips did break into a smile—beautiful and corrupt. "You speak your mind, ma'am. How refreshing. Tell me, have you a protector?"

Oh, dear God, she'd rather bed a snake. Not to mention the insultingly frank way he'd made his proposition.

She smiled again—though it was becoming harder and

harder to keep her expression polite. "Your Grace flatters me with his attention, but I have no wish for a protector."

"Don't you?" He let his gaze travel skeptically over the falling-down theater she lived in. "But no doubt you know best your own circumstance." His voice was politely doubtful. "I have another use for your, er, *person* that you might find more to your liking: an acquaintance of mine is hosting a house party in a few weeks and is planning to stage an especially written play as part of the festivities. He has engaged a theatrical troupe of players, but the lead actress has unfortunately found herself unable to play." He made a slight moue. "A delicate indisposition, you understand."

"I do indeed," Lily said coolly, feeling pity for the actress who had discovered herself with child and thus out of work. She hoped the poor woman had someone to care for her. Without Maude she wasn't sure what she would have done when Indio arrived. "But I'm surprised, Your Grace."

He tilted his head, his blue eyes sparkling with interest. "Indeed?"

"I would think the arranging of a simple house party play quite beneath your attention."

"Ah." He smiled almost to himself. "I find I do like doing the occasional favor. It makes the receiver so much more in my debt."

Lily swallowed. Would the duke consider *her* in his debt now? Probably, but it really didn't matter: she needed the work. Private theatricals were quite popular, but naturally expensive to produce and thus few and far between. She was lucky to have the offer. "I'd be pleased to act in the play."

"Wonderful," the duke said. "I'm told that rehearsals won't begin for another fortnight or so, as the play isn't finished yet. I'll contact you at the appropriate time, shall I?"

"Thank you."

He smiled slowly. "Your talents are very much praised, Miss Goodfellow. I find myself looking forward to the party—and the play—with unforeseen anticipation."

Lily was still considering the proper reply to such a complicated comment when a muddy whirlwind burst from the blackened trees, followed closely by a tumbling ball of red-and-black mud. "Mama! Mama! You'll never guess—"

Indio skidded to a stop as he caught sight of their guest, falling abruptly silent.

Sadly, Daffodil had no such impulse. The little greyhound halted by her friend and began yapping shrilly, the force of her barks making her front legs bounce off the ground.

The duke narrowed his eyes very slightly at the dog and Lily suddenly felt an irrational fear for her pet.

Maude came out of the theater and snatched up Daffodil, who decided to turn affectionate, laving the maidservant's face with her pink tongue.

"Enough of that now," Maude scolded. "Come here, Indio."

She held out her hand for the boy and Indio started forward.

"A moment," Montgomery drawled. He halted the boy with a touch of his hand to Indio's shoulder. The duke glanced at Lily. "This is your son?"

Lily nodded, her fingers balling into fists in her lap.

She didn't know why the duke should take an interest in Indio, but she didn't like it. Not at all.

Montgomery placed a long forefinger under Indio's chin and tilted his face up, staring at his curious eyes for several heartbeats.

"Fascinating," the duke drawled softly at last, "the dissimilar colors of his eyes. I believe I've only seen the like once before."

And he turned and smiled his beautiful snake smile at Lily.

THE BOY WAS watching him again.

It was late afternoon a day later and the sun was giving up the struggle behind a barrier of gray clouds as Apollo examined the ornamental pond. He and the other gardeners had spent the last three days dredging the stream that fed the pond, clearing it of debris so the pond might once again be filled with freshwater. It had been filthy, muddy work, but the result was already apparent: the water level in the pond was rising. An old stone bridge arched to a little island in the middle and Apollo raised both hands, palms out, fingers together and pointed up, thumbs at right angles, making a frame for the view between.

Nearby the bushes rattled as the boy shifted—and then froze like a hare hiding from a fox.

Apollo was careful to show no sign that he'd noticed the child.

He considered the picture within his frame. Originally he'd thought to tear the bridge down—it was much the worse for wear from the fire—but looking at it now, he thought it might become a rustic ruin with the right plantings around it. Perhaps an oak at the near shore and a grouping of reeds or a single flowering tree on the island.

He sighed and dropped his hands. Trees were his most pressing problem. Most hadn't survived the fire, and of course for one to mature took many years. He'd read about transplanting fully grown trees—the French were said to be able to do so—but he'd never tried it himself.

Time enough to worry about that. For today he still had to pull yet another dead tree from the ground. He pivoted—and exhaled hard as his right foot slid on the slippery pond bank. Apollo caught himself and grimaced down at his boot, covered with the stinking green slime that still lined the bank where the pond had retreated from the original shoreline.

From the bushes came a gasp, presumably at his near fall. What the child found so fascinating about him, Apollo had no idea. His work was the same as the other gardeners'—tedious and wearying—yet the boy seemed to spy only on him. In fact, Apollo had noticed that Indio's hiding place became closer every day, until today the boy was only feet away. He was beginning to wonder if the boy *wanted* to be noticed.

Apollo bent to pick up his long-handled adze. He swung it over his head and then down into the soft ground at the root of a stump. The heavy adze hit with a satisfying *thump* and he could feel that he'd struck one of the main roots.

He wiped his brow with the sleeve of his shirt and heaved the adze free from the stump. Then he swung again.

"*Daff*," came a hiss from the bushes.

Apollo's lips twitched. Indio hadn't chosen a particularly adept spy-mate. The greyhound obviously didn't understand his young master's need for stealth. Even now she was wandering out of their hiding place, nose to the ground, more interested in some scent than Indio's frantic call. "Daff. *Daffodil*."

Apollo sighed. Was he really expected not to notice the dog? He was mute, not blind—or deaf.

Daffodil ambled right up to his feet. She'd apparently lost her fear of him in the last week of spying—or perhaps she was simply bored of sitting still. In any case she sniffed the tree stump and the adze, and then abruptly sat to scratch one ear vigorously.

Apollo extended a hand for the little dog to sniff, but the silly thing jumped back at his movement. She was quite near the pond bank and her sudden leap caused her back legs to slip in the mud. She tumbled down the bank and into the water, disappearing beneath the surface.

"Daff!" The boy ran from his hiding place, his eyes huge with fear.

Apollo put out his hand, blocking him.

The boy tried to dart around his outstretched arm. "She'll drown!"

Apollo seized him and swung the boy off his feet and then set him down firmly, placing his hands on his shoulders and bending to stare into his eyes. He narrowed his eyes and *growled*, never so frustrated by his loss of speech as now. He couldn't argue with the child— tell him what he meant to do and instruct him to *obey*, and thus he was reduced to animal grunting. Better the boy should fear him, though, than drown trying to rescue his pet.

Indio gulped.

Apollo stepped back, keeping his eye on the boy, and

pulled off his shoes, waistcoat, and shirt. He hesitated a moment, staring suspiciously at the boy.

Indio nodded. "Yes. *Please*. Please, help her."

Without waiting further, Apollo turned and waded swiftly into the water. The little dog had reemerged at the surface, but she was thrashing in panic instead of trying to swim.

Apollo grabbed her by the scruff of the neck and lifted her clear from the pond. She hung pathetically, water streaming from her rat-thin tail and drooping ears. He turned and waded back to the shore.

The boy hadn't moved from where Apollo had stopped him. Indio watched him intently.

Apollo picked up his shirt and wrapped the shivering greyhound in it before handing the little dog to the boy.

Indio clutched her to his chest, his eyes swimming in tears as the dog whimpered and began to lick his chin. He looked from the pet in his arms up at Apollo. "Thank you."

Daffodil coughed, choked, opened wide her narrow mouth, and vomited up a thin trail of pond water all over the shirt.

Apollo winced.

He turned and found the worn cloth bag he'd brought his lunch in. Fortunately, he'd placed his notebook in it earlier, so that at least wasn't wet. Apollo repressed a shuddering shiver as he crouched and rummaged in the sack. Earlier he'd eaten his luncheon—a pork pie—and wrapped a leftover piece in a cloth. Apollo rose with the bundle and the little dog immediately leaned from her master's arms, sniffing eagerly at the cloth. Apollo unwrapped the morsel and broke off a piece, holding it out. Daffodil snatched it from his fingers and gulped it down.

Apollo almost laughed.

"She likes piecrust," the boy said shyly.

Apollo merely nodded and fed Daffodil another bit.

"'Course she likes bread and sausage and chicken and green beans and apples and cheese as well," Indio continued. Not so shy after all, then. "I gived her a raisin once. She didn't like that. Is that your dinner?"

Apollo didn't answer, simply offering the last of the pie to Daffodil. She gobbled it and then began nosing his hand, looking for crumbs. She seemed to have forgotten her unexpected swim already.

"It's kind of you to give it her," Indio said, stroking Daffodil's head. "D'you...do you like dogs?"

Apollo glanced at him. The boy was staring up at him hopefully and for the first time Apollo noticed that his eyes were of different colors: the right blue, the left green. He turned away to stuff the bit of cloth back into his bag.

"Uncle Edwin gave me Daffodil. He won her in a game of cards. Mama says a puppy is a silly thing to wager for. Daff's an Italian greyhound, but she didn't come from Italy. Mama says Italians like skinny little dogs. I named her Daffodil because that's my favorite flower and the prettiest. She doesn't know to mind," Indio said sadly as Apollo rose.

Daffodil wriggled and the boy set her cautiously on the ground. The greyhound struggled from the folds of the shirt, shook herself, and then squatted, watering the ground—and a corner of the shirt.

Apollo sighed. He really was going to have to wash that shirt.

Indio sighed as well. "Mama says I ought to train her to sit and beg and most 'portantly come when we call her, but"—he took a deep breath—"I don't know how to."

Apollo bit his lip to keep down a smile. It was too bad that he'd already fed all the scraps to the dog. He glanced at the boy.

Indio was staring at him frankly. "My name's Indio. I live in the old theater." He pointed in the direction of the theater with a straight arm. "My mama lives there and Maude, too. She's a famous actress, my mama, that is. Maude's our maidservant." He chewed on one lip. "Can you speak?"

Apollo shook his head slowly.

"I thought not." Indio dug into the mud with the toe of one boot, frowning down. "What's your name?"

Well, he couldn't answer that, could he? Time he was back at work, anyway. Apollo reached for his adze, half expecting the boy to run away at his movement.

But Indio simply stepped back out of his way, watching with interest. Daffodil had wandered several feet away and was now digging energetically in the mud.

He was wet and chilled from the air, but work would soon fix that. Apollo took another swing at the tree stump, hitting it with a *thwock!*

"I'll call you Caliban," Indio said as Apollo lifted the adze again.

Apollo turned and stared.

Indio smiled tentatively. "It's from a play. There's a wizard who lives on a island and it's all over wild. Caliban lives there, though he *can* speak. But he's big like you, so I thought... Caliban."

Apollo was still staring helplessly at the boy through

this explanation. Daffodil had paused to sneeze and glance at them. Her nose was adorned with a clot of mud.

There were dozens of reasons to refuse the boy. Apollo was in hiding, a price on his head, wanted for the most awful of crimes. The boy's mother had already made plain that she wanted him nowhere near her son. And what did he have to offer the boy after all, mute and over-worked and on the run?

But Indio smiled up at him with mismatched eyes and cheeks made red from the wind, and an air of sweet hope that was simply impossible to refuse. Somehow, against his better judgment, Apollo found himself nodding.

Caliban. The illiterate knave from *The Tempest*. Well, he supposed he could've done worse.

Indio might've chosen *A Midsummer Night's Dream*— and named him Bottom.

Chapter Three

*The black bull was without mark, both beautiful
and terrible, and it opened its jaws and spoke in the
language of men: "You have overthrown my island,
but I will have my price."
When the king awoke he marveled on the oddity
of his dream, but thought no more of it...*
—From *The Minotaur*

"Indio!"

Lily paused and glanced around the blackened garden
an hour later. She hated to keep Indio locked inside the
old theater, but she was going to have to if he insisted on
disappearing like this. The sun would soon be setting.
The garden held all manner of dangers for a little boy—
and that was without the interest the duke had shown her
son yesterday afternoon. Lily hadn't liked that comment
Montgomery had made about Indio's eyes.

Not at all.

A sense of urgency made her cup her hands around her
mouth to shout again. "*Indio!*"

Oh, let Indio be safe. Let him return to her, happy and
laughing and covered in mud.

Lily trudged onward toward the pond. Funny how she'd learned to pray again when she'd become a mother so suddenly. For years she'd never thought of Providence. And then she'd found herself whispering beneath her breath at different, frightening points in Indio's short life:

Let the fever break.

Don't let the fall be fatal.

Thank you, thank you, for making the horse swerve aside.

Not the pox. Anything but the pox.

Oh, dear God, don't let him be lost.

Not lost. Not my brave little man. My Indio.

Lily's steps quickened until she found herself almost running through the charred brambles, the clutching branches. She'd never let him out again when she found him. She'd fall to her knees and hug him when she found him. She'd spank him and send him to bed without his supper when she found him.

She was panting as the path widened and she came to the clearing by the pond. She opened her mouth to call yet again.

But she was struck dumb instead.

He was there—Indio's monster. He was in the pond, his back to her.

And he was quite nude.

Lily blinked, frozen in place. The garden was all of a sudden eerily still as the day made its last farewell. His massive shoulders were bunched, his head lowered as if he saw something in the water. Perhaps he was struck by his own reflection. Did he know himself when he saw that man beneath the water—or was he frightened at the sight? She felt a flash of pity. He could not help his own huge size—or the deformity of his brain. She ought to speak, ought to make her presence known, ought to...

All thought left her head as the giant plunged beneath the water.

Lily's mouth half opened.

The setting sun broke through the cloud cover and bathed the pond in golden light, reflecting off the ripples left by his movement. He burst from the water. He was facing her now. The muscles bunched on his arms as he slicked his wet, shoulder-length hair back from his face. The mist swirled amber over the surface of the water, adorning his gleaming skin as if he were the tributary god of this ruined garden. Her pity evaporated, burned away by the sudden realization that she had it all wrong.

He was...

She swallowed.

Good Lord. He was *magnificent*.

The water trickled down his chest, trailing through a diamond of wet, dark hair between his beaded nipples, down over a shallow, perfectly formed navel, and into a dark line of wet hair that disappeared—rather disappointingly—into the concealing misted water.

She blinked and glanced up—only to find that the giant, the beast, the monster was looking directly back at her.

She ought to be ashamed. He was a mental defective and she was ogling him as if he were able to reciprocate any feeling she might have...except his expression didn't seem stupid now. He almost looked *amused* by her stare.

Not defective at all.

And an awful, terrible, *mortifying* thing happened: she felt herself grow wet.

Just yesterday she'd had tea with the most beautiful man she'd ever seen. The Duke of Montgomery had aristocratic cheekbones, sapphire-blue eyes, and shining, golden hair—and he'd moved her not at all.

Yet this...*beast* before her, this man with his wild muddy-brown hair, his animallike shoulders, his big, knobby nose, his wide, crooked mouth and heavy brow. *Him* she found attractive.

Obviously she needed to take a new lover—and soon.

He began wading to the shore, his leaden expression returned. Had she imagined the look of intelligence, supplying one where none existed?

Lily squeaked as he neared, but sadly, did *not* turn her back.

She had a moral defect—a despicable personal flaw— for she simply could *not* look away. Her eyes dropped to the wet black tangle between his legs as he strode toward her, the water swirling about his muscled thighs. There was a hint of the flesh below, crude and male and—

"Mama!"

Lily jumped, whirling, her hand on her heart, which surely had stopped, poor, worn thing.

"Indio!" she gasped, rather breathlessly, for her wretched son had chosen *this* moment to emerge from the shrubbery. He was standing on the path she'd just come from, a leaf stuck in his curly black hair. Daffodil, looking even muddier than usual, capered up to her and planted filthy paws on her skirts.

"Mama, can Caliban come for supper?" Indio asked, his mismatched eyes wide and entirely too innocent.

"I...*what*?" Lily asked weakly.

"Caliban." Indio gestured behind her.

She glanced over her shoulder to find—to her mingled relief and disappointment—that the man was slowly buttoning the falls of a ragged pair of breeches. The setting sun limned the wet slope of his shoulders, but his big fingers fumbled on the buttons. Whatever intelligence she'd imagined in his eyes was gone. But then it'd probably never been there in the first place.

She looked back at Indio, brow knitted. "Caliban? *That's* Caliban?"

Her son nodded. "I named him just today."

"You..." She shook her head. She'd found—shortly after Indio learned to talk—that letting him lead a discussion could result in a tangled web, incomprehensible to anyone over the age of seven. Sometimes one must simply cut through the tangle. "Indio, it's suppertime and Maude is waiting for us. Let's—"

"Please?" Indio came closer and took her hand, pulling her down to whisper in her ear, "He hasn't anything to eat and he's my *friend.*"

"I—" She looked helplessly back at Caliban.

He'd donned his shirt and was staring at her with his mouth half open. As she watched he scratched his... well, his *male parts*, quite obliviously, just as a half-wit might.

Her eyes narrowed. He'd not looked half-witted at all a minute ago. Perhaps she'd imagined it. Perhaps she'd wanted to condone her own baser impulses by giving the object of her thoughts reason that simply wasn't there.

And perhaps she was dithering over the matter too much.

She glanced back at Indio's pleading face and made her decision. She straightened and said loudly, "Of course, darling, let's invite your friend to supper."

A choking sound came from behind her, but when she turned, Caliban's face was stupidly blank. He snorted, hawked, spat into the pond—ew!—and scrubbed his hand across his mouth.

She smiled widely. "Caliban? Would you like to eat? *Eat?*" She mimed lifting a spoon to her mouth and then chewing. "Eat. With. Us." She pointed back along the path. "At the theater. We have *good* food!"

Her exaggerated miming was ridiculous—and if he *wasn't* mentally defective, it was insulting. She watched him closely to see if he'd break—change expression, show in any way that he did harbor normal intelligence.

But he simply stared back blankly.

It certainly wasn't the first time she'd misread a man. Sighing—and telling herself firmly that she most certainly *wasn't* disappointed—Lily began to turn away.

Indio started forward and took the big man's hand as naturally as he'd taken his mother's. "Come on! Maude's making roast chicken and there'll be gravy and dumplings."

Caliban looked at the boy and then her.

She raised an eyebrow. She'd already pled her piece—she wouldn't do so again. Not for a lackwit.

Was there something behind the muddy-brown eyes? A glimmer, a glint of challenge? She couldn't tell, and in any case she was no longer certain of her own perception.

But it didn't matter. Caliban nodded slowly.

Lily turned and started back up the path, Daffodil

scampering ahead. Her heart, that silly, mercurial thing, was beating in double time.

This was going to be interesting.

THIS WAS A very bad idea.

Apollo followed Lily Stump, watching her skirts sway from side to side as she walked. Her back was rigidly straight, but the nape of her neck was soft and unguarded, trails of dark hair curling down from the knot at the crown of her head. He had an animal urge to set his teeth against her nape, test the tender flesh, taste the salt on her skin.

He swallowed, glad the cool evening air kept him from embarrassment. There was no reason for him to have accepted her offer of supper. He had another cold pork pie safely stowed in the ruins of the musician's gallery where he'd set up camp while he worked in the garden. He was tired and sore and still damp from washing off the sweat and mud of the day. His recently rinsed shirt clung, wet and uncomfortable, to his shoulders.

Everything—*everything*—he'd worked for would be forfeit if anyone discovered who he really was.

And yet he was holding the hand of a little boy and trailing the boy's exasperating mother. Perhaps he was lonely. Or perhaps it was the look in her eyes when he'd emerged from the pond and found her watching him that urged his footsteps on. It had been a long time—a very, *very* long time—since a woman had last looked at him like that. As if she saw something she liked.

As if she might want more.

He'd spent four years in Bedlam, most of them chained in a stinking cell. He'd escaped last July, but in the months since, he'd been in hiding—not a situation conducive to finding a willing wench. And of course there'd been that last beating—the one that had stolen his voice. The prison guard had reached for his falls. Had—

But he wouldn't think of that now.

Apollo inhaled, shoving aside a black mass of shame and anger.

Indio looked up at him. "Caliban?"

Apollo realized he'd squeezed the boy's hand. Deliberately he made himself relax his hold and shook down his shoulders. Stupid for a man as big as he to feel such wretched fear. He was out of Bedlam. He'd made sure—*damned* sure—that guard was no longer a threat to anyone.

He was free.

Free.

Free.

He tilted back his head, watching the sun cast her flame-colored skirts upon the sky as she set over his ruined garden. Beyond the theater, between the tops of blackened and burnt trees, one could just make out a glitter that was the mighty Thames.

This had once been a lovely pleasure garden. When he was done with it, it would be a wondrous pleasure garden, even better than before.

But right now they were nearing the theater.

Apollo assumed the blank expression that he wore around the other gardeners—and only just in time. The door flew open and a tiny, gray-haired woman stood in the opening, arms set akimbo on hips.

"What," she barked, "is that?"

"We have a guest for supper tonight," Miss Stump

replied, and as she glanced back at him he thought he saw a mischievous glint in her eye. "Indio's monster, in fact—though Indio now calls him Caliban."

"Caliban?" Maude narrowed her eyes, cocking her head as she examined him critically. "Aye, I can see that, but is he safe in the theater with us is what I'm wanting to know?"

Apollo felt a tug on his hand. He looked down at Indio, who whispered, "She's nice. Truly."

"Don't fuss, Maude," Miss Stump murmured.

"He's my friend," Indio explained earnestly. "And he fed Daff all his dinner."

At the mention of her name, the little dog ran over and, growling in what she no doubt considered a ferocious manner, began to worry the ragged hem of Apollo's breeches.

"Humph," Maude said, her tone as dry as dust. "If that's the case, better come inside, all of you."

Indio bent and rescued Apollo's breeches by picking up Daffodil, who immediately began bathing his face with her tongue. He laughed and trotted past Maude. His mother gave Apollo an indecipherable look and motioned him in ahead of her. Apollo ducked his head and entered the charred theater, trying to quell his unease. There was no reason to think she'd seen through his subterfuge.

The last time he'd been in the building was on the night the garden had burned. Asa Makepeace was an old friend and the only one Apollo had trusted to keep his whereabouts secret when he'd been rescued from Bedlam. He'd hidden in the garden for only a day before the place had burned down. Then the theater had been smoldering and had stank of smoke and devastation.

Now there was still the faint smell of charred wood, but there were other changes. Miss Stump had obviously attempted to make the place more comfortable—a table and chairs were in the center of the room, and a print of ladies in bright dresses hung on the wall. A fire crackled on the grate, and a rack had been erected nearby to dry clothes. Someone had been knitting, for two knitting needles and a half-finished sock were stuck in a ball of gray yarn on a stool near the hearth. A tiny side table held a messy sheaf of papers, a corked bottle of ink, and a chipped mug with several quills. On the mantel sat a single, rather ugly black-and-green enameled clock—working, unlike Makepeace's. Before the fire was an incredibly plain purple settee, one corner propped up with several bricks.

It wasn't much—certainly not as grand as some of the houses he'd once seen as a young buck new to town, before his fall from grace—but it was homey. And that was all that mattered.

"Well?" Maude demanded, pointing to one of the chairs at the table. "Have a seat, milord."

For a terrible second Apollo couldn't breathe. Then in the next moment he realized that the honorific had been meant sarcastically. He nodded, hoping his face hadn't betrayed his surprise, and pulled out a chair to sit.

Maude was still scowling. "What's wrong with him? Can't he talk?"

"No, he can't," Indio said simply, saving Apollo from having to do his dumb show.

"Oh." Maude blinked, obviously taken aback. "Has he had his tongue cut out?"

"Maude!" Miss Stump cried. "What a horrible thought.

He has a tongue." Her brows knit as if from sudden doubt and she peered worriedly at Apollo. "Don't you?"

He didn't even bother resisting the urge. He stuck out his tongue at her.

Indio laughed and Daffodil began barking again— obviously her first reaction to nearly everything.

Miss Stump stared at Apollo for a long second and he was aware that his body was heating. Carefully he withdrew his tongue and snapped his mouth shut, giving her his most uncomprehending face.

She *humph*ed and abruptly took her seat.

"It's a fair enough question, it is," Maude defended herself. "Why can't he talk, then, if'n his tongue works well enough, I'd like to know?"

"I don't know why he can't talk." Indio took the chair next to Apollo. "But he saved Daff from drownding today."

"What?" Miss Stump paused in the act of reaching for the plate of sliced chicken on the table. "You're not to go near the pond, you know that, Indio."

"*I* wasn't near the pond," Indio explained with a boy's complicated logic. "*Daff* was. Caliban went in and took her out and wrapped her in his shirt. And then Daff spewed on his shirt."

Both women swung their heads to eye his shirt askance.

Apollo repressed an urge to lift his arm and sniff to see if the shirt still stank of dog vomit.

Miss Stump blinked. "*Spew* isn't a nice word, Indio, I've told you before."

"Then what is?" Indio asked—rather reasonably, in Apollo's opinion. "Can I have some of the chicken now?"

"Yes, of course." Miss Stump began to serve the chicken, the skin crisp and brown, the meat tender and moist. "Actually, we don't talk about such things at the dinner table."

"Never?" Indio looked very puzzled.

"Never," his parent said quite firmly.

"But if Daff eats an earthworm like she did last week, how—"

"So how did Caliban come to be nearby when Daffodil went into the pond?" Miss Stump asked loudly.

"He was chopping at a stump with a funny-looking ax," Indio said, and Apollo wanted to tell him, *adze*, but instead he took a bite of the chicken. "And me an' Daff were walking. But not," he added, "*to* the pond. We was walking *not* near the pond."

Apollo chanced a glance at the ladies and winced. Neither woman had swallowed that particular story.

"Then he's a gardener." Miss Stump picked up her wineglass and eyed him with far more interest than was safe.

"Not just *any* gardener," Indio said. "He tells all the other gardeners what to do."

At which point Apollo nearly swallowed his bite of chicken the wrong way. He choked and gasped and Miss Stump pounded him hard on his back.

"Does he indeed?" she asked, with a pointed look at him.

How the hell did the boy know that? Not even the other gardeners knew he'd designed the garden. He had a rather complicated method of leaving written instructions for the lead gardener—a slow but methodical man named Herring—so that none of them realized their employer was working right under their noses.

"Why do you think that?" Maude asked interestedly.

Apollo flicked his wrist and knocked his plate to the floor. It was a sad waste of good roast chicken, but not to be helped. The plate smashed on impact, shards skidding across the charred boards, gravy and meat oozing everywhere. Daffodil rushed over and began gobbling chicken as Indio and Maude tried keep her from inadvertently eating a piece of crockery.

In the melee Apollo looked over and met Miss Stump's gaze. Her green eyes were narrowed speculatively on him and he felt a thrill shoot through him, low and visceral.

The feeling might've been simple fear, but on the whole he thought it was something far, far more dangerous.

MAUDE AND INDIO were shouting, grappling with Daffodil and the mess on the floor, but Lily was frozen, staring into murky brown eyes. Not eyes the color of coffee or chocolate or that lovely China tea that came in a little red paper packet and that she could no longer afford. No, Caliban's eyes weren't like any delicious beverage. They were simply *brown*. As dull and uninspiring as a dumb animal's.

Except…

Except that they were surrounded by the lushest lashes she'd ever seen on a man: short, black, and thick, and exotically beautiful in their own way. Why hadn't she noticed before? Caliban's eyes were simply breathtaking.

But what was more disturbing, there was a glimmer, somewhere in the muddy-brown depths, that made Lily draw in her breath. It was a glimmer of intelligence—sharp intelligence—and it made her afraid. Because if Indio was right, if this man—this *stranger*—was not just a simple gardener, but was somehow in charge of the other gardeners, then he wasn't at all what she'd first taken him for. She was aware, suddenly, of how huge he was, of how *male*. He was in her home, with her little boy and an old woman, and they had no defenses.

She knew all too well what destruction a big man could wreak.

She drew a shaky breath as Indio sat back down again, between Lily and Caliban.

Indio leaned close to the giant and whispered, "You can have some of mine."

Lily swallowed, gripping her apprehension firmly. Perhaps Indio had misunderstood something he'd seen. Surely a mute couldn't be the head gardener? Surely Caliban was exactly what he'd seemed when she'd first come upon him in the garden?

"That's quite all right, Indio," she said evenly. "Maude can serve him another portion."

Her former nursemaid shot Lily a quick look, but said nothing as she fetched the only other plate they owned and began filling it.

"Indio," Lily said carefully as she touched her wineglass. Her own appetite had fled completely. "Tell me about how Daffodil fell into the pond?"

Her little boy crinkled up his nose. "We-ell, we was walking, me an' Daff, and then Daff sort of skidded."

She waited, but Indio was looking at her with an expression of suspicious innocence.

"Indio," she started, but her son took that as a prompt to speak again.

"He was real quick, Caliban was. Fished Daff out of the water like a...a...well. A drownded rat. Sorry, Daff."

Indio looked apologetically at the dog. Not that there was any need. Daffodil wasn't paying her master any mind. She sat nearly under Caliban's chair. Apparently her tiny little brain had decided that Caliban was the God of All Fallen Food.

"Hmm," Lily murmured. "I trust that won't happen again?"

"No, Mama," Indio said, ducking his head.

"Indio."

He raised his head, looking at her pleadingly from his beautiful eyes.

She hardened her heart. "I mean it. I don't want you near that pond again—with or without Daffodil." She inhaled and said more softly, "Think what might've happened had Caliban not been there to save Daff."

He looked again at the little dog—who had one delicate paw on Caliban's solid thigh—and swallowed. "Yes, Mama. I mean, I won't go there again."

"Good." She blew out a breath. Hard to tell if he'd remember his promise the next time the water sang its siren song to him, but she had to hope. Deliberately she lightened her tone. "What else did you do today? I vow, I haven't seen you since luncheon."

"Me an' Daff comed back for tea. Don't you remember?" Indio had pulled his legs into the chair and was kneeling on it again—a habit that she really ought to stop someday. "You was writing on your—"

He abruptly stopped speaking and cast a guilty glance at the behemoth beside him. Fortunately, Caliban was taking a bite of Maude's excellent dumplings and didn't seem to be paying any attention to their discussion.

"Mmm," Lily murmured, covering for him. "And then what did you do?"

"We went to the old musician's gallery but," he added hastily as her brows began to lower, "we *didn't* go *in*. An' then Daff found a toad."

Lily glanced at the little dog in alarm. Daffodil now had both paws on Caliban's thigh and was giving him a tragically pleading look. She really was terribly spoiled. "She didn't catch it, did she?"

Daffodil routinely found the most disgusting things edible.

"No," Indio said sadly, "It got away. But we *did* catch a cricket. I was going to keep it in a cage as a pet, but Daff swallowed it before I could. I don't know why. She didn't seem to think it tasted very good."

Maude snorted. "That might explain the spewing."

"Not *spewing*," Lily murmured to her, sotto voce.

Maude rolled her eyes. "You prefer *retch*?"

"I prefer not discussing it at the dinner table, but nobody seems to be paying me much mind." Lily turned to Indio. "Now then, I see you've finished your supper. I think it's time for your bath."

"Maa-*ma*," he whined in the disappointed voice every boy used at the notion of cleanliness. "But Caliban isn't done eating."

She smiled tightly. "I'm sure he'll be fine with Maude."

"And you aren't done eating, either," he pointed out earnestly.

"I'll finish the rest of my meal later."

She rose and walked to the small fireplace, where

a kettle had been set long before supper. It was gently steaming now. She caught up a rag and reached for the handle, but another, much bigger, hand got there first.

Lily gave a tiny jump, watching wide-eyed as Caliban picked up the hot kettle as easily as lifting a twig. At least he'd had enough sense to shield his palm from the heat with a rag.

He stood blank-faced until she pulled herself together.

"In here." She stepped gingerly around his bulk and led him into the little bedroom. A tin hip bath was waiting, laid beside the bed on some old cloths. It was already half full of cold water. "You can pour it in there."

He lifted the hem of his shirt to hold the bottom of the kettle and she caught an unsettling flash of his stomach.

Hastily she looked away, her cheeks heating.

"Mama?" Indio stood in the doorway.

"Come in," she said briskly to her son, and then to the man: "Thank you for your help. You can go back to the table."

Without a word he turned and left the tiny room, closing the door behind him.

Indio stuck a finger in the bathwater and swirled it around. "Why d'you talk to Caliban like that?"

Daffodil trotted over and placed her front paws on the rim of the tub to peer in.

"Like what?" Lily asked absently. She rolled up her sleeves and tested the water with an elbow, making sure it was neither too hot nor too cold. The bath was barely more than a shallow basin. She could use it herself by standing or crouching in it, but she missed the bigger copper half-bath they'd had to sell.

"Like he can't understand," Indio said.

"Start undressing," she reminded him.

Indio sighed heavily. "He *can*."

She placed her hands on her hips and raised an eyebrow.

"Caliban's smart," Indio insisted, his voice only slightly muffled by the shirt over his head. He pulled it all the way off, making his hair stand on end, and looked at her.

She bit her lip. "How do you know?"

Indio shrugged and sat on the floor to push off his stockings. "I just do."

She frowned, thinking. Caliban had presented himself as dull-witted the first time she'd seen him. Was it a ruse? And if so, whyever would...?

"*Ma*ma," her son said with all the exasperated patience of a seven-year-old. He'd somehow taken off everything but his smalls while she was woolgathering.

"Yes, dear."

"I'm old enough to bathe myself."

That was actually debatable, since though Indio *could* wash the more obvious parts of himself—such as his feet—he had the tendency to forget anything *else*, such as his neck, face, knees, and elbows.

But she sighed and gave him a kiss on the cheek. "I'll check back in a bit, then, shall I?"

"Yes, please," he said, scrambling out of his smalls.

Daffodil immediately attacked them as Indio got in the bath.

Lily opened the door. "Maude, would you—"

She cut herself off. Maude was nowhere in sight, but Caliban was across the room, holding a page of her play to the light of the fire. His eyes were intent, his brow slightly creased—and he was quite obviously *reading* the page.

Quietly she closed the door behind her and folded her arms on her chest as her heart began to beat faster.

She lifted one eyebrow. "Who are you?"

Chapter Four

*Nine months later the queen was brought to bed with
the king's firstborn. But the child was horribly deformed,
with the head, shoulders, and tail of a bull, and
the remainder of his body human, the skin overall as
black as ebony. When the queen looked between
her bloodied thighs at the monster she'd birthed,
she fell insensible, never to fully recover her wits
thereafter...*
—From *The Minotaur*

Apollo turned slowly and stared blankly at Miss Stump.
He'd been so enthralled by the wit of the play—a play he
suspected she'd written—that he hadn't heard the door
open until it was too late. Perhaps if he made no reaction
to her words...

She huffed and crossed her arms. "*I'm* not an idiot,
you know. If you're reading *that*"—she tilted her chin at
the sheet of paper still in his hands—"you're no half-wit.
Who are you and why have you been pretending to be
mute and a fool?"

Well, it'd been a last-ditch effort anyway—and not a
very good one. He let the paper drop to the small side table

and crossed his own arms, looking back at her. Whatever she might think, he really *couldn't* talk.

She frowned—rather ferociously for such a small thing. "*Tell* me. Are you in hiding from creditors or the like? What's your name?"

That was perilously close to the truth. Best to divert her before her imagination ran wild. He sighed and uncrossed his arms to draw out his notebook. He flipped to a blank page and wrote, *I can't speak.*

He handed the notebook to her.

She glanced at it and snorted. "Truly?"

He nodded once and held out his hand for the notebook. She gave it to him. "Then tell me your name at least."

He wrote again and showed her the notebook. *Caliban will do.*

She studied his writing, her brows knit. "You really can't speak?" She looked up. Her voice was softer now, more curious. She handed him back the notebook.

He shook his head as he wrote. *I mean you and yours no harm.*

When he glanced up again, she was watching him intently, and for a moment he stilled. Her lichen-green eyes reflected the candlelight, the light flickering deep within their depths, and it struck him suddenly and without warning how beautiful she was. Not in the common way, with soft cheeks and rounded mouth, but with a sharp little chin and intelligence that fairly radiated out of those light-green eyes.

If only this were another life—one in which he might impress her with his title or his own verbal wit.

He blinked and looked down at the notebook in his hand. The page had wrinkled beneath the clench of his fingers. He was in hiding, his title of no consequence under the circumstances, and *he couldn't speak*.

She'd tilted her head to read the notebook, seemingly unaware of his thoughts, and for a moment she was very close to him.

He inhaled the scent of her hair: orange and clove.

She glanced up and took a step back, suddenly wary. "You still haven't said *why* you're here."

He sighed. *Indio was correct: I'm a gardener.*

She took the notebook to read his writing; then, before he thought to stop her, she was flipping back through the pages.

"You're more than a simple gardener, aren't you?" She sank into the old settee, seemingly not noticing how the thing rocked unsteadily beneath her.

Apollo wasn't going to risk the fragile piece of furniture beneath his weight. He crossed to the round table and brought back one of the chairs. She was examining his sketch of the pond with the bridge in the background when he returned. He placed the chair across from her and sat.

She turned the page slowly, tracing her fingers over the next sketch: a study of an ornamental waterfall. "These are lovely. Will the garden really look like this when you've finished with it?"

He waited until she glanced at him, then nodded.

Her brows knit as she turned another page. The next one showed a wide, craggy oak at the foot of the bridge. "I don't understand. Where did Mr. Harte find you? I think I would've known if there were a mute gardener of your talents in London."

There was no way to answer that without giving himself away. She waited a beat and then turned the page again. The drawing here caught her eye, and she pivoted the notebook, examining the sketch. "What is it?"

Parallel lines took up both pages across the open notebook, some intersecting, some leading nowhere. A few of the lines were wavy. Here and there a circle or square sat in spaces between the lines.

He leaned closer, inhaling orange and clove, and wrote along one side of the page, next to the sketch, *A maze.*

"Oh! Oh, I see." She cocked her head, examining the diagram. "But what are these?" She pointed to a square and then a circle.

Follies—places for lovers to sit or amusements like the waterfall. Things to gaze upon and amaze the viewer.

"And these?" She traced the wavy lines.

He inhaled quickly, excited that she was interested, frustrated that he couldn't just *tell* her.

Quickly he reached over and flipped through the pages of the notebook still in her hands. He found a blank one and ripped it out, then turned back to his diagram of the maze. He wrote swiftly on his knee, the pencil nearly poking through the paper in several places. *The wavy lines are the parts of the hedge that I can salvage from the fire. The plants that are still living.*

He showed her his words, waited while she read, her brows knit, and when she looked up, snatched the paper back before she could say anything.

The solid lines will be new plantings. The maze will be the centerpiece of the new garden. The pond on one side, the theater on another, so that from the theater one will look across the maze to the pond. There may be viewing places in the theater itself so that visitors may see the maze and those within it. It will be—

The pencil finally broke through the paper at this point. He balled his fist, frustrated, the words bottled up inside him.

Slim fingers covered his fist, cool and comforting.

He looked up.

"Beautiful," she said. "It will be beautiful."

His breath seemed to stop in his lungs. Her eyes were so big, so earnest, so completely captivated by his trifling drawings, his esoteric work. So few were interested in what he did—even Asa began to fidget after only minutes if Apollo tried to explain his plans for the garden.

Yet this gamine woman looked at him as if he were a sorcerer.

He wondered if she had any idea how seductive her very interest was.

She blinked and drew back as if conscious that she'd let too much show. "And amazing. And wonderful. I'll look forward to wandering your maze, though I'm sure I'll never figure it out—I'm terrible at puzzles. I'll need to bring a guide, I think. Perhaps—"

The outer door opened at that point and Miss Stump jumped up from the settee. "Oh, Maude, wherever have you been?"

"Down to the dock to get those eels the wherryman promised me." Maude set a basket—presumably containing the aforementioned eels—on the table. "Missed me, did you?" Her brows rose as she glanced at the notebook Apollo had reclaimed. "What's that?"

Miss Stump sent him an ironic glance. "Caliban isn't nearly as foolish as he was making us believe."

"Then he can talk?"

Both women looked at him and Apollo could feel the heat burn his neck.

"No, he can't." Miss Stump cleared her throat. "Indio's in his bath. I'd better see if he's remembered to wash his ears—or if he's flooded the floor again."

She hurried into the back room.

Maude began unpacking her eels. "Brought back some water from the river to wash the dishes. It's by the door, if'n you want to bring it in."

Apollo pocketed his notebook and went to fetch the water. Had he known that they needed it, he'd have offered to go down to the river.

He set the bucket of water by the fireplace to warm, conscious that the old woman was watching him.

When he turned she pinned him with a gimlet gaze. "You've got a tongue and my Lily says as how you're not stupid, so you mind telling me why you can't speak?"

He opened his mouth—even after nine months it was an automatic reaction. After all, he'd spent eight and twenty years opening his mouth and having speech emerge—without thought or effort. Such a simple thing. A mundane, everyday thing, speech, the thing that set men apart from the animals.

Lost—perhaps forever—to him now.

So he opened his mouth and then didn't know what to do, for he'd tried before, tried for days and weeks, and all that had occurred was a damnably sore throat. He thought of that day, of the boot shoved into his neck, of the Bedlam guard leering down at him as he threatened hell, and he could actually feel his throat closing, cutting off hope and humanity and the power of *speech*.

"Maude!" Miss Stump was there now and he had

no idea what she saw on his face, but she was frowning fiercely—at the maidservant. "Stop badgering him, please. He can't talk. Perhaps it doesn't really matter why."

It might make him a weakling, but he took her defense gratefully. A part of him railed against his own cowardliness. A man—even a man without the power of speech—shouldn't hide behind a woman's skirts. Apollo ducked his head, avoiding both women's gazes as he strode to the door. This had been a mistake—he'd known it from the first. He should never have given in to the temptation to come here. To try to associate with other folk as if he were a normal man still.

A small, damp hand caught Apollo as he made for the door, and such was his disquiet, he nearly pulled away.

But he remembered in time and stopped.

Indio looked up at him, his hair in wet spirals, dripping onto his nightshirt. The boy had his brows drawn together, but underneath his stern expression there was hurt. "Are you leaving?

Apollo nodded.

"Oh." Indio let go of Apollo's hand and chewed his bottom lip. "Are you coming back? Daff wants you to."

Since Daffodil was presently asleep on the hearth, this seemed extremely unlikely.

Apollo frowned, not knowing how to reply. He shouldn't return. It was a danger to himself—and not only in the sense that his identity might be discovered.

"Please do." Miss Stump's voice was quiet, but when he glanced at her, her expression was firm.

He held her green gaze a moment more and then looked back at the boy and nodded.

The reaction was immediate and overwhelming. Indio's

face was taken over by his grin and the boy surged forward as if about to hug him. Only at the last minute did he pull himself back and hold out a hand instead.

Apollo's palm engulfed the boy's but he shook Indio's hand as if he were a duke in velvet instead of a seven-year-old in damp linen, with bare feet.

He wished he could say something, but in the end all he did was nod again and walk out the door.

Still, he heard the old maidservant as she spoke to Miss Stump: "You're a fool."

THE PROBLEM WITH writing witty dialogue, Lily thought bitterly the next afternoon, was that ideally one should actually *be* witty in order to *write* wittily.

At the moment Lily felt about as witty as Daffodil—who was chasing a fly. As Lily watched, the little dog jumped on the old settee and snapped at the fly, missed—*again*—and nearly toppled off the back.

Lily groaned and laid her head in her folded arms. It was a sad thing indeed when one felt as intelligent as Daffodil.

"Uncle Edwin!" Indio had for once stayed close to the theater and his shout of ecstasy could be clearly heard through the door.

Lily hastily tidied her writing table, straightening the papers and picking up a quill that had fallen to the floor.

A second later the door to the theater burst open and Edwin Stump ducked inside, a wrapped parcel under his arm. He didn't duck because he was so very big—he stood but a few inches taller than Lily herself—but because he was carrying his nephew on his shoulders.

Maude trailed behind with the remains of their washing in a basket. The maidservant glared sourly at Edwin.

"Oof!" Edwin exclaimed as he tumbled Indio onto the settee and set his package by it. Daffodil immediately leaped on the boy, licking his giggling face. Edwin turned to Lily, his hand pressed dramatically to the small of his back. "I think he's put on a stone or more since I last saw him."

"Mayhap you should visit more often," Lily said, rising. She crossed to hug her brother and then stood back to examine his face.

Edwin Stump was eight years her senior, and looked nothing like her. This was probably the result of their having different fathers. Mother had been in her heyday as a leading actress when she'd started increasing with Edwin. He was the result of a happy liaison with the younger son of an earl. Eight years later, gin and happenstance had taken their toll on Lizzy Stump. By that time her beauty had been ravaged by drink and disappointment, the earl's younger son was long gone, and she no longer commanded the lead—or even a secondary role—in plays. As a result Lily had been conceived after a night of drinking with a common porter—a fact her mother was apt to bring up in moments of high emotion.

Edwin had a long, thin face, dominated by black arching brows that stood out like signposts of his temperament in his fair complexion. His smile was a V of merriment with more than a dash of mischievousness, completely impossible to ignore. His black eyes could dance with joyous spirits or glower with ill intent—and they were quick to change. Lily had more than once heard Maude muttering under her breath that Edwin was the Devil's bastard—as much fey as mortal. Lily had to admit that if she believed in such nonsense she'd think Edwin a magical creature herself.

He had, after all, saved her on more than one occasion from her mother's drunken neglect when she was a girl.

"Would you like some tea?" Lily asked.

"Have you anything stronger?" Edwin threw himself on the settee beside Daffodil and Indio.

The settee wobbled ominously and Lily sent it a worried glance. "We have wine," she said reluctantly. Edwin's jaw was unshaven, his bristles in dark contrast to his snowy wig.

"Then pour me a glass, there's a lass." He smiled at her winsomely.

She went to where the bottle stood on the mantel, ignoring Maude's tutting.

"Thank you," Edwin said when he took the glass from her fingers. He swallowed a sip and winced. "Good Lord, that tastes like—"

Lily widened her eyes and looked pointedly at Indio.

"A mud puddle," Edwin finished smoothly.

"Ick," Indio said with interest. "Can I taste it?"

Edwin tapped him on the nose. "Not for another year at the very least."

Lily cleared her throat.

Edwin rounded his eyes at Indio. "Maybe even *two*."

"Bollocks," her son said, making Lily choke in shock. "Indio!"

But Edwin was laughing so hard he was spilling his wine, much to the delight of Daffodil, who was lapping it up off the settee.

"Here now." Thankfully Maude intervened. "Best come outside, Indio, you and Daffodil."

"Aw!"

"I seem to remember…" Edwin looked theatrically about the room. "Ah!" He picked up the parcel he'd earlier left by the settee. "This might be for you, young nephew."

Indio eagerly took the parcel and unwrapped it, revealing a toy wooden boat, cloth sails and all.

Indio looked up, his mismatched eyes shining. "Thank you, Uncle Edwin!"

Her brother waved a hand magnanimously. "Think nothing of it, scamp. No doubt you'll want to try it out in that pond I saw."

"But only with Maude nearby," Lily said hastily.

"Or Caliban?" Indio asked.

Lily hesitated for a moment, but the big man had been exceptionally gentle with her son last night. "Or Caliban," she agreed.

"Huzzah!" Indio rushed from the theater, chased by a barking Daffodil.

Maude gave her a look that promised a talk later on and then followed her charge.

Lily sighed, taking a seat on one of the wooden chairs from the table. "You shouldn't have spent so much on him."

Her brother shrugged carelessly. "It was hardly a king's ransom."

And yet the money could've been better spent on clothes or food. Lily pushed the thought aside. Edwin had never been frugal with his money and a boy needed a treat once in a while as much as clothes and food.

He grinned at her as if he could tell the path of her thoughts. "Who is Caliban? An imaginary friend?"

"No, he's quite real."

"And Caliban is truly his name?" Her brother's eyebrows were high arches of curiosity.

"Well, no—not that we know of, anyway. He's a gardener here. Indio has taken to following him about."

But Caliban was much more than that, Lily realized as she pleated her skirt between her fingertips. She remembered those huge hands, deftly holding his pencil as he impatiently wrote. Those beautifully airy sketches in his notebook. It was laughable, really, that she'd at first taken him for an idiot. It was only the day after his confession and she couldn't think of him as anything but intelligent. *Wonderfully* intelligent.

And for some reason she didn't want to discuss the big, gentle gardener with her sometimes devious brother. She glanced up at him. "Will you sup with us?"

His own look was swift and calculating, but he took her abrupt change of subject meekly enough.

"I'm sorry, no." Edwin got up to pour himself more wine. "I have an appointment I must keep this evening." He took another swallow of the wine and then turned one of his most charming smiles on her. "I came to see how the play is going."

"Terribly." She groaned and slumped in her chair. "I can't think how I ever wrote dialogue before—it's so wooden, Edwin! Perhaps I should burn it and start over."

Usually this was the point at which her brother teased her out of her doubts, but he was oddly silent.

She straightened, looking at him.

He was grimacing into his wineglass. "As to that…"

"What is it?"

He shrugged. "It's nothing really, but I promised to have the play done by next week. I have a buyer who wants to use it for a house party theatrical."

"What?" She gasped, feeling her chest tighten. For a moment she wondered if the house party the play was intended for was the same one she herself was to act at, but then sheer panic swamped the thought. However was she to finish in a *week*?

Edwin grimaced, his mobile mouth stretching into a comical shape. "It's just that I've had a bit of bad luck at cards lately. I need my portion of the play proceeds and this is a quick sale. Apparently the buyer had originally engaged Mimsford to write the play, but the old sod has fled London and his creditors."

They'd made a bargain years ago, when Lily had started writing plays: Edwin would take the plays and sell the works under his name. He was both a man and a much better salesman than she. He knew how to float on the fringes of aristocratic society—something Lily had never wanted to do—and thus had myriad associates. Their arrangement had worked very well in the past. She and Edwin had made a tidy sum together. But now she was at the end of her resources and had begun to wonder if she should try selling her plays herself. Of course that wasn't very fair to Edwin...

She shook her head, trying to think. "Whom do you owe, Edwin?"

"Don't take that tone with me." He stood suddenly and tossed back the rest of the wine in the glass. "It's insulting." He glanced slyly at her. "*And* it reminds me of our dear mother."

That sent a guilty chill down her spine. "But—"

He darted over and knelt in front of her chair, taking her hands. "Darling, it's nothing to worry about, truly. Just finish the play, hmm? Quick as you can." He squeezed her hands and bussed her cheek. "You know you're the best. *Far* better than that hack Mimsford, and he's had two smash hits in a row at the Royal."

"But Edwin," she said helplessly, "what if I can't write that fast?"

She saw his eyes darken before he dropped his gaze. "Then I'll have to find some other means of ready blunt. Perhaps Indio's father—"

"No." It was her turn to squeeze his hands. Her heart had begun to beat in terror against her rib cage. "Promise me you'll not approach him, Edwin."

"You must allow he's very rich—"

"Promise."

"Very well." He made a discontented moue. "But I need to pay my creditors somehow."

"I'll finish the play," she said, dropping his hands.

He looked up at her through his eyelashes. They really were quite long, she thought absently. They almost gave him an innocent demeanor.

Almost.

"By next week." His voice was light, but no less hard for it.

"By next week," she agreed.

"Splendid!" He kissed her again, on both cheeks, and rose to dance across the room, his good humor restored. "Thank you, darling. That's a load off my mind. Now I really must dash. I'll be back next week to pick up the manuscript, shall I?"

And he was out the door before she could say anything.

Lily stared stupidly at the door. However was she to finish her play in a week?

"WHY," ASKED ARTEMIS Batten, the Duchess of Wakefield, "are we hiding in a ruined musician's gallery?"

Apollo grinned fondly at his twin sister. A duchess only five months and she swanned about as if born to the role. She wore some type of dark-green costume with wide lace ruffles at the sleeves that even he could tell was outrageously expensive. Her brown hair was bound up neatly at her nape and her dark-gray eyes were calm and happy—a wonderful improvement over the four years when she used to visit him in Bedlam.

Then her eyes had been filled with sick despair.

He took out his notebook and wrote, *Don't want you to be seen by the other gardeners and Indio.*

She frowned over his words as he dug into the wicker basket she'd brought with her: a new shirt—thank God—some socks and a hat and a smaller, cloth-wrapped parcel filled with lovely food.

After Bedlam, he'd never take any sort of food for granted again.

"Who's Indio?" Artemis asked, quite reasonably, as he bit into an apple.

He held the apple between his teeth—ignoring his sister's wrinkled nose—as he wrote: *Small, very inquisitive boy with a dog, a nursemaid, and a curious mother.*

Her eyebrows shot up as he crunched the apple. "They live here?"

He nodded.

"In the *garden*?" She glanced around at the charred,

crumbling walls of the musician's gallery. In front of the gallery was a row of marble pillars, which had once supported a roof over a covered walkway. The roof had caved in during the fire, leaving only the crumbling pillars. Apollo had plans for those pillars. With a little scouring, and a judicial blow from a mallet here and there, they would become very picturesque ruins. Right now, though, they were just gloomy, blackened fingers against the sky.

He'd commandeered one of the rooms behind the gallery, where once the musicians, dancers, and pantomime players had prepared for their performances. Here he'd propped a big, oiled tarp over one corner to keep out the rain and wind, and brought in a straw mattress and two chairs. Spartan accommodations, certainly, but there were no fleas or bedbugs, which made this heaven compared to Bedlam.

Apollo took back his notebook and scrawled: *They live in the theater. She's an actress—Robin Goodfellow. Harte has given her his permission to stay here for the nonce.*

"You know Robin Goodfellow?" For a second Artemis's ducal dignity fled her and she looked as awed as a small lass given a halfpenny sweet.

Apollo decided he needed to find out more about Miss Stump's acting career. He nodded warily.

Artemis had already recovered her aplomb. "As I remember, Robin Goodfellow is quite young—not more than thirty years, certainly."

He shrugged carelessly, but alas, his sister had known him for a very, *very* long time.

Artemis leaned forward, her interest definitely engaged.

"She must be witty, too, to play all those lovely breeches roles—"

Breeches roles? Those tended to be risqué. Apollo frowned, but his sister was nattering on.

"I saw her in something last spring, here at Harte's Folly with Cousin Penelope. What was it?" She knit her brow, thinking, then shook her head. "I suppose it doesn't matter. Have you talked to her?"

Apollo glanced pointedly at his notebook.

"You know what I mean."

He skirted the truth: *My circumstances don't lend themselves to polite social calls.*

Artemis's mouth crimped. "Don't be silly. You can't continue to hide forever—"

He widened his eyes incredulously at her.

"Well, you *can't*," she insisted. "You must find a way to live your life, Apollo. If that means leaving London, leaving *England*, then so be it. This"—she gestured to the tarp and chairs and straw mattress—"this isn't living. Not truly."

He grabbed the notebook and scribbled furiously. *What would you have me do? I need the money I invested in the garden.*

"Borrow from Wakefield."

He scoffed, turning his head aside. The last thing he wanted was to be in debt to his brother-in-law.

Artemis raised her voice stubbornly. "He'll gladly lend you the money you need. Leave. Travel to the continent or the Colonies. The King's men won't pursue you so far, not if you take another name."

He looked back at her and wrote angrily, *You would have me abandon the name I have?*

"If needs be, yes." She was so brave, his sister, so determined. "I hadn't wanted to mention this before, but I think I might've been followed."

He looked at her in alarm. *Followed here today?*

"No." She shook her head. "But on other days I've come to visit you. Once or twice I thought a man was following me." She grimaced. "Never the same man, mind, so it may be I've entirely made the thing up."

He frowned at her.

"Don't give me that look," she said. "I wasn't sure— I'm still not sure—but don't you see? If I *was* followed, if someone were to discover your hiding place... Apollo, you simply can't stay here. You must leave the garden. Leave England. For your own safety."

He blinked and stared down at his notebook, the paper smudged from his hand. He wrote carefully, *I cannot. I didn't do it, Artemis.*

"I know," she whispered. "*I know.* But you don't have any way of proving it, do you?"

He was silent—which was answer enough, he supposed.

She placed a hand on his arm. "This stubborn refusal to leave England will be the death of you or worse." She leaned forward. "Please. You're kind and smart and... and *wonderful*. You didn't deserve Bedlam and you don't deserve this awful half life. Please don't let—"

He turned his shoulder to her, but that had never stopped his sister when she was on a tear.

"Apollo. Please don't let obsession or... or revenge consume you. A name is important, I know, but it's not nearly as important as *you*. Don't let me lose my brother."

At that he did look up to see—oh, God, no—that her eyes were glittering. That he simply could not stand. He reached out and took her hand in his, the feel of it familiar and calming.

She inhaled. "Just promise me you'll not give up on life."

He pressed his lips together, but nodded firmly.

She smiled tremulously. "Besides, perhaps with this Robin Goodfellow about you'll find something else to find interest in. She's quite pretty, isn't she?"

Pretty wasn't the right word. *Gamine, sly, seductive*... his brain stuttered on the last and for a moment he thought he'd give himself away. How fortuitous that he'd been practicing a dumb face. Apollo used it now on his sister, who retaliated by laughing and flinging an apple at him.

He caught it deftly and wrote, *How is His Grace the Ass?*

She frowned over the notebook as he'd known she would. "You really must stop calling him that. He did, after all, save you from Bedlam."

He snorted and wrote, *And then chained me in his sinister cellar. I'd be there still if you hadn't released me.*

She sniffed. "'Tisn't sinister—especially now that he's using most of it to store wine. *Maximus* is well, thank you for inquiring. He sends his regards."

He gave her a look.

"He does!" She tried to appear convincing, but he merely shook his head at her. Had it not been for Artemis's persuasion—and Wakefield's regard for her—Apollo would still be languishing in Bedlam. Wakefield had certainly not freed him because he thought Apollo sane—or innocent.

Artemis heaved a sigh. "He's not nearly as awful as

you make him out to be—and I love him. For my sake, you ought to take a more charitable disposition toward my husband."

Apollo privately wondered how many times Wakefield had heard the inverse of this little speech, but he nodded at his sister anyway. There really was no point in arguing the matter with her.

Her eyes narrowed for a moment as if she found his capitulation too easy, then she nodded in return. "Good. Someday I'd like you two to be friends, or," she added hastily as he cocked an incredulous eyebrow, "at least *polite* to one another."

He didn't bother replying to that. Instead Apollo rummaged in the bundle of foodstuffs further. There was a big loaf of bread and he brought it out and set it on a piece of wood to slice.

"There's actually another matter I needed to talk to you about," his sister said, her voice unusually hesitant.

Apollo looked up.

She was turning an apple around and around in her fingers. "Maximus heard it from someone—I suspect Craven, because for a valet, he certainly seems to know everything about everyone. It's just a rumor, of course, but I thought I should tell you anyway."

He abandoned the bread and placed a fingertip under her chin to make her look at him.

He cocked his head in question.

"It's the earl," she said, meeting his eyes.

For a moment his mind went blank. *What* earl? Then, naturally, it came to him: the unsmiling old man in a black full-bottomed wig who'd come to see him once— only once—to inform him that as the man's heir he was to be sent away to school. The old man had stunk of vinegar and lavender and he'd had the same eyes as Apollo.

Apollo had loathed him on sight.

He stared into his sister's eyes—thankfully the dark gray of their mother's—and waited.

She took both his hands, giving him strength as she said, "He's dying."

Chapter Five

*The king saw what his wife had birthed and drew back
his arm to kill the monster, but his priest stayed his
hand. "It is rumored that the people of this island once
worshipped a god in the shape of a great black bull. Better,
my liege, to let this thing live than risk offending such an
ancient power."…*
—From *The Minotaur*

Captain James Trevillion glanced at the small brass clock
on the table next to his chair. Four fifteen. Time to return
to his charge. Carefully he placed a lopsided cross-stitch
bookmark between the pages of the book he was reading: *The History of the Long Captivity and Adventures of
Thomas Pellow.* He picked up his two pistols and shoved
them securely into the holsters of the wide leather bando-
liers that crisscrossed his chest. Then he reached for the
cane.

The damnable cane.

It was plain, made of hardwood, with a wide head.
Trevillion leaned heavily on the cane, bracing his crip-
pled right leg as he heaved himself to his feet. He paused
a moment to adjust to standing, ignoring the ache that shot

through the leg. The ache was bone-deep, which made sense, since it was a bone of that leg that'd been broken—not once, but twice, the second time catastrophically.

It was the second break that had cost him his army career in the dragoons. The Duke of Wakefield had offered him another job instead—although Trevillion still wasn't entirely sure if he should be grateful for that offer or not.

He glanced out the window as he waited for the ache in his leg to die down. He could see several gardeners laboring over a crate in the back garden. As he watched, the top was pried off, revealing rows of what looked like sticks packed in straw.

Trevillion raised his brows.

He pivoted gingerly and limped out his door and into a hallway in Wakefield House—the duke's London residence. His room was at the back of the house, at the end of one of the corridors. Not a servant's room, certainly, but not a guest's, either.

Trevillion's mouth quirked. He lived in a strange limbo between.

It took him five excruciating minutes to negotiate the stairs down to the floor below. Just as well that the duke had been so generous with his living situation.

The servants had the topmost fifth floor of Wakefield House.

He could hear feminine laughter now as he laboriously approached the Achilles Salon. Quietly he pushed open the tall, pink-painted doors. Inside, three ladies sat close together, the ruins of a full tea service on the low table before them.

As he began limping toward them, the youngest, a

pretty, plump, brown-haired girl, turned in his direction a full second before the other ladies looked up as well.

He marveled at how Lady Phoebe Batten was always the first to be aware of his presence. She was blind, after all.

"My warder comes for me," she said lightly.

"Phoebe," Lady Hero Reading whispered, chiding. She was the middle Wakefield sibling—younger sister of the duke, elder of Lady Phoebe—but the two women looked nothing alike. Lady Hero was taller than her sister, with a willowy figure and flame-colored hair. No doubt she thought he couldn't hear her undertone, but alas, he could. Not that it mattered. He was fully aware of what his charge thought of him and his duties.

"Won't you have a seat?" the third member of the tea party asked kindly. Her Grace the Duchess of Wakefield, Artemis Batten, was an ordinary-looking woman—excepting her rather fine dark-gray eyes—but she held herself with all the command of a duchess. If one were unaware of her history, one would never guess that she'd served as an impoverished lady's companion to her distant cousin until her marriage to the duke.

A formidable lady indeed.

"Thank you, my lady." Trevillion nodded and chose a chair a discreet distance from the trio. However much she hated it, it was his job to watch over and protect Lady Phoebe. Obviously he wasn't needed when she was with her sister and sister-in-law—or indeed anywhere in Wakefield House—but should she wish to go out after tea, he was bound to accompany her.

Whether she liked it or not.

Lady Hero rose. "I ought to get back to Sebastian anyway. No doubt he's woken from his afternoon nap."

"So soon?" Lady Phoebe pouted, then immediately brightened. "We'll take tea next week at your house—preferably in the nursery."

Lady Hero laughed gently. "I fear taking tea with an infant and a small child in leading strings is a messy business at best."

"Messy or not, Phoebe and I look forward to seeing our nephews," the duchess said.

"Then please come." Lady Hero smiled ruefully. "But don't say I didn't warn you when you leave with mashed peas in your hair."

"A small price to pay to spend time with Sweet William and baby Sebastian," Her Grace murmured. "Come, I'll see you to the door. I'll be leaving shortly anyway."

"You will?" Lady Phoebe's eyebrows drew together. "But you were gone this morning as well—quite mysteriously, too. Where are you off to now?"

It was small, but Trevillion caught it—a slight waver in the duchess's gaze, swiftly corrected before she replied. "Just to visit Mrs. Makepeace at the orphanage. I shan't be long—I'll certainly return by supper, if Maximus ever emerges from his study and wonders where his wife has gone."

"He spends entirely too much time in there. Truly Parliament won't fall apart if he takes one day away." Lady Hero bent to buss her sister on her cheek. "Next week, then? Or shall I see you at the Ombridges' soiree?"

Lady Phoebe sighed heavily. "Maximus says I can't attend. Too crowded, it seems."

Lady Hero darted a glance at the duchess, standing behind Lady Phoebe. The duchess's mouth flattened as she shrugged.

"It's sure to be a terrible bore," Lady Hero said cheerfully. "A crush like that. You wouldn't like it anyway."

Trevillion felt his own mouth tighten as he looked away in irritation. Lady Hero was trying to soften the blow, he knew, but she was going about it in the wrong way. He'd not been serving as Lady Phoebe's bodyguard for long—only since just before Christmas—but in that time he'd come to realize that the girl loved social events. Musicales, balls, afternoon tea parties, anything with people. She lit up when she was at these gatherings. But her elder brother, Maximus Batten, Duke of Wakefield, had decreed that such outings were too dangerous for Lady Phoebe. Thus she went to very few social events outside her family—and those were carefully vetted.

Trevillion shifted, scraping his stick against the floor. Lady Phoebe swiveled her head, looking in his direction.

He cleared his throat. "I believe, my lady, that the rose canes you ordered have arrived. I noticed the gardeners unpacking them. I don't suppose they need your supervision, but if you have an opinion on where they're planted—"

"Why didn't you say so at once?" Lady Phoebe was already moving, her fingertips trailing and tapping lightly along the backs of chairs as she walked. She halted at the door and half turned, not quite looking in his direction. "Well? Do come on, Captain Trevillion."

"My lady." He rose as briskly as he was able and limped toward her.

"Good-bye, dearest." Lady Hero touched her sister's shoulder as she passed by Lady Phoebe on the way out the door. "Try not to be so impatient."

Lady Phoebe merely rolled her eyes.

The duchess tucked her chin as if hiding a smile. "Enjoy your roses."

Then both she and Lady Hero were gone and he was alone with his charge.

She tilted her head, listening as he drew near. "They're in the back garden? How did the canes look?"

"I saw them from my window, my lady," he said as he drew abreast of her. "I couldn't ascertain their condition."

"Hmm." She pivoted and began walking toward the stairs, her fingertips trailing along the wall.

He always felt a twinge of fear when she neared the staircase—it was wide and curving, and made of highly polished marble. But he'd learned after a few brief spats early in his employment that Lady Phoebe did not wish to be helped down the stairs. Indeed, despite his qualms, she'd never so much as faltered on them in his presence.

Still, he watched intently as she began her descent, ready to grab her arm should she waver.

"You're hovering," she said without turning.

"Hovering is my job."

"That's debatable."

"No, actually, it isn't," he said, flatly.

"Humph." They'd reached the ground floor now and she turned to walk toward the back of the house.

He grimaced as he took the last step overly hard on his bad leg.

She didn't turn, but he noticed that she slowed her pace for him.

He limped grimly after.

Outside, a wide, paved terrace ran along the entire back of the house. Beyond was a formal garden, the flower beds mostly dormant at this time of year. There were two gardeners plus the young boy who helped them. All three came to attention as Lady Phoebe appeared.

"M'lady," the eldest, a gnarled specimen of a man, called to give her their direction.

"Givens," Lady Phoebe said. "Never tell me you're planting without me."

"Nay, m'lady," the other gardener replied. He could've been Givens's twenty-years-younger twin, they looked that much alike. In fact, Trevillion suspected that they were in some way related. He made a mental note to find out how.

"We was jus' lookin' over the canes," Givens said.

"And how are they?" Lady Phoebe started forward. The canes had been laid out on the lawn between the flower beds.

Trevillion cursed under his breath and lengthened his stride, his stick thumping on the paving stones. He caught up to her just as she neared the shallow steps that led down to the garden.

"If you don't mind, my lady." He took her arm without waiting for her reply.

"And if I do?" she murmured.

There was not much point in answering that question, so he merely said, "The grass begins here."

She nodded, keeping her head high as he led her toward the gardeners. "A pity that Artemis couldn't stay to help me."

"Yes, my lady." He glanced down at her, eyes narrowing. "Strange that you were unaware of where she went this morning."

She frowned. "I don't know what you mean."

"Don't you?" he asked softly. "I've noticed the duchess often makes mysterious errands."

"Whatever you're implying, Captain Trevillion, I don't think I like it."

He sighed silently as they made the gardeners and she pointedly turned her attention to them and the rose canes.

He watched, leaning heavily on his walking stick, and wondered if she really had no idea. Lady Phoebe was close to her sister-in-law—very close. She must know that the duchess had a twin brother, Apollo Greaves, Lord Kilbourne, who had recently escaped from Bedlam—and was still on the run from the King's men.

Did she know, however, *why* Lord Kilbourne had been committed to Bedlam? Did she know about the bloody triple murder that had been hushed up when the aristocrat was locked away? Perhaps she'd never heard—she was a sheltered lady, after all. Or perhaps she knew and had chosen to forget the four-year-old scandal.

Trevillion found it impossible to forget. Four years ago he'd arrested Lord Kilbourne.

And Kilbourne had been drenched in the blood of his friends.

HE COULD NEVER claim the title if he was wanted for a murder he hadn't committed.

The next day Apollo hacked savagely at a small tree with his curved pruning knife, welcoming the stretch and burn of his muscles. Why should it matter? The title had never been important to him. If anything, it had meant separation from his sister—his family—when he was a schoolboy. Apollo snorted. The earl hadn't cared if his son's family ate or had proper clothes, but by damnation his son's heir—and thus his own—would be expensively educated.

He paused to wipe away the sweat on his brow. There was no logical reason for him to care about the title. Except…

Except that it was one more thing stolen from him because of the murders.

He grunted and had lifted his arm to attack the tree again when he heard it: a gruff voice mumbling.

Apollo raised his head, glancing around. He was on the far side of the pond, in quite a deserted area of the garden. The other gardeners had been set the task of clearing dead trees near the musician's gallery. He'd been half expecting Indio and Daffodil to find him today, but so far they hadn't.

And the voice didn't sound at all like Indio's.

Curious, he stuck the pruning knife into the wide belt at his waist and crept around the tree he'd been assaulting. He and the other gardeners had made some headway on the area of the garden between the pond and the theater, but here, on the far side of the pond, all was still wild chaos. Clumps of burned trees stood here and there, with the remains of hedges trailing throughout. The voice was growing louder as he neared, and appeared to be coming from behind one of the few hedges still growing.

Cautiously he ventured nearer, peering around the remains of a big tree.

"'…Or consider yourself a knave, my lord,'" Miss Stump was muttering to herself in an artificially low voice. She paced before a fallen tree on which a flat board had been laid. On top of the board were paper, a small bottle of ink, and a quill—obviously a makeshift desk.

"Bollocks," she muttered to herself in her own voice.

"*Knave*. Knave. Knave. *Completely* the wrong word. Oh, of course!"

She bent to the paper and scribbled furiously for a few minutes, and then stood. All at once her demeanor changed. Her shoulders squared, she widened her stance, put her fists on her hips, and Lily Stump became a broad-shouldered man. "You'll pay your chits, if you're a gentleman at all, Wastrel."

"Shall I, my lord?" Her voice was still low, but it had a sort of fey quality to it now, her head tipped coquettishly to the side. "Do you judge a gentleman by his *bits*, my lord?"

He realized suddenly that though she was playacting a *man*, she was doing it as a *woman*. No wonder she was known for her acting. She wore none of the trappings of the theater—neither wig nor costume nor paint on her face, and yet as she strutted around her writing log he knew immediately which character she played.

Apollo must've made some sound, for Miss Stump spun, staring in his direction with wide green eyes. "Who's there?"

Damn. He hadn't meant to scare her. Apollo stepped from behind the tree.

"Oh." She glanced around, her brows drawn together. "Is this your place? I can move elsewhere. I didn't mean to disturb your work..."

He'd started shaking his head with her second sentence. She finally seemed to notice, winding down her protests until they trailed away into silence. For a moment they simply stood, staring at each other, alone in this ruined garden. A breeze rattled the thin branches of the bushes and blew a lock of her dark hair across her mouth to catch in the seam of her plush lips. She pushed it behind her ear, her gaze still tangled with his.

He didn't want her to leave, he knew it suddenly. He talked to Artemis, to Makepeace—and to no one else. There *was* no one else—save her, now. She'd found his secret, knew he wasn't just a hulking mute, devoid of brain or soul. And more—she stirred something deep within him, something he'd thought had been beaten out of him in Bedlam.

Carefully he took a step back, hoping she'd understand that he was ceding the ground to her.

"Stop!"

They both started at her voice.

Miss Stump cleared her throat and said in a lower tone, "That is . . . I mean, if you'd like to stay and continue your work, I . . . I don't mind."

He nodded once and turned.

"Wait!" He heard her call from behind him, but there was no point in trying to explain when actions were simpler.

He jogged back to the tree he'd been trying to take down earlier and picked up his shovel and his satchel before returning.

Miss Stump was bent over her papers again, but he made sure to make enough noise that he wouldn't startle her.

"Oh," she said, straightening. "You've come back."

Was that relief in her voice?

His mouth twisted wryly at himself. She was a lauded actress, vivacious, quick, and pretty. Even when he'd been able to speak, most of his feminine company had been bought. He wasn't a comely man. Quite the opposite, in fact.

Yet she seemed happy that he'd returned, and that simple fact made his chest bloom with joy.

He dropped his satchel and took up the shovel, sticking it into the base of one of the dead bushes, striking at the root mass. The blade only went halfway into the soil, so he jumped with both feet on the shoulders of the blade, driving it the rest of the way down. He could feel as the blade sliced through the roots and he grunted with satisfaction. He'd spent part of the previous night sharpening the shovel to do just that. Gingerly he began prying with the handle—too hard a movement and he'd snap it, or worse, the iron blade itself. He'd already lost two shovels this spring.

"You don't mind if I continue?" he heard Miss Stump ask. "It's just that I need to finish writing this soon—*very* soon."

He glanced up curiously at that, wondering at the worried line between her brows as she stared down at her manuscript. Makepeace had said she couldn't get acting work at the moment. Perhaps this was her only means of making money.

He shook his head in reply.

"I'm only in the third act," she said absently. "My heroine has gambled away all her brother's money because, well, she's dressed *as* her brother."

She glanced up in time to catch his raised eyebrows.

"It's a comedy called *A Wastrel Reform'd.*" She shrugged. "A complicated comedy because right now no one knows who anyone is. There's twins—a brother and sister—named Wastrel, and the brother has convinced his sister—her Christian name is Cecily—to pretend to be *him* so that he might seduce Lady Pamela's maid, and he's engaged to her—Lady Pamela, *not* her maid."

She took a breath and Apollo slowly smiled, because against all odds, he'd understood everything she'd just said.

Miss Stump grinned back. "It's silly, I know, but that's what comedy is, really—a lot of silly things happening, one after another." She glanced down at her play, running her finger down the page. "So Cecily, dressed as Adam—that's the brother—has lost terribly at a hand of cards to Lord Pimberly. Oh! That's Fanny—the maid's—father, and Lady Pamela's scorned suitor. Although of course no one knows that Pimberly is Fanny's father, otherwise she wouldn't be a lady's maid, now would she?"

Apollo leaned on his shovel and cocked an eyebrow.

"Kidnapped at birth, naturally," she replied. "But fortunately she has quite a distinctive birthmark. Right here." She tapped the upper slope of her right breast.

Apollo defied any man not to follow the direction of her finger. She had a lovely breast, gently swelling above the severe square neckline of her dress and modestly covered by a filmy fichu.

"Yes, well." Her husky voice made him raise his gaze. Her cheeks had pinkened, but that might've been the wind. "In any case, I'm writing a scene between Cecily and Lord Pimberly in which Pimberly demands his money and Cecily doesn't *have* it. And naturally he's begun to realize he's attracted to her at the same time."

She cleared her throat.

He nodded, messing a bit with his shovel to look as if he were still working. Actually, he was beginning to fear that the blade was stuck in the roots.

Miss Stump glanced at her manuscript and slipped

back into what he now knew was Cecily—the sister dressed as her brother. "Do you judge a gentleman by his *bits*, my lord?"

She turned and placed her fists on her hips again, in the wide-legged stance. "Pardon me, but I said *chits*."

Turn. Her hands dropped. "And yet, 'tis still your manly *bits* we discuss." She glanced at him out of the corner of her eye. "No?"

He screwed his mouth to the side and reluctantly shook his head.

"Blast!" she exclaimed under her breath, bending to the paper. She scratched out something and then froze, obviously thinking.

He wasn't even pretending to work anymore.

She gasped and then hunched over her manuscript, scribbling furiously before straightening, a gleam of triumph in her eye.

She tossed her head as Cecily. "Indeed, and would you know a *chit* should you see one?"

Now she was a baffled Pimberly. "Naturally."

"Oh, my lord?" She turned her head and looked over her shoulder through lowered lashes at the imaginary Pimberly, all daring flirtation. "And how is that, may I ask?"

"*How?*"

"*How* does a gentleman of your unsurpassed perception differentiate a *chit* from a *bit*?"

And she batted her eyelashes.

The juxtaposition between the ribaldry of her words and the innocence of her expression was so silly, so utterly enchanting, that Apollo couldn't help it: he threw back his head and laughed.

*   *   *

LILY STUMBLED AT the sound, entirely forgetting both Cecily and pompous Pimberly, forgetting her play and everything else, really, and simply stared.

Caliban was laughing.

Deep and full, a masculine laugh, his shaggy head thrown back, eyes closed in mirth and crinkling at the corners, straight white teeth flashing. He wore a white shirt topped by a brown waistcoat missing two buttons. The sleeves were rolled to just below his elbows, revealing strong brown forearms lightly sprinkled with dark hair. His breeches were grayed black and over his worn shoes he wore stained buff gaiters. A red kerchief was tied loosely at his neck and he'd wrapped a wide leather belt around his waist to hold his pruning knife. She'd seen innumerable laborers in her lifetime, but she'd never really *looked* at them. Now she gazed her fill at Caliban and thought how terribly, *awfully* appealing he was: physically strong, yet able to critique her play, and with a sense of humor to boot. He was so much more than a simple laborer.

But that thought was followed quickly by another: if he could *laugh*, then why could he not *speak*? She felt rather stunned, watching the strong cords of his throat work as he laughed. It made no sense to her, for surely he was using his voice to laugh?

He opened his eyes, his laughter dying, as he met her gaze, and Lily realized that she'd stepped closer to him in her fascination. She stood almost touching him, his heat, his masculinity like a magnet to her. He dipped his head, watching her, traces of his amusement lingering on his face. She couldn't help it: she reached out and touched his face, her fingertips running lightly down his lean cheek, feeling the catch of invisible stubble. He was so hot, so *alive*. She stood on tiptoe, her hand slipping to the back of his neck, beneath the wild tumble of his brown hair, to pull his homely face down to hers. She just wanted to *see*, to capture some of that vitality and find out if it tasted as sharp as it looked.

She was so absorbed, in fact, that the male voice, when it came from behind her, nearly startled her out of her skin.

"I've come to bring you back."

She jumped, whirling to see who had invaded their Eden, but she wasn't as fast as Caliban.

He shoved her to the side—not gently—and charged the stranger. Caliban's head was down, massive shoulders bunched like a bull's. He caught the other man about the middle, his momentum sending both men skidding to the ground, the stranger on the bottom. Caliban growled, slamming his fist at the stranger. But the other man was swift, pulling his head to the side and avoiding what surely might've been a disabling blow.

The stranger was in his prime, dressed all in black, wearing his own dark hair pulled back into a braided queue. A tricorn hat had been knocked from his head and she saw that a walking stick had also fallen to the side.

"Stop!" she cried, but neither man paid her the least mind. "Stop!"

The stranger wrapped one leg over Caliban's, heaving to displace him, but the mute must've outweighed him by a couple stone or more. Caliban, meanwhile, hit the man repeatedly in the side, each blow earning him a grunt of pain from his adversary.

Metal flashed between them, and Caliban reared back, grabbing for something. Oh, dear God, the other man had a pistol! Both men had a hand on it. They strained in ghastly embrace, each trying to turn the barrel to the other's face. The stranger's fist shot out and struck Caliban square in the jaw. His head whipped to the side with the blow, but he didn't let go of the awful pistol. Lily wavered, afraid to venture nearer, afraid to leave the scene. She wanted to help, but couldn't think how. If she tried to strike the other man, she'd merely interfere with Caliban—and any distraction could prove fatal.

A flash and a horrific *bang*.

Lily screamed, half-crouching in reaction, her hands over her ears.

She started forward, afraid she'd see blood—afraid to see Caliban's dynamic face rendered slack by death—but the men were still struggling. Somehow the shot had missed them both.

"Mama?"

Indio's voice was high and scared, his eyes fixed on the men wrestling on the ground. Lily thought her heart would beat right out of her breast. She flew to her son, catching him up in her arms even though she hadn't carried Indio for years. She turned with him clutched to her chest, in time to see the stranger draw a *second* pistol. Caliban grabbed the other man's wrist and glanced up, as if searching for her.

Their eyes met, and she didn't know what he saw in hers, but his face was distorted in a scowl, his visage war-like and grim.

A man like this could kill, she thought, somewhere in the back of her mind where she was still sane. *I should be afraid of a man like this.*

Then he jerked his chin, sharply, and the message was clear: he wanted her and Indio gone.

A better woman might've stayed, might've argued or in some way helped him, but evidently she wasn't that better woman.

Lily turned and fled, stumbling, sobbing, clutching Indio.

And as she did she heard the second shot.

Chapter Six

So the king took the baby and walled him up in
an impenetrable labyrinth at the center of the island.
There the monster lived and grew, unseen by any human.
But on certain nights there could be heard a mournful
lowing such as a bull might make, and on those nights the
people of the island shivered and shuttered
their windows…
—From *The Minotaur*

Trevillion stared up into Kilbourne's bloodied face and knew he was about to die of hubris.

The first pistol shot had missed Kilbourne completely, the second had bloodied his thick skull but hadn't seemed to slow the man down at all. Maybe nothing would. Maybe Kilbourne was like some mindless beast, driven into a killing rage, unfeeling of any pain.

It was pure, stubborn hubris for a cripple to come after a fully capable man—especially a man as large and muscled as Kilbourne. Hubris to announce his presence to his quarry instead of disabling him first.

Hubris to think he was the man he'd been before the accident.

Trevillion continued to struggle, even though he'd discharged both pistols, his leg was screaming, and he had no hope of overpowering Kilbourne. He might be a prideful bastard, but he was a *stubborn* prideful bastard and if this was to be his last hour, then by damn, he'd go down fighting.

Kilbourne's forearm was across his throat, pressing down, stealing the air from his lungs. In the giant's other fist was a hideously curved knife. Trevillion expected to feel the hooked blade sinking into his skull at any moment.

Black spots floated in Trevillion's vision and he wished viciously that he'd drawn both his pistols *before* he'd called to Kilbourne. He'd've at least had the chance to shoot when the big man charged. He'd worried about the woman getting caught by a shot, though...

His leg stopped hurting. That was worrying.

Blackness closed in, narrowing his vision.

Then suddenly light, air, and pain returned.

He rolled, coughing violently as his lungs drew air, his leg spasming torturously. Trevillion threw out his hand, grasping blindly for any sort of weapon. The pistols were already discharged, but if he could at least reach his walking stick, perhaps he could crack it over Kilbourne's head.

He looked up.

Kilbourne was squatting nearby like some hulking native, his hands hanging between his knees, the hooked knife dangling from one. The left side of his face was painted red with blood and he looked a veritable savage.

Except for his eyes. He was simply watching Trevillion struggle—warily, to be sure, but in no way threateningly.

Trevillion narrowed his own eyes, glancing around. "You're expecting someone to come to your aid."

Kilbourne blinked and at last an expression showed in his blank face—sardonic humor. He shook his head.

"What then?" Trevillion had managed to prop himself on his elbows, but with his leg in such pain he wouldn't be standing anytime in the next half hour. "What are you waiting for?"

Was the man a sadist to draw out death so?

Kilbourne shrugged and pushed his knife into his belt, then reached to the side for something, making Trevillion tense.

The other man handed him his stick.

Trevillion glanced incredulously between his walking stick and the murderer before snatching it out of the other's hand. "Why don't you answer me? Can't you talk?"

Again the sardonic half-smile and Kilbourne simply shook his head.

Trevillion stared. He was on his back, unarmed except for a *walking stick*, and pathetically helpless, and Kilbourne had made no move against him.

Worse, he'd *helped* him.

Trevillion cocked his head, the thought arising, simple, organic, and patently true. "You never killed those men, did you?"

APOLLO STARED AT the man on the ground, ignoring the stinging of his scalp. He'd recognized him at once. Captain James Trevillion. He knew the soldier's name now— he'd learned it years ago in Bedlam—but on the morning he'd been arrested, the other man had just been a dragoon in a red coat. The herald to his coming downfall.

Now Trevillion wore unrelieved black, wide belts crisscrossing his chest, the holsters empty. The other man's pistols lay in the dirt. A pity. They were rather fine, decorated with silver repoussé caps on the grips.

This man had wanted to arrest him. To take him back to the hell that was Bedlam. He ought to kill the dragoon—or at the very least render him unable to ever come after him again. He'd known men who would do the same and never think on the matter after.

But Apollo was, for better or for worse, not one of those men. He'd had more than enough violence crammed down his throat in Bedlam. On the whole he preferred more civilized methods of solving dilemmas.

He opened his satchel, took out his notebook, and wrote, *I didn't kill them.*

Trevillion, from his position prone on the ground, craned his neck to read and huffed out a breath. "You certainly looked like you'd killed them that morning—you were covered in blood, clutching the knife, and not in your right mind."

His words were accusatory, but his tone was curious.

Apollo began to feel a small, curling shoot of hope. He shrugged cautiously and wrote, *Drunk.*

Trevillion's right leg seemed to be bothering him, for he was kneading the calf muscle. "I've seen plenty of men after a night of drinking. Most have some kind of method to their madness. You didn't make any sense at all."

Apollo sighed. His scalp stung from the bullet crease, his head hurt, and the blood from the wound was beginning to soak into his shirt. But worse, he could still feel Miss Stump's cool, slim fingers on his cheek. So close, so intimate. The other man had ruined that fragile moment.

She'd looked absolutely terrified when Apollo had warned her away with the boy. He wanted to find her and assure himself that she was safe and unafraid.

That her look of terror had been caused by the situation, not *him*.

Apollo almost rose and left Trevillion lying there in the mud. But the soldier *knew* him and had discovered him—somehow that must be dealt with.

And, too, Trevillion was the first in a very long time to actually listen to his side of events about that morning.

So instead of stomping off he picked up his notebook again and wrote carefully, *I remember sitting down with my friends, remember drinking the first bottle of wine... and nothing after.*

While Trevillion read that, Apollo removed both waistcoat and shirt and wrapped his shirt around his bleeding head like a Turk.

The soldier looked up. "Drugged?"

Apollo tilted his head and shrugged, hopefully conveying, *Probably.* He'd had time to think the matter over in Bedlam—long, long years of regret and speculation. The idea that the wine had been drugged seemed more than obvious after the fact.

He stood and held out his hand to the other man.

Trevillion looked at his hand so long, Apollo nearly withdrew it.

The other man grimaced at last. "I suppose you could've killed me by now anyway."

Apollo cocked an eyebrow at that, but heaved Trevillion up when he took his hand. The soldier's body was stiff. He didn't utter a sound, but it was quite apparent he was in pain.

Trevillion leaned on his cane, but Apollo kept his arm around the other's shoulder—and since the soldier didn't complain, it was evident his help was needed. Apollo guided him the few steps to the fallen tree Miss Stump had used as a writing desk. The soldier gingerly lowered himself, wincing as he did so, his right leg held rigid and straight before him.

Trevillion eyed him as Apollo squatted before him. "Why can't you speak?"

He wrote one word in the notebook. *Bedlam.*

The soldier frowned over that, his fingers tight on the notebook's edges. He looked up, his eyes sharp. "If you didn't kill those men, then someone else did—someone who never paid for his murders. I arrested the wrong man. I *condemned* the wrong man."

Apollo simply looked at him, fighting to keep his lip from curling. Four years. Four years of starvation, beatings, and boredom, because some other man had killed his friends. Any regret seemed long past due.

All at once he opened the door and let them in from that black room at the back of his mind:

Hugh Maubry.

Joseph Tate.

William Smithers.

Maubry, with his intestines spilling on the tavern's sawdust floor. Tate entirely intact, save for a wound high on his chest and three missing fingers. Smithers, his boyish face surprised, eyes open, throat cut.

He hadn't known them particularly well. Maubry and Tate had been at school with him, Smithers had been some distant relation of Tate's. They'd been jolly fellows, good for a night of drinking—before he'd woken to a nightmare.

Apollo blinked, pushing back the images, the terrible memories, and looked at Trevillion.

The soldier stared back, his spine straight, his expression grim and resolute. "This is an injustice that must be righted—that *I* must right. I'm going to help you find the real murderer."

Apollo grinned—though not in mirth. He took up his pencil and wrote, his words so angry that the point gouged the paper in places: *How? I was in Bedlam four years and in that time no one doubted my guilt. You yourself thought me guilty when you attacked me just now. Where will you find the man or men who actually did the crime?*

Trevillion read that and said drily, "In point of fact, *you* attacked *me*."

Apollo snorted and waved aside the other's reply. *Besides, won't your superiors resent your time spent away from the dragoons?*

The other man's face went blank. "I am no longer a dragoon."

Apollo stared at that. Even in his unrelieved black, Trevillion looked every inch the dragoon captain. He glanced at the leg and wondered when the injury had happened. In his hazy memory of that awful morning, he didn't recollect the other man's being so badly lamed. He had a feeling, though, that any questions would not be welcome.

Instead he wrote, *My point remains: how do you expect to find the murderer after so long?*

The former soldier looked at him. "You must have some idea, some suspicion, about who could've killed your friends?"

Apollo's eyes narrowed. He had, in fact, spent hours—days—meditating on this very subject. He wrote cautiously, *Our purses were taken.*

"A large amount?"

Apollo twisted his mouth. *Not on my part—I'd already paid for the room and wine. I doubt the others had more than a guinea or two between them. Tate had a rather fine gold watch, though—his late father's. That was stolen.*

"Not a large haul for three men dead," Trevillion said softly.

Men have been killed for less.

"True," the soldier replied, "but not usually so methodically." He stared for a moment at nothing, absently rubbing his calf. Then his gaze sharpened. "Who were they, the men who were killed? I was told at the time, but I've forgotten since."

Apollo listed the names.

Trevillion pursed his lips over the notebook. "How well did you know them?"

They were men I liked, men I drank with, but I was not especially close to any of them. Smithers I had only met that night.

And yet his boyish face was now imprinted on Apollo's mind forever.

"Were they rich? Had they enemies?"

Apollo shrugged. *Maubry was the third son of a baron and doomed to the church. Tate was his uncle's heir, I believe, and would've come into a comfortable sum—or so the rumors went at school. Whether they were correct or not, I cannot say. Smithers seemed to have no blunt at all, but he was dressed well enough, certainly. As to enemies, I do not know.*

Trevillion read carefully before looking up, his eyes intent. "Had *you* enemies?"

He wrote with a wry twist to his mouth, *Until that night I would have said no.*

Trevillion glanced at his words and nodded sharply. "Very well, then. I shall investigate the matter and return when I can to consult with you."

The man got laboriously to his feet. Apollo moved to help him once and was met with a furious scowl.

He didn't again.

When Trevillion was at last upright, his face was reddened and shone with sweat.

"Be careful, my lord," the former soldier said, for the first time giving him the courtesy of his title. "If I could find you, others might do so as well."

Apollo glared at him. *How did you find me?*

"I followed your sister," Trevillion said drily. "Her Grace is very discreet, very circumspect, but I noticed that she made regular errands. None at Wakefield House knew—or at least would *admit* to knowing—where she was going. I decided to follow her secretly, though it was some time before my employment would allow the opportunity. Today is my day off."

Apollo raised his eyebrows. The former dragoon knew an awful lot about Wakefield House and its inhabitants. He wrote hastily, *How are you employed?*

"I guard Lady Phoebe," the other man said simply.

He bent and, one at a time, picked up his pistols and placed them once more in the holsters on his chest. *If his bearing weren't so military, he'd look like a pirate*, Apollo thought in some amusement.

"Good day, my lord." Trevillion nodded his head.

"Please do heed my warning. Should the King's men find you before I can prove your innocence, I think you know well what would happen."

He did: death. Or worse, Bedlam.

Apollo nodded stiffly in return.

He watched Trevillion make his way slowly down the path toward the Thames and then picked up his satchel, stowed his notebook, and turned in the opposite direction.

He was feeling light-headed now with an unpleasant tinge of nausea, no doubt the result of his head wound, but he simply couldn't wait to discover if Miss Stump was all right.

Apollo picked up his pace, breaking into a jog along the path, trying to ignore how his movements worsened his headache. She'd looked at him with such wonder before, as if he might be something special, almost lovely. No one had ever looked at him in such a way, especially no woman.

When he burst into the theater at last, the first thing he saw was Miss Stump and the maid, Maude, bent over Indio. The boy was eating a biscuit smeared liberally with jam and seemed quite all right.

The second thing he saw was Miss Stump's look as she straightened and turned to him.

Stark fear.

CALIBAN CAME CRASHING through the theater door and Lily thought, *Thank God*—for he was at least alive—followed very quickly by *Dear God*, for his face was streaked with gore and his head was wrapped in a bloody rag. Also, and this was of course not *nearly* as important as the fact that he was *hurt*, he'd somehow lost his shirt again, and his bare, muscled chest was rather distracting.

"Remember Kitty," Maude hissed like some dolorous chorus at her shoulder, and Lily felt a very strong urge to slap her beloved nurse.

"Heat some water," she snapped instead to the older woman.

Maude muttered to herself, but turned to the hearth.

"What's wrong?" Indio said at the same time. "Why is Caliban all over blood? Did he kill that other man?"

He sounded elated rather than frightened, and Lily could only stare in horror at her son.

Caliban came closer, bloodied head and distracting chest and all, and knelt at Indio's feet. He shook his head and took out his notebook from a battered cloth bag. *It was a misunderstanding between friends.*

Lily read the notebook aloud and stared at him incredulously. Not even Daffodil was naïve enough to believe *that* explanation.

The mute swayed where he was squatting and she rushed forward to take his upper arm—his very *hard* upper arm—and help him into a chair. If he fainted on the floor, he'd have to lie there, for there was no way she and Maude could lift him.

"Is he gone?" she asked urgently. "That other man?"

Caliban nodded wearily.

She leaned closer and whispered, "Is he dead?"

His mouth twisted wryly at that, but he shook his head slowly. His eyes were beginning to droop and his skin, usually a lovely golden color, was going gray.

She hurried to the mantel and snatched down their one bottle of awful wine. In the state he was in, he was unlikely to notice the quality—and in any case it was for medicinal purposes at the moment.

She poured him a glassful and pressed it into his hands. "Drink this." She glanced over her shoulder. "Maude, the water?"

"'Tis only God can make water boil faster," the maid muttered sourly.

"He's hurt, Maude," Lily chided and got to her feet. "Don't move," she said sternly to Caliban, for she wouldn't put it past him to try to stand.

She crossed swiftly to her room. She had an old chemise tucked away and she scooped it up and brought it back into the main room.

Indio was now off his chair and peering into Caliban's face while Daffodil licked the boy's sticky fingers.

"Indio, don't crowd him," she said gently, and unwrapped the rag from Caliban's head.

She had to lean close to do so and she could feel the heat radiating off him, smell his male musk. Her arm accidentally brushed his shoulder and that little contact made her shiver.

He sat docilely, letting her do as she would. The rag turned out to be the remains of his shirt, now entirely ruined, and she wondered if he had another. Maybe he'd have to go naked from the waist up, except for his waistcoat, as he labored about the garden. That would be a distracting sight: his huge arms flexing as he wielded a shovel or his savage hooked knife. She fancied she could charge ladies a shilling to come sit by the theater and sip tea as they watched him work—and wasn't that a silly idea?

Frowning to bring her wayward thoughts under control, she carefully pried the last of the shirt from his head. The blood had begun to dry, sticking the material to his hair and scalp. She winced as fresh scarlet stained the tawny strands.

"An' here's the water," Maude said, bringing over the steaming kettle and setting it on a cloth on the floor. She bent to peer at Caliban's head as Lily began delicately washing the clotted blood from his hair. A seeping furrow appeared, about three inches long, running along the top of his head, slightly right of center.

Maude grunted and straightened. "Creased from a bullet, he is."

She went to the corner where she kept her trunk.

"Cor!" Indio exclaimed, and for once Lily didn't correct his common expression.

She frowned over the bleeding wound. "Shall we have to stitch it closed?" she called to Maude.

"Nay, hinney. Not much point since it's so shallow." The maidservant returned with a rag. "Pour a bit of wine over this and press it to the wound."

Lily raised her eyebrows doubtfully, but did as she was told.

As soon as the cloth met his head, Caliban's eyes widened and he grunted in pain.

"It hurts him!" Lily took away the rag.

"Aye, but the wine'll help it heal, too." Maude put her hand over Lily's and pressed the rag back. "Now hold it there." She carefully poured a little more of the wine onto Caliban's scalp, ignoring his wince.

Indio, watching closely from the side, giggled. "He looks silly. Now his hair is red and brown and black."

Caliban's mouth lifted in a wan smile.

Lily frowned, concerned. "How do you know about such things, Maude?"

"Been around theater folk a long, long time," the maid replied. "A right quarrelsome bunch, they are. Patched up more'n my fair share of young men after an argument got out of hand."

Indio seemed deeply interested in this bit of information. "Has Uncle Edwin ever been shot in the head?"

"'Fraid not, lad. Your uncle is good at wriggling out of such things—likes to keep his skin whole, he does." Maude tapped Lily's hand to get her to lift the cloth, and inspected the still-bleeding wound. She nodded her head. "We'll use your old chemise to wrap this, hinney."

They tore the chemise up and while Lily held a folded pad over the wound, Maude wrapped strips around Caliban's head to hold it in place. By the time they were done, he looked as if he'd been shrouded for burial and Indio was in fits of laughter.

"He looks like an old man with a toothache!"

Daffodil yipped and jumped up to nip at her giggling young master, and even Maude broke into a reluctant smile.

The maid hastily repressed it, though. "I'll have you know, young Indio, that this here is the finest of nursing work."

"Yes, Maude," Indio said, more soberly. "Will he be all right?"

"O' course, lad," Maude said stoutly. "Best your mother helps him to her bed, though, because he looks like he could do with a nice long sleep." Her voice softened just a fraction. "Poor man probably hasn't a decent

bed to sleep on, wherever he takes his rest. Come, you an'
I will start the supper."

Indio leaped at that, always eager to be allowed to help
in grown-up endeavors, and both maid and boy went to
the fireplace, trailed by a curious Daffodil.

Lily looked into Caliban's face. He had his eyes closed
and was listing slightly in his chair. "Can you walk to
the bed?"

He nodded and opened his eyes. They were duller than
she was used to now. It reminded her uncomfortably of
the time when she'd thought him mentally incompetent.
How strange that idea seemed now.

"Can you stand?" she asked softly.

He answered by rising like a drunken behemoth and
she hastily dipped a shoulder to bring it under his arm.
It wasn't that she could physically hold him up—he was
much too big—but she helped guide him as he stumbled
unsteadily toward her little bedroom.

Inside was her bed—a narrow, pathetic thing—and she
helped him climb in, drawing the coverlet over his chest.
He looked as if he lay in a child's cot. His feet hung off
the end and one arm dangled almost to the ground from
the side.

Caliban seemed comfortable enough—his eyes already
shut. Was he asleep? She bent over him, whispering
urgently, "Caliban."

He opened his eyes, and though the color hadn't
changed from ordinary brown, they were somehow more
dear to her now.

"Who was that man?" she asked. "Why did he attack
you?"

He shook his head and closed his eyes again. If he was

feigning sleep, he was better than many actors Lily had known.

She blew out a frustrated breath and went around to the foot of the bed. His gaiters and shoes were quite muddy and she wrinkled her nose in disgust, but got gamely to work. She unlaced his gaiters and then unbuckled his shoes, marveling at their size before setting them neatly beneath the bed. Then she found another blanket and pulled it over his upper half, for the one on the bed didn't come close to his shoulders.

With a last look, Lily shut the bedroom door and went out into the main room.

Maude and Indio were by the hearth as Maude supervised the boy in stirring something in a bubbling pot.

She cast a look over her shoulder at Lily's entrance. "There's tea on the table, hinney. Take a seat and have a cup, but first you'll want to scrub your hands. Go on, then."

Lily nodded wearily and crossed to the outside door. It was oddly comforting to have Maude instructing her as the older woman had when she was a little girl. As Lily herself did now with Indio.

Outside, the sky had begun to gray and Lily blinked at the passage of time. She'd been so fearful for Indio, then so concerned about tending to Caliban, that she hadn't noticed.

She went to the barrel of water they kept beside the door, removing the wooden cover and dipping out some water with which to scrub the blood and mud from her hands. She watched the pinkish water run into the dirt at her feet, making little runnels, and remembered another time she'd scrubbed blood from her hands. Kitty's dear face had been so swollen she couldn't open her eyes, her mouth turned into an obscene, bloodied mass.

All because of a big, violent man.

Lily watched the last of the water run off and recalled Maude's words—*Remember Kitty*—and wondered if she was making a very foolish—and perhaps fatal—mistake.

Chapter Seven

*The king sat in his golden castle and brooded. He
fathered no more children, and as he aged he
grew bitter that others might have lovely offspring
but he, the ruler of the island, had sired only a monster.
So he made an awful commandment: every year the
people must send into the labyrinth the most beautiful
youth and the most beautiful maiden on the island
as sacrifice to his terrible son...*
—From *The Minotaur*

Apollo woke in the dark the next morning to two immediate realizations: one, he was in a bed—a real bed—for the first time since before Bedlam, and two, he hadn't written and set out the day's instructions for the gardeners. He groaned silently at the last thought. The fellows Asa had hired were a competent enough lot, but with no instruction they had a tendency to mill around without doing any useful work.

But the bed—the lovely, lovely bed—made it hard to feel put out by the matter. The bed wasn't big, but it was soft and clean with a proper mattress—*not* stuffed with scratchy straw—and it was comfortable. He was tempted to go back to sleep.

Except the thought hit him of *whose* bed he must be in: Miss Stump's.

He sat up, jostling his head, which promptly began to complain about the matter. The room was dark—it had no windows—but he knew from the internal clock his body had kept since he was a boy that it was morning, probably six or seven of the clock.

Where was Miss Stump?

Cautiously he lowered his foot to the floor and only then realized he was missing both shoes and gaiters. His brows shot up. Had elegant Miss Stump removed them? It took a few minutes of feeling about, but he eventually discovered his shoes under the bed and donned them.

He felt his way to the door and cracked it.

Immediately he was set upon by Daffodil, who appeared to be the only one of the household awake. She spun at his feet, yipping excitedly.

Apollo bent and picked up the little dog to keep her from waking everyone.

When he straightened he saw Indio, sitting up from a nest of blankets on the floor. He and his mother appeared to be bedded down together, while Maude was in the cot. Both women still slept.

Apollo had only a moment to sneak a glimpse of Miss Stump's mahogany hair, down and spread like a silken skein over her pillow, before the boy yawned and rose. "Daff says she has to go out an' so do I."

Apollo looked with alarm at the wriggling dog in his arms.

The boy had worn his shirt to sleep in. He donned a pair of breeches and trotted over.

Apollo opened the outer door.

Outside, the morning had dawned sunny and glorious. He set Daffodil on the ground and she immediately squatted.

Indio was making his way around the back of the theater and Apollo followed him. The boy stopped at one of the few trees still living—a great gnarled oak—and began fumbling with the fall of his breeches.

He glanced up, grinning, as Apollo halted beside him. "I like to try an' hit that knot." He nodded at a knot in the tree, about three feet off the ground.

Apollo smirked back and unbuttoned his own breeches.

The two streams of urine hit the knot and steamed impressively against the morning cold of the tree trunk, Apollo's lasting a bit longer than the boy's.

"Cor!" Indio said as he shook off his little prick and began righting himself. "You're dead good at that. Took me days to hit it the first time."

Apollo tried not to let the compliment go to his head. Precision pissing was, after all, a sadly underrated skill among most of society.

"Indio!"

Miss Stump's call echoed through the garden.

Indio's eyes widened. "That's my mama. She'll be wanting us to come in for breakfast."

Apollo followed the boy back around the theater to find Miss Stump standing in the doorway, her arms crossed over a wrap.

She raised a hand to her unbound hair when she caught sight of him. "Oh, Caliban. I didn't know you were up yet. Good morning."

He nodded, watching as she pushed her hair behind her ears. The sad female creatures of Bedlam had often had their hair down, but theirs had been dirty and tangled, the result of unsound minds no longer caring about their toilet.

Miss Stump's unbound hair was an intimate sight— a sight such as a lover or husband might be privy to. It shone, waist-length, heavy, and straight, and he fought the urge to take it between his fingers to test its weight and feel the silky texture.

Perhaps some of his desire revealed itself on his face because she stepped back into the theater, glancing nervously at him from the corners of her eyes. "Have you washed, Indio?"

"Nooo." Indio drew out the reluctant syllable.

Apollo tapped him on the shoulder and nodded at the water barrel. No doubt he could do with a bath as well.

Miss Stump disappeared for a moment and then returned with several cloths. The boy stripped off his shirt, shivering in the morning air, his arms wrapped over his skinny chest.

Apollo smiled and uncovered the water barrel to dip a cloth in. He handed it to the boy before wetting his own washcloth. Normally he'd simply have sluiced himself with the water dipper, but he had a feeling Miss Stump would not appreciate his undoing all her hard work in dressing his wound.

So instead he washed his face and neck briskly, then poured fresh water over the cloth and wiped his arms, underarms, and chest. He pivoted as he did so and saw that Miss Stump stood in the doorway to the theater, watching him.

He met her eyes and became conscious for the first time that he was half naked and performing a private act before her. Bedlam had stripped him of modesty. There the cells had never been entirely shut off, never entirely private. The most basic of human activities had, at times, been done before an audience of other inmates or uncaring guards. He might as well have been a horse in a stable—save that most horses were better treated than the patients at Bedlam.

But Miss Stump didn't look at him as if he were an animal. She looked at him as a woman does a man she finds attractive.

Perhaps even arousing.

Her eyelids were half lowered, her cheeks flushed, and as he watched, her pink tongue ran slowly over her bottom lip.

He was aware suddenly of his nipples, pulled exquisitely tight on his chest, of his cock, pumping full of hot blood.

"Am I c-c-clean now, Mama?" Indio's high voice chattered behind him.

"What?" Miss Stump blinked. "Oh! Erm, yes, quite clean, Indio. Come inside before you catch your death of cold."

The boy darted past Apollo, his shirt clutched in his hand, and Daffodil, who had been milling about, sniffing at dead vegetation, barked and happily raced after.

Apollo followed more slowly, watching Miss Stump as he did. She was bustling about the room, settling her son at the table, instructing Maude, and then disappearing abruptly into the bedroom he'd taken last night.

When she reappeared, her hair was dressed—much to his regret—and she bore a thin blanket. "Caliban, would you like this until you can find another shirt?" She held out the blanket and then her brows knit. "You *do* have another shirt, don't you?"

He gave her a sardonic glance that made her blush and then nodded.

"I hope you like tea, because we don't run to coffee," Maude said, and banged a teapot down on the table.

That apparently was the signal to sit for breakfast, and so Apollo did.

The table held bread and butter and a plate of cold sliced meat. There wasn't a lot of anything, and he was reminded of Makepeace's words. Miss Stump was out of work.

Apollo was careful to take only one slice of bread and only a little meat. He knew what it was like to be without food. He'd often been weak with hunger in Bedlam, despite Artemis's heroic attempts to keep him supplied with food. Hunger was an affliction worse than beatings. It made the mind narrow to only that one point: food and when one would next be able to eat. Damnable to reduce a man to the state of a starving dog.

Once he'd been lower than a starving dog, mindless with want.

So he was careful now to eat in slow, moderate bites, as a gentleman should, for he was, beneath everything else, a gentleman.

The tea was weak but hot and he drank two cups of it, watching Miss Stump nibble at her own bread. She caught his eye once and bit her lip, as if hiding a secret smile. All the while Indio chattered about everything from the sparrows he'd seen in the trees the day before to the dead snail Daffodil had attempted to eat the previous week.

But pleasant as the morning meal was, it wasn't long

before Apollo recollected that he must be at work—and to do that, he'd have to fetch his only other shirt from the musician's gallery.

He pulled out his notebook and, turning to a new page, wrote, *Thank you—for the meal, the physicking, and the bed—but I must be off to my labors.*

Miss Stump blushed when she read it and gave it back. "We were glad to help."

Indio, who had been watching the exchange, slumped in his chair. "Aww! Must Caliban go? I wanted to show him my new boat."

"He's a man grown, dearest, and must be about his job. But perhaps"—she cleared her throat, peeking at him beneath her lashes—"we could take Caliban a picnic luncheon?"

"Yes!" Indio was so excited he knelt up on his chair as he turned to Apollo. "Say yes, pleeeease?"

Apollo's lips twitched as he inclined his head.

"Huzzah!" Indio cried, making Daffodil leap and twirl in excitement. "Huzzah!"

"Sit down afore you spill your tea, lad," Maude said gruffly, but even she had a smile upon her face.

Apollo walked out into the garden feeling better than he had in months—even *with* the headache. He could hear chopping coming from somewhere in the garden, so at least *some* work was being done—whether it was the correct work might be another matter. He hurried to the musician's gallery.

It was as he was buttoning his waistcoat—sadly he'd only the one, and that was now stained and slightly damp from lying on the ground all night—that he heard the distinctive sound of Makepeace's voice raised in ire.

Hastily he finished his crude toilet and jogged in the direction of the yelling, which became comprehensible as he got nearer.

"If you think I'll take on some wet-behind-the-ears, overeducated, *dilettante* architect to design and rebuild *my* bloody garden just because you met him at some aristocratic ball in Sweden—"

"Switzerland," drawled an obnoxious, familiar voice.

"Bloody *Switzerland*," Makepeace amended without even taking breath, "than you've lost your blasted ducal mind. This garden is going to be the most wondrous pleasure garden in all of London, which might as well be the *world*, and to do that we need an experienced, *working* architect, not some silly aristocrat who's decided that he'd play with blocks and see if he could build something that wouldn't fall down after three damned *minutes*."

By the time Makepeace had come to the end of his loud and foul objections, Apollo had rounded a corner and caught sight of him.

Makepeace was standing in the middle of the ruined path that led to the dock, hair on end, hands on hips, glowering thunderously at the Duke of Montgomery, who didn't seem to realize the mortal peril he was in.

Indeed, as Apollo came to a stop beside the two men, the duke flicked open a jeweled snuffbox and smiled slyly at him. "Why, Mr. Makepeace, I'm surprised you have such objections to the blood of my architect, considering you're such good friends with Viscount Kilbourne."

Apollo froze. They'd never made mention of his real name or rank in front of Montgomery. The man was supposed to have been out of the country for *years* until last summer. How in hell had he figured out who Apollo was?

His gaze met Makepeace's and he saw equal baffled fury there.

Montgomery sneezed into an enormous lace-edged handkerchief. "Now then, gentlemen," he said after he'd stowed both the snuffbox and the handkerchief in his pocket. "Let us begin this discussion again on a more congenial note, shall we?"

"What do you want, Montgomery?" Makepeace all but growled.

The duke shrugged delicately. "As I've said: to employ an architect of my own selection to design and build the theater and musician's gallery and various other follies I might like in the garden. I shall, naturally, be paying him from my own pocket. Come now, it's not as if you have a choice."

At that, Makepeace *did* growl.

"Fascinating," Montgomery drawled, cocking his head as he watched Makepeace simmer. Apollo wondered if the man had *any* sense of self-preservation. "But I shall take that as agreement."

He turned and strolled leisurely away.

"We can't trust him, 'Pollo," Makepeace said, abruptly and low. "We couldn't trust him before, but now he knows your *name*."

And Apollo couldn't help but agree.

"HE'S JUST A gardener," Maude muttered later that day as she watched Lily dither over the picnic luncheon she was packing. "Well, that's what he told you, anyway."

"Do you think he'd like roast chicken or boiled eggs better?" Lily had spent the morning frantically writing so that she might take a few hours' break in the afternoon, which meant she had only minutes to pack the picnic luncheon. "And he isn't *just* a gardener, he's the head gardener—he's designing the entire pleasure garden, as far as I can tell."

"Hinney, a man as big as that, working hard all day, will eat anything and everything you set in front of him," Maude opined. "If he's the head gardener and such an important man as all that, why is he livin' rough in the garden and wearing such common clothes?"

"I don't know, Maude." Lily put both the eggs and the leftover roast chicken securely in the basket. It was normally used for Maude's knitting and she'd been none too pleased to have her work dumped out on the table so Lily could commandeer the basket. "Perhaps he's down on his luck. Or maybe he likes to stay at the garden he's working on. Or…" But her imagination had run out. There really wasn't an explanation for Caliban's many strange habits.

"And the fact he won't tell you his real name or that he let you think he was stupid when you first met, can you explain that, my girl?"

Lily couldn't, so she just kept her head down and wrapped a half loaf of bread securely.

"You can get any man you want," Maude said. "I've seen them look at you when you're prancing about the stage—and off—from footmen to bejeweled lords, they all fancy you. Why not let one of them take you out?"

"I'm not interested in lords, bejeweled or otherwise," Lily said lightly.

"I'll give you that," Maude said, "but there's plenty o' other men. Why bring a picnic lunch to a great brute you know nothing about?"

Why indeed? Lily's hands stilled as she tried to

explain, both to herself and to Maude. "He's big, but he's gentle."

"He was fighting some stranger just yesterday!"

"I know!" Lily took a breath and said more quietly, "I know." She met her old nursemaid's eyes. "I don't know why Caliban fought that man, but I know he felt he had to."

"Hinney..." Maude's old face seemed to have grown lines.

Lily caught her hands, squeezing gently. "He looks at me in admiration, but not like those other men—as if I'm an object he wants to have, for other men to admire. When he looks at me I think he sees a woman he likes, a woman he wants to talk to. And I want to talk to him, Maude. I want to learn what he thinks about when his lips turn up, and what he sees when he looks at his garden, and what he'll be doing tomorrow and the next day." She stopped because she knew she'd lost any hope of eloquence. "I can't explain it. I only know I want to spend time with him. When I'm with him, the minutes, the *hours*, fly by so fast and I hardly notice."

She blinked and stared helplessly at Maude.

"I don't want you hurt, hinney." Maude's voice softened, turned pleading. "I can't get Kitty's face out of my dreams, I can't. She haunts me at night and I think it's a warning, I do. Remember she was so taken with that man, so sure he would be kind to her."

"He was different," Lily muttered. "He wasn't nearly as nice as Kitty thought and we all knew it, even from the first. We told her not to go with him."

"As I'm telling you not to go with this Caliban fellow," Maude said. "Think, dear one, what do you know of him?

What has he told you of his family, his life outside this here garden?"

"Nothing," Lily said. She didn't want to face it, but it was true: Caliban was hiding who he was. "But Maude, he isn't violent—not to us. You've seen how gentle he's been with Indio."

"And what if that's just a false face?" Maude's voice quavered. "*He* was sweet at first, too. I couldn't bear to lose you, hinney, I just couldn't."

Lily finally looked up to see to her horror that Maude's eyes were misted. Impulsively she hugged the older woman tight and whispered in her ear, "You'll never lose me, Maude, not even if you try."

"Oh, get on with you," Maude said, pulling away as if embarrassed at her own show of emotion. She swiped at her eyes with the corner of her apron. "Just be careful. Promise me."

"I promise," Lily said solemnly as she picked up the basket and left before Maude could make any more arguments.

She found Indio outside kicking at a charred stick, breaking it to bits, while Daffodil nosed at a clump of violets. Indio held his precious boat in his arms.

He looked up eagerly as she came out the theater door. "Did you bring the boiled eggs?"

"Yes." Lily fell into step with him.

"And the jammy tarts Maude made?" Indio asked, skipping beside her.

"Of course."

"Huzzah!"

She smiled down at him and then nodded as they passed a group of gardeners. Two of the three men stopped and doffed their hats, making her feel quite fine. They hadn't seen many of the gardeners beside Caliban, as most of the work seemed to have been away from the theater thus far. It was inevitable, she supposed, that their restoration would eventually reach the theater, though she was not looking forward to the loss of their privacy. Stepping outside to find strange men would be a bit disconcerting. Lily wondered if she ought to ask Mr. Harte for some sort of lock for the theater door.

Abruptly she realized that she didn't know where Caliban was working today. She looked down at her son, happily skipping with his boat cradled in his arms. "Do you know where Caliban has gotten to?"

"He's by the pond, digging a hole in the ground," Indio said promptly.

Lily raised her eyebrows. "Is he? Whatever for?"

"Dunno," Indio said, unconcerned. "But it's a big 'un—bigger than any *I've* ever dug before."

He sounded admiring. Of course to a little boy the adventure of digging the hole was probably reason enough for the labor.

They came to the pond and began walking along it as best they could given there wasn't a path. Several times they had to dodge away from the pond to go around debris, but at last they found Caliban.

He was a terrifically dirty mess, shoulder-deep in a hole that was indeed quite big. Daffodil ran to the edge and barked at him until he placed his hands on the side and levered himself out. He wore a bandage on his head to cover his wound, but it was much smaller than the one she'd dressed it with the night before.

He grinned at the small dog and Indio, who showed

him the boat, and then looked at Lily. Even with his face and hair dusted with dirt, his shirt near brown from the silt, her heart gave a little jump. Like Indio when he was excited.

She shook her head at herself and called, "You need to wash before luncheon."

He looked down at his muddy hands and nodded. Then he simply took off his shirt and knelt by the pond to scoop water over his shoulders and face. The man had no modesty at all, it seemed.

Lily busied herself spreading a blanket on a dry patch of ground and unpacked their picnic. Daffodil immediately galloped up at the sight of food and attempted to steal a tart.

"No, Daff!" Indio cried. The tarts were rather dear to his heart. "Have this instead." And he handed her the fatty chicken tail they'd saved for her.

Daffodil scurried off with her prize. Lily hoped fervently that the little dog wouldn't decide to bury the chicken tail, for she'd done so in the past with what she considered delicacies and the results had been rather messy when disinterred for later leisurely enjoyment.

Caliban sat down, his shirt pulled over his head, but left loosely unlaced.

Lily looked away primly, her heart beating fast. He'd slicked back his wet hair and he was, if not handsome, certainly compelling.

Hastily she took one of the plates from the basket. "Would you like a chicken leg? Oh, and a hard-boiled egg?"

He nodded, his broad mouth slightly curved as if he was amused.

"*I'd* like an egg," Indio reminded her.

"Guests first, Indio," she said gently, and put a generous helping of everything she'd packed on a plate for Caliban before handing it over to him.

He lounged on his side, like a Roman aristocrat, carefully picking up a small piece of meat to eat.

She watched him out of the corner of her eye as she served Indio and then selected an egg and some bread for herself. She sat back, her legs curled to the side under her dress, and tilted her face to the sun—it was quite welcome after the dreary weather they'd had lately.

Daff came back, proudly bearing her chicken tail, and Caliban smiled at the little dog.

Which reminded her.

Lily cleared her throat as she tore off a bit of her bread. "I noticed yesterday that you laughed."

He looked up, his head cocked in obvious inquiry.

"It's just…" She gestured with the bit of bread before realizing and placing it carefully on her plate. "Well, it was out loud. I wondered, well, if you can laugh…"

He was still staring at her, his expression hard to decipher.

She inhaled and just blurted it out. "When was the last time you tried to speak?"

He reached over and picked up his cloth bag, opening the flap and taking out the notebook. He bent to write and then showed her the notebook. *Months ago. I assure you nothing happened*.

She licked her lips. "How long ago did you lose your voice?"

He frowned and wrote. *Nine or so months ago*.

"So recently!" She looked up in excitement. "That's

less than a year. Don't you see? Your infirmity might not be permanent."

"What are you talkin' about?" Indio asked, scrambling to his knees. "What's a 'firmity?"

"It's like an illness or a sickness." Lily glanced at Caliban and saw that his face had closed. His eyes flicked to her and then to Indio and she took the hint, though she was determined to continue the discussion later. "What are you digging the hole for?"

Caliban sat up at that, and Indio edged closer to look at his notebook as he wrote. *I intend to plant an oak tree here.*

She looked between his writing and the huge hole. "That's a big hole."

His mouth quirked as he wrote and she knew even before she read his words that he'd had a quick rejoinder.

She was correct: *It's a big tree.*

"But how can you plant a big tree?" she asked as she cracked her egg. "Won't it die when it's dug up from where it originally grew?"

He began to write furiously at her question. She ate her egg as she watched him, marveling at how deeply involved he was in his profession. Indio lost interest in the discussion and delved in the basket for a jammy tart.

At last Caliban showed her the notebook and she saw a full page of writing. He came to sit beside her as she read: *It's a very difficult job to move a large tree, for the roots mirror the tree above. Thus, as tall as the tree might be, so far below the ground do the roots reach. Of course one cannot move such a mass of earth, for there is no machine to dig so far nor one to move it could it be dug up. But . . .*

She marked her place with her finger and looked up. "But if you can't dig up the roots, how—?"

He rolled his eyes and leaned forward, tapping the page below her finger.

"Oh." She bent over the notebook, continuing to read, aware that he was looking over her shoulder now, reading his explanation along with her.

But as a tree's branches might be cut—quite sharply sometimes—and the tree still live, indeed thrive, it is believed that the roots as well might be cut. In this way a tree can be moved with its roots in a ball of dirt that, in comparison to the tree's height, is quite small indeed.

Lily turned her head—to find that his face was quite close to hers. She blinked, for a moment forgetting what her question was. Then it came to her. "You say here in comparison to the tree's height. But the earth and roots might still be quite big, mightn't it?"

He smiled slowly, as if particularly pleased with her question, and she couldn't help smiling in return.

He reached around her, his arms nearly embracing her, and wrote in the notebook on her lap, *Very good. Yes, the root ball should be quite big, even so.*

"Should be?"

His breath was warm against her ear. *I confess. I've never attempted to transplant a fully grown tree. I shall do so, however, this afternoon. Would you like to watch?*

If someone had asked her a fortnight ago if she'd like to watch a tree being planted, she would've looked at the questioner quite pityingly. But right now, this moment, she was rather excited at the prospect.

Perhaps too many viewings of Caliban's nude chest had addled her brain.

In any case she gazed into his thickly lashed brown eyes and smiled brilliantly. "Yes, please."

His grin was quick and all-encompassing and, she couldn't help but think, solely for her. As she watched, it faded a bit and his gaze dropped to her mouth. Her lips parted almost unconsciously, and she leaned a little forward, her own eyes on that wide, masculine smile.

"Mama," Indio interrupted, his cheeks smeared with the remains of a jammy tart. "Can I show Caliban my boat now?"

Lily jerked back from Caliban, feeling her cheeks heat, and caught the amused glance he gave her as he turned more leisurely to the boy.

"Yes, of course," she replied, repressing the urge to stick her tongue out at the maddening man. He'd started it—whatever *it* might've been—after all.

She watched as Indio eagerly crawled over with the boat. Caliban held it carefully, seeming to understand how important the toy was to her son, as Indio pointed out its best features and Daffodil poked her nose eagerly into the matter.

When at last they rose by some unspoken male accord, she noticed with a pang that Indio came only to Caliban's waist. The man towered over the boy, so much taller and broader that his gentleness was all the more moving as a result. They walked to the pond's bank and Indio launched his boat. Caliban restrained Daffodil from jumping in after.

This man was not at all like Kitty's husband. Not at all.

APOLLO WATCHED THAT afternoon as the machine containing his oak tree was hauled into the garden. Elegant in its simplicity, it was a sort of modified cart, and indeed two dray horses labored to pull the contraption in from the dock. Two wheels were at one end with a flat bed where the tree's huge roots lay. The bed narrowed into a long tongue that held the tree's trunk and was supported by a smaller single wheel. The horses were harnessed to the root end, where the bulk of the weight rested.

The entire thing had been brought down the Thames on a barge. Tree and machine had been especially ordered from a fellow garden architect whom Apollo had been corresponding with under the pseudonym Mr. Smith. He'd been quite specific in his order, including both diagrams and copious notes, and was pleased with the result before him: his oak lay like a colossus fallen, the roots spidering out from the earth-encased base.

Now all they had to do was get the tree in the ground without mishap.

Lily stood to one side with Indio and Daffodil capering at her feet. The gardeners had apparently become used to their presence in the garden, for there had been no questions when they'd stayed to watch.

Apollo almost literally twitched with the desire to direct the operation himself. Herring, the head gardener, was a good Yorkshireman, able to read and follow Apollo's written instructions, but he was plodding and not much of a thinker. He had a hard time compensating when something didn't go as planned.

And many things might not go as planned with the oak tree.

Two of the gardeners—dark-haired brothers from Ireland—steadied the cart while a third man—a short, wiry Londoner, new to Harte's Folly just this week—led the horses. Herring shouted orders while Apollo, igno-miniously demoted to dullard while in the company of the other gardeners, stood by with a shovel.

"Hold it there!" Herring called, and studied the notes Apollo had left him the week before. "Says here that the master wants the cart pulled to near the hole, then the horses to be unhitched there." He nodded to himself. "Makes sense, that."

The horses were dutifully unhitched and Apollo, along with the Irish brothers, put his back into hauling the tree the remaining few feet over the hole. If he'd measured the hole correctly and his correspondent had followed his measurements, the wheels should be just wide enough to straddle it.

He watched as the cart trundled into place and felt a surge of satisfaction in a job well done.

"Pretty as a lamb at its ma's tit, that," Herring said admiringly, then seemed to remember Miss Stump. "If'n you'll pardon an old countryman's expression, ma'am."

She waved cheerily. "Not at all, Mr. Herring."

She exchanged an amused glance with Apollo and then he turned back to the work. The root ball now lay over the hole with the tree trunk extending to one side, parallel to the ground. Daffodil was nosing about the hole, as curious as usual, and Apollo gently toed her aside. Awful if the little dog should be stepped on as the men labored. All that was needed now was to haul the tree upright, cut its ropes and drop it—gently—into the waiting hole.

"Stand back, you," Herring ordered Apollo. "Let the ones with some wits attach the ropes or we'll have it all down around our ears and I don't know what we'd do then."

Apollo feigned patience, standing by as the other men tied the ropes. He winced as one of the Irish brothers drew a rope over-tight about the oak's trunk and hoped the man hadn't damaged the bark.

He took one of the ropes as one of the Irishmen and the small Londoner took the other.

"All together now," Herring called. "And don't be hasty. Slow and steady'll get us there faster."

At Herring's signal, Apollo and the other two men pulled on their ropes, hand over hand, hauling the tree upright. The tongue and the bed of the cart pivoted as one on the two big wheels as the smaller wheel left the ground. Two ropes were needed for stability and to keep the tree from falling to one side or the other. Now that Apollo was actually pulling the oak tree upright he was beginning to think that three or even four ropes might have been better. Well, he'd experiment with the next tree they transplanted into the garden.

Sweat stung as it dripped into his eyes. Out of the corner of his eye he noticed that Daffodil was back, peering interestedly into the hole, but he couldn't move to shoo her away. His muscles strained and he could hear the loud grunts of the other men. Slowly the tree rose, majestic and tall. It would be lovely at the side of the pond and in a hundred years, when it had spread its branches over the water, it would be magnificent.

He felt the sudden, sickening slackening of the rope first, followed closely by a hoarse shout from one of the gardeners on the other rope. That rope was whipping through the air, free of the men's hands. Apollo looked up and saw the great oak shudder and then begin falling toward him.

At the same time, Indio darted between him and the cart as Daffodil slipped and slid helplessly into the tree hole.

The sound ripped from him, like a thing outside himself, a beast that'd been bound inside his gut and would no longer stand to be caged.

The shout burned as it roared through his throat.

"INDIO!"

Chapter Eight

*Now it fell one year that the maiden chosen as
sacrifice was named Ariadne. She was the only child
of a poor wise woman, and her mother wept bitter tears
at the news. Then the wise woman dried her cheeks
and said to her daughter, "Remember this: when
you are presented to the court, curtsy not only to
the king, but to the mad queen as well, and ask her
if there is anything you may take to
her son."...*
—From *The Minotaur*

Lily heard Indio's name shouted and then all was drowned
in the roar of the oak crashing down.

Down where Caliban had stood.

Down where Indio had darted.

The men were yelling. The horses bolted, dragging
their harness behind, and where Apollo's planting hole
had been was only wreckage and a cloud of sooty dust.

She ran forward, pushing against smashed tree branches,
fighting the man who tried to restrain her. He had to be
in there somewhere, perhaps with only a broken limb or
a bloodied back. Her lips were moving, muttering, as she
bargained with whatever deity would listen. The tree was

big, the branches lying shattered and sticking up every-where and in her way.

"Let me go!" she screamed at the arms holding her.

She couldn't *see* them. Even in the mess of demolished branches, there should be some sign—Indio's red coat or Caliban's white shirt.

Then in the shouting she heard it: a yip.

"Quiet!" she called, and wonder of wonders, the men actually listened.

In the sudden silence Daffodil's high, hysterical bark-ing was quite clear—and coming from *inside* the hole.

"I'll be," Mr. Herring said, amazement in his voice.

She turned and looked. At first she saw only the mess of roots. There wasn't space in there, surely, for a small dog, let alone a man and boy. But as she watched, a huge hand slapped down on the edge. She started for the hole even as Caliban emerged, head and broad shoulders blackened, clutching Indio to his chest like Hephaestus rising from his underworld forge.

She'd never seen such a wonderful sight.

He tossed a very dirty Daffodil over the edge of the hole. The little dog tumbled, righted herself, and shook vigorously, and then she ran to Lily, tail wagging as if nothing especially remarkable had happened.

Lily ignored the greyhound in favor of her son. Caliban had set him on the edge of the hole before heaving him-self over.

"Mama," Indio said, and then burst into tears.

She knelt in front of him, feeling his body with trem-bling hands. He had a bloody nose and a scrape on his chin. His hair was quite filthy with dirt, but otherwise he was sound.

She clutched him to her chest and looked over his little shoulder at Caliban. "Thank you. I don't know how you did it, but thank you for saving my son."

That seemed to bring Indio out of his shocked tears. "He caught me, Mama!" he said, looking at her with his mud-and-salt-streaked face. "Caliban caught me and pushed me an' him in the hole and the oak tree comed down on us, but it didn't really because the machine was on the outside, see?" And he pointed to where the tree had landed on top of the hole instead of in it.

Lily shuddered at the sight, for if one of the wheels of the machine had slid, the entire root ball would've fallen on them instead of merely tilting half in the hole. But she smiled for Indio.

"Yes, I see, but there mustn't have been very much room down there."

"No, there wasn't," Indio assured her earnestly. "And Caliban lay on top of me an' Daff." He leaned close to whisper in her ear. "He's very heavy. Daff squeaked. I think she was nearly squashed."

Lily laughed through her tears at this bit of information, for she understood as her son seemed not to that Caliban had covered Indio to protect him from the tree roots.

She glanced again at Caliban as she said, "You and Daffodil were very brave."

"And the best part, Mama," Indio said, tugging her hand to get her attention, "the *best* part is Caliban spoke. Did you hear him? He shouted my name!"

"What?" Lily stared at Indio's filthy little face and then back up at Caliban. She absently noted that he had a bleeding scratch on his cheek. That shout right before the accident—had that been him?

Caliban looked away from her, his face pale, and she immediately wanted to get him alone so that she might find out if he could truly speak.

"I'm glad your boy's safe, ma'am." Mr. Herring's words were kind but he was looking worriedly at the wreckage of the tree and machine.

"Thank you," she said. "I'll be taking him back to the theater for a bath and to patch up his scratches. And I'll do the same for...erm..." Good Lord, what did the other gardeners call Caliban? She gestured vaguely at him.

"What?" Mr. Herring glanced at her in alarm. "But I've already lost the new man—ran off who knows where. I'll be needing Smith."

Smith? Lily drew herself up. "I'm afraid I must insist, Mr. Herring."

"Oh, very well." The head gardener waved her off wearily. "Probably won't get much work done the rest of the day anyway. Don't know what I'll be tellin' the master."

"I have a feeling that won't be a problem," Lily muttered under her breath, ignoring Caliban's warning glare. She turned to Indio. "Can you walk to the theater, love?"

The question seemed to prick her son's male pride—a fickle, easily provoked thing—and he snapped back, "Of *course*, Mama."

His hauteur was rather ruined, though, by the drooping of his shoulders. Now that the excitement was past it was evident that the accident had taken its toll upon Indio's stamina. He yawned widely even as he stumbled down the path. In another few steps Caliban scooped him up without a word.

The thought made Lily eye the big man carrying her son on his shoulder. He could talk—or at least he had spoken.

One word, true, but surely where there was one there were more? Lily spent the rest of the walk to the theater with myriad questions swarming her brain.

Maude was away shopping for the afternoon, so the theater was empty when they arrived.

She waited until they were safely inside before turning to Caliban and demanding, "*Can* you talk?"

He opened his mouth and for a terrible moment nothing happened, but then sound emerged, creaking and halting. "I think...yes." He swallowed and winced, as if the words physically hurt.

"Oh," Lily whispered, pressing her fingertips to her trembling mouth. "Oh, I *am* glad."

"Told you," Indio said sleepily from Caliban's shoulder.

"So you did," Lily replied, wiping at her eyes with her fingers. She was turning into a veritable watering pot. She inhaled to steady herself. "I think you need a nap, little man."

It was a measure of how exhausted Indio was that he didn't even protest that he was now much too old for naps. Lily relaxed her cleanliness standards far enough to simply insist she wash his face for him before laying him down, already mostly asleep, in her own bed.

She gently shut the door to her bedroom and looked up to find Caliban reading her play in the outer room.

He set down the sheet he'd been holding and cleared his throat. "It...is...good." He looked at her. "Very... good."

His voice was naturally deep, but there was a strained, hoarse quality about it that suggested damage.

"Thank you." She'd had compliments on her plays, but they'd always been filtered through Edwin. No one had told her in person that they liked her writing. "It's not done, of course, and I need to work quite hard on it if I'm to get it finished in time—I've only a week—but I think it might well be one of my better ones. That is, if I can do something about Pimberly. He's rather priggish at the moment. But"—she reeled in her wandering words with a deep breath—"you don't want to hear about—"

"I do," he said, interrupting her.

"Oh." She stared and then had to look down shyly— she was *never* shy! "That's good. I mean...I'm glad, but you'll be wanting to wash your face and see to your wounds right now, surely?"

He nodded, perhaps saving his voice, but he kept his gaze on her, watching her as she fetched water and cloths. She came to where he sat at the table and placed the basin there.

"May I?" she asked, surprised at how husky her voice was.

He nodded again, tilting his face up.

First she peeked beneath the bandage on his head. The wound was scabbing over and didn't look damaged, so she replaced the bandage and left it as it was. In the silence she dipped a cloth in the water and wrung it out, then gently patted at his face. Up close she could see it was badly scraped in several places, and she thought of his bearing the brunt of that tree for her son.

She rewetted the cloth. "How is your back?"

"It's...fine."

She smoothed over his right cheekbone where the bloody cut was. "I'll check it after I've washed your face."

"There's no...need."

She smiled, sweet but insistent. His back would've

been the hardest hit when he'd covered Indio and Daffo-dil. "I want to."

He made no reply to that, so she continued, gently wiping around his nose, over the broad brow, and up the craggy cheekbones. Not a handsome face. Not pretty or comely. But it was a good face, she thought. Certainly masculine.

Certainly one she was attracted to.

She paused, swallowing at the thought. She did not know this man. She knew *of* him—knew that he would without hesitation fling himself into a filthy hole to save her son, knew he was kind to silly dogs and quarrel-some old women, knew he could, with a single, certain look, make her insides heat and melt—but she did not know him.

She straightened, concentrating as she wetted the cloth again, watching her fingers wring brown water out. "How did you lose your voice, Caliban?"

When she turned back to him, his face was closed, his eyes shuttered.

"Please," she whispered. She had to find out something—some small thing about him.

Maybe he understood her plea. Or perhaps he was so tired he could no longer fight her.

"It was a...beating," he said, his voice croaking. He cleared his throat, but it sounded the same when next he spoke. "He...a man stood...on my neck." He touched his hand to his Adam's apple.

She stared. He was big and brave and she knew he could move swiftly. How could he have been bested in a fight? Unless...

"How many were there?" she whispered.

His eyes flicked to hers, sardonic acknowledgement in them. "Three."

Even so... "Were you drunk or asleep?"

He shook his head. "I was..."

He looked away from her as if *ashamed*. Her eyes narrowed. What had happened to put that look on Caliban's face?

He cleared his throat and tried again. "I...was... chained."

Chained. She blinked. The only persons she knew who might be chained were prisoners.

Suddenly she felt much better. A man might be imprisoned for many things—debt chief among them. Edwin had spent an uncomfortable month in Fleet Prison several years back.

She bent to wipe his chin, the cloth catching at stubble. "And you couldn't speak after?"

"No." He frowned. "I could...not..." He inhaled sharply as if in frustration. "I...was knocked out... they...the three of them..." He swallowed, grimacing, and she realized with sudden comprehension that there might be more to the story.

A big, powerful man chained, made helpless. She'd seen boys poke at a chained bear—a beast they'd run screaming from were it free to do as it would. Little boys—and weak men—fancied themselves brave in the face of such helplessness. It made them giddy with false power. And they were apt to wield that power in terrible and cruel ways.

Had such a thing been done to her Caliban?

The thought made her light-headed with rage. *No one* had the right to bolster his own feeble manhood by tearing down Caliban's.

She took a deep breath, knowing that pity was the last thing he'd want. "I see," she said, her voice level.

He shook his head, his mouth twisting. "It was... months...ago."

And his simple bravery, his quiet pride, finally broke her. She let the cloth slip from her fingers and bent down to kiss him.

His reaction was immediate and decided. He wrapped his strong arms around her waist and pulled her into his lap, forcing her to straddle his legs. He cradled the back of her head in the spread of his fingers, angled his head for a better fit, and opened his mouth over hers.

And, oh, the man knew how to kiss.

His tongue licked into her mouth, tasting of wine and want, sure and in no hurry. He explored her thoroughly, sliding against her own tongue, taunting before withdrawing. He caught her bottom lip between his teeth, worrying gently, and chuckled low in his throat when she moaned and arched into him. Her skirts were caught between their bodies and naturally he still wore his breeches, but she could feel a hardness there—big and powerful. Her breasts ached against her bodice and she suddenly wished all their clothes vanished—that she could discover him for who he was.

She must've gone a little mad then, for she found her fingers threaded in his still dusty hair, tugging at it, demanding something that she couldn't articulate.

It was he who had to break from her, and only then, as she was glaring at him for the interruption, did she hear Maude *humph* behind her.

"Far be it from me to interrupt, hinney, when you're a-wallowin' in the mud with a man, but I've supper to put on."

*   *   *

"But *why* are we going to Harte's Folly?" Lady Phoebe asked late the next morning, wrinkling her nose, presumably at the stink of the Thames, although for all Trevillion knew it was at his continued presence in her life. "I understand the theater and garden are quite burned to the ground."

"They are, my lady." Trevillion glared at the wherryman who'd been unashamedly listening in. The wherryman hurriedly bent to his oars. "But the garden is in a state of renovation and I thought you'd be interested. Also," he added very drily, "I have business there, and since my job is to guard you and you insisted on going out today, I couldn't very well make the journey without you."

"Oh," she said, her voice small, as she let her fingers trail in the water.

The wherryman scowled at him.

Trevillion sighed and turned to watch the Harte's Folly dock draw near. The pleasure garden had been a very popular attraction before the fire, and the dock had once been wide and well maintained. Now it was half fallen into the Thames, only a narrow part shored up and rebuilt with new wood. Behind the dock the burnt and ruined vegetation looked positively grim—not at all like a frivolous pleasure garden. 'Twas said that Harte intended to rebuild the garden entirely, but Trevillion thought it an almost impossible goal, attainable only with a tremendous outlay of money, and then the end result still uncertain.

But that was hardly his concern.

The wherryman caught at the dock, pulling the small

boat close enough to fling a rope over one of the wooden posts on the side.

"We're here, my lady," Trevillion said to Lady Phoebe, although she probably knew from the lurch of the boat. "There's a ladder to your right, just past the gunwale of the boat."

He watched as she felt for the rough wooden ladder with her fingertips.

"Now take my hand, my lady." He lightly pressed against her forearm so she'd know where his hand was.

"I have it," she said impatiently, taking his hand nevertheless as she gingerly climbed out.

He made sure to hold her firmly until she was standing on the dock. He followed as swiftly as possible, despite being hampered by both lame leg and cane.

"Wait for us," he ordered the wherryman, tossing him a coin.

"Aye," the wherryman muttered, pulling his broad-brimmed hat over his face as he lounged back in his boat. No doubt he meant to fill the time with a nap.

"This way, my lady," Trevillion said to Lady Phoebe, giving her his left arm. He leaned heavily on his cane with his right hand. A crude path had been cleared, leading from the dock into the garden, but debris still littered the ground. "Mind your step. The ground is uneven."

She turned her head from side to side as they walked, sniffing the air. "It still smells quite strongly of the fire."

"Indeed," he replied, guiding her around a charred lump—perhaps a fallen tree, though it was hard to tell. "The ground is blackened and what trees remain are scorched."

"How sad," she murmured. "I did so love this place."

Her brows were knit, her plump lips drooping.

He cleared his throat. "There are a few signs of rebirth," he remarked, feeling a fool even as he said it.

She perked up. "Such as?"

"Some green blades of grass. And the sun is shining," he said lamely. He caught sight of something. "Ah. There's a sort of small purple flower off to the left as well."

"Is there?" She brightened. "Show me."

He took her hand and carefully pulled it down to the pathetic little flower.

She felt it so gently the petals weren't even bruised.

"A violet, I think," she said at last, straightening. "I'd pick it to smell, but with so few survivors I don't want to steal it away."

He forbore to say that one violet hardly made a garden.

She sighed as they continued. "Very few signs of rebirth indeed. I wonder how Mr. Harte will ever rebuild it?"

Privately he thought the matter a lost cause, but he decided not to share that thought with her.

They were nearing the theater and Trevillion frowned. He'd not thought this out well enough. He hadn't made specific plans with Lord Kilbourne about where or when to meet. The man might be anywhere.

When they came within sight of the theater, however, his problem was solved. Lord Kilbourne was digging a hole some yards from the theater while a small dark-haired boy sat nearby, apparently chatting with him.

Trevillion felt his brows lift. Where had the boy come from? There were no residences for a half mile at the least in any direction.

The boy had a small, thin dog lying curled at his side,

and the creature raised its head at their approach. In a blur it was up and racing over, yapping wildly.

Trevillion scowled at the beast. It was jumping excitedly at Lady Phoebe's skirts. "Down, you."

"Oh, Captain, I don't think I need be protected from a lapdog," Lady Phoebe said, and before he could ascertain if the animal was friendly or not, knelt before the thing.

Immediately it began pawing at her and licking her face.

Lady Phoebe laughed, hands outstretched, but the dog was too excited to hold still so she might pet it. Her round face was positively lit with joy. "What kind is it?"

"I don't know," he replied, looking away from her. "Something small, thin, and hysterical."

"Daffodil's an Italian greyhound," the boy said, having trotted after his dog. "You can pet her if you like. She doesn't bite, although," he added, entirely unnecessarily, "she *does* lick."

"I can feel that," Lady Phoebe replied, smiling. Her face was tilted toward the sky. "I once had a friend who had an Italian greyhound. What color is she?"

"Red," the boy said, adding with the frankness of the young, "can't you see?"

"*Lady* Phoebe is blind, boy," Trevillion said sharply.

His charge winced and turned a glare on him, which was quite effective, unseeing or not.

The child shrank back at his tone, and Trevillion noticed his eyes were mismatched: one blue, one green. "Oh. I'm sorry."

"There's no need to be," Lady Phoebe said gently. "What's your name?"

"I'm Indio," he said. "That's Caliban, my friend"—he

pointed to Lord Kilbourne, which made Trevillion's eyebrows rise farther—"and my mama is in the theater."

Lady Phoebe turned her head at that as if she could look about. "We're near the theater?"

"Yes."

"But I thought the theater burned?"

"Well it did, mostly," Indio replied. "But part of it's good. That's where we live."

Her brows knit. "You live here?"

He nodded, apparently having already forgotten that she couldn't see him. "My mama is a famous actress. She's Robin Goodfellow."

"Is she?" Lady Phoebe breathed, evidently delighted. "Might I meet her? I'm a great admirer."

And within minutes Lady Phoebe had somehow become fast friends with Miss Goodfellow and was taking tea with her at a table brought out to the garden.

"Did…they already…know each other?" Lord Kilbourne asked.

He and Trevillion had taken themselves far enough from the theater that they couldn't be heard by the ladies, but were close enough for Trevillion to keep an eye on his charge. Kilbourne had glanced once at his cane and suggested a fallen log to sit on. Trevillion had been too grateful for the respite for his leg to worry about his pride.

Somehow, in the days since Trevillion had seen him, the viscount had miraculously regained the power of speech, though his words were slow and his voice quite rough. There was a story there, Trevillion knew, but it didn't concern him at the moment.

"Not at all," Trevillion said, watching as Lady Phoebe laughed at something Miss Goodfellow told her.

"You're sure."

"Quite."

"Simply . . . marvelous," Kilbourne muttered, sounding nonetheless confused. His gaze, Trevillion noticed, lingered a fraction too long on the actress.

"If you say so, my lord."

The other looked at him at that and Trevillion noticed that the viscount was sporting a series of new scratches across his face.

"I do," Kilbourne replied coolly. "I collect . . . you have some . . . information for me?"

Trevillion straightened. "Yes, my lord. I've made some inquiries into the histories and situations of your friends who died that night. Maubry, as you said, was destined to become a churchman. According to his remaining friends he had no enemies and wasn't in debt, nor had he offended anyone in the months before his death. I think we may consider him a blameless victim."

Kilbourne nodded, looking grim. He was watching the ladies again.

Trevillion turned to look as well, observing as Lady Phoebe discreetly felt the tartlet on her plate with her fingertips before taking a bite. She was very deft at living with her infirmity, he mused.

"Mr. Tate was indeed his uncle's heir," he continued. "At Tate's death, a very distant cousin became heir and eventually inherited the uncle's estate of some two thousand pounds per annum—not a fortune, but by no means an insignificant sum. However, the cousin in question lived in the American Colonies until only a year ago. While he might certainly have sent agents to murder his cousin, it seems, on the surface at least, unlikely."

"I agree," Kilbourne replied, sounding a little absent-minded.

Miss Goodfellow was at that moment licking her lips of some tartlet crumbs.

Trevillion cleared his throat. "As for Smithers, the last man, there I did find something of interest."

Kilbourne looked at him sharply. "How...so?"

"Unlike the rest of you," Trevillion said, "he *was* in debt—and for quite a large amount, to a rather nasty sort—men running a gambling den in the stews of Whitechapel."

"Then that was...it?" Kilbourne's face was stoically blank.

"I don't think so," Trevillion said reluctantly. "His creditors didn't recoup their money on his death, nor was it widely known that he owed them." He shrugged. "Murdering Smithers along with two other gentlemen would've been a poor business decision, and these villains are, if nothing else, quite sharp men of business."

A muscle in Kilbourne's jaw flexed and he glanced away—for the first time *not* at Miss Goodfellow. "Then... you have nothing."

"Not quite, my lord," Trevillion replied softly.

Kilbourne merely stared at him stonily, as if he'd let hope seize his emotions too many times in the past to permit it free rein again.

Trevillion met his gaze and said bluntly, "Your uncle is in debt, my lord, to your grandfather, the earl's, estate—and has been for at least a decade. If you inherit the title, I suspect he would find himself in a very awkward position, for he doesn't have the monies to repay the estate. Had you died that night, he would've inherited the title—and the money that goes with it upon your grand-father's death. He would never have to repay the debt and wouldn't fear the courts or debtor's prison."

Kilbourne's expression didn't even flicker—proving that he was as intelligent as Trevillion had suspected. "But I...*didn't* die. Instead...apparently I...was drugged."

"Think," Kilbourne murmured low, for if what he suspected was true, they had a powerful man as an enemy. "Had you been murdered then, had not a common thief or some such been apprehended, your uncle, as the next heir to the earldom, would've been the natural suspect. *But* if you were drugged and your friends killed instead, *you* are made the murderer, and must perforce be brought to justice—and the hangman. A scandal, surely, but in no way your uncle's fault—and with the same result as if he'd murdered you himself: your death. It was," he added thoughtfully, "a rather elegant scheme, you must admit, my lord."

"You'll...forgive me if...I *don't*," Kilbourne replied drily. "I would've...been dead these four years...had not my distant...cousin, the Earl of...Brightmore not been so horrified...at the thought of a relation...of his being tried for...murder that he bundled...me away in Bedlam instead." He paused, swallowing, after such a long speech. "Scant...comfort though...that was at the time. I think...I might've preferred...the noose."

Trevillion reflected sardonically that he must be grateful, then, to Brightmore, for he'd saved Trevillion from indirectly sending an innocent man to his death.

"Why..." Kilbourne started, and then had to cough and clear his throat. "If your...theory is true, why... wouldn't my...uncle have had me killed in Bedlam?"

"Perhaps he thought you would die there, my lord." Trevillion shrugged. "Many do."

Kilbourne nodded, contemplating that for a moment, or perhaps letting his throat rest. He said abruptly, "My grandfather…is dying…or so my sister informs me."

"Then your uncle will want you dead as well," Trevillion replied. "He made some very unwise investments in the last year and his debt has doubled just in the last five months."

Kilbourne stared at him, frowning.

"His need has become acute, I think." Trevillion met his gaze and once again noticed the scratches on the other man's cheek. "Where did you get those scratches, my lord? You're looking much the worse for wear since I saw you last."

"Yesterday…" Kilbourne coughed, raising a hand to finger the scratches. "I nearly died…from a falling tree…that was to…be planted. There…was a new… gardener…he is…missing today."

Trevillion pivoted to face the other man fully, leaning on his stick urgently. "You've been discovered, my lord. If I could follow your sister, so, too, could your uncle's men."

Kilbourne shook his head violently, coughing. "Accident," he gasped.

"You don't think that yourself or you wouldn't have told me," Trevillion said impatiently.

At the same time a voice called, "Hullo! Hullo! I say, can anyone tell me where Mr. Smith is?"

They both pivoted to see a red-haired young man, not more than five and twenty, blinking in the sunlight far too close to the ladies, and already being assaulted by the little dog.

"Damnation," Trevillion muttered. It seemed their tête-à-tête was over. "Listen to me, my lord. You must leave the garden. Find some other place of hiding until we can devise a plan to find evidence against your uncle."

Kilbourne was still shaking his head, though more slowly now, his eyes fixed toward the theater. "Can't."

Trevillion followed the direction of his gaze—naturally to where Miss Goodfellow was rising to meet the newcomer. "Can't—or won't?"

Kilbourne never took his eyes from her, but his face hardened with determination. "Doesn't matter."

Chapter Nine

*The next morning Ariadne journeyed to the golden
castle. There the king sat on a jewel-encrusted throne
with, beside him, his mad queen, spinning red wool with
a wooden distaff and spindle. The youth chosen with
Ariadne made a low bow to the king and then turned aside.
But Ariadne, remembering her mother's warning, curtsied
to the king and then the queen and inquired politely of her
if there was aught she might bring her son. Without a
word the queen handed her spindle to the girl . . .*
—From *The Minotaur*

Lily met Caliban's gaze across the clearing and felt heat
climb her cheeks. His eyes were hot and intent.

He looked at her as if with a single kiss he'd already
claimed her.

She glanced away, inhaling. It *had* only been one kiss
and they hadn't had a chance to speak properly since. Last
night there'd been Maude, sharp and sarcastic and disapproving, and this morning Indio had been excited and
scampering about. And that had been before Lady Phoebe
and Captain Trevillion showed up.

"Who is it?" that lady asked, facing in the direction
of the young man advancing toward them. Daffodil had

finished welcoming him and was now dashing off to her master. Indio had previously wandered away from their tea party and was playing by the corner of the theater in what looked suspiciously like a mud puddle.

"I've no idea," Lily replied, hoping she didn't sound as irritable as she felt. Good Lord, Harte's Folly had become like a county fair—a veritable crossroads of visitors. Belatedly she remembered her manners and tacked on, "My lady."

Lady Phoebe smiled and asked softly, "What does he look like?"

Of course Lady Phoebe had no idea of the aspect or even the age of the man approaching them.

"He's a young man with bright red hair and a comely face," Lily answered quietly and quickly. "Wearing a black tricorn and an acorn-brown suit. The waistcoat is a lighter shade, more tan than brown, and trimmed in a fine scarlet ribbon. Not expensive, but well cut." She cocked her head, considering. "He's quite handsome, actually."

"Oh, good," Lady Phoebe said with some satisfaction, sitting back.

Lily only had time for a glance of amusement at the other woman—she really was quite delightful—before the gentleman was upon them.

"Good morning," he called in a faint Scottish accent. He came to a stop, swept his hat from his head, and gave a lovely bow. "I am Mr. Malcolm MacLeish. Whom might I have the honor of addressing?"

"I am Miss Robin Goodfellow," Lily said as she curtsied, "and this is Lady Phoebe Batten."

"Good Lord!" Mr. MacLeish exclaimed, his bright-blue eyes opening wide as he staggered dramatically back. "An honor indeed, ladies! I had the privilege of attending a production of *As You Like It* a year or two ago, Miss Goodfellow, in which you were a most magnificent Rosalind."

She curtsied again, amused at his profusion. "Thank you, sir."

"And my Lady Phoebe," Mr. MacLeish said, turning to her, "I am in awe of your presence."

"Indeed, sir," Lady Phoebe replied, cocking her head, with a trace of a smile playing about her mouth. She didn't look quite in his direction. "At my mere presence?"

"Y-yes, my lady," he replied, obviously uncertain if she teased or not. He darted a quick glance at Lily, but she decided to leave him to his own devices since he'd dug the hole for himself with his enthusiasm. "Your beauty alone is enough to put wonder in my gaze."

Lady Phoebe burst into laughter. From any other lady it might've been taken as an insult or at the very least a gentle belittlement—but from her it was simply a sign of joyous amusement.

Lily couldn't help grinning in sympathy—the other woman's laughter was that infectious.

"But Mr. MacLeish," Lady Phoebe said, bringing her mirth under control, "I've been told that you are yourself quite an ugly specimen of manhood."

The young man's eyes widened as sudden realization washed over his features, but to his credit he recovered quickly—and without insulting Lady Phoebe's intelligence. "But my lady, I do protest. I am accorded one of the finest-looking gentlemen in England, with milk-white skin, straight teeth, blue eyes . . . and shining golden hair."

Lady Phoebe shook her head. "Lying to a blind woman,

Mr. MacLeish? I've already heard you have bright-red hair."

"My lady, you wound me," the young man exclaimed, hand to heart, though Lady Phoebe couldn't see the gesture. "I vow I've had many a lady at my feet."

"And elsewhere?" she asked, her eyelashes lowered.

"You shouldn't tease the boy, my lady," Captain Trevillion said as he limped to the table. Caliban was by his side, his eyes alert, Lily noticed. He gave her one blazing glance and then focused on the newcomer.

The captain's words fell awkwardly on their light flirtation, breaking the effervescent mood.

Lady Phoebe stiffened.

Mr. MacLeish sobered immediately, eyeing the pistols strapped across Captain Trevillion's chest. "And who might *you* be, sir?"

Before the man could reply, Lady Phoebe said, "This is Captain James Trevillion, who has been set to guard me by my brother, like a dog chained before a tasty pork pie."

"I think of you, my lady, as more of an apple tart," Captain Trevillion murmured. He turned to the younger man. "And you are?"

"Mr. Malcolm MacLeish," the Scotsman replied, and Lily was glad to see that he didn't look at all cowed by the former dragoon's stern manner. Caliban had explained that Captain Trevillion was some sort of business acquaintance, but she *had* seen the soldier try to kill him, and only recently, so she thought she might be forgiven a bit of prejudice. "I've been commissioned as architect for the rebuilding of Harte's Folly by His Grace the Duke of Montgomery. He informed me that the garden designer, a Mr. Smith, was to be found here."

Caliban had stilled during this little speech and at the end of it he nodded. "I am...he."

Mr. MacLeish brightened. "Very good to meet you, sir." He held out his hand and for a moment Caliban looked at it as if it were a strange and foreign thing before he seemed to recollect himself and shook hands with younger man. "If you'll show me the grounds and what you yourself have planned, I would be most grateful."

Captain Trevillion's eyes narrowed and he exchanged some type of significant glance with Caliban.

Lily sighed. She really was getting quite tired of not knowing what was going on.

And apparently she wasn't the only one.

"Your pardon," Lady Phoebe said, suddenly sounding every inch the daughter of a duke, "but I don't think you introduced me to Mr. Smith, Captain. I confess myself curious to meet the man you were so eager to see today."

Lily could tell by the stiffening of Captain Trevillion's back that he did not care for Lady Phoebe's interruption, but for the life of her, she couldn't understand why.

Yet he said politely enough, "My lady, may I present Mr...."

"Sam," Caliban supplied. "Just Sam Smith."

"Mr. Sam Smith?" Captain Trevillion continued smoothly. "Mr. Smith, Lady Phoebe Batten, the Duke of Wakefield's sister."

Lady Phoebe held out her hand imperiously and Caliban was forced to take it, bowing over it as he said in his broken voice, "My lady...I am most...pleased to meet you."

She cocked her head at his voice. "Have you a cold, Mr. Smith?"

"No...my lady," he said so gently that Lily felt an unfamiliar pang of jealousy. "I recently...injured my throat and...as a result...my voice."

She nodded. "I see."

He tried to extricate his hand from hers, but she seemed to hold him fast. "Tell me, Mr. Smith, and know that it is a mortal sin to lie to a blind woman: have we met before?"

The strangest expression crossed Caliban's face. Lily wasn't entirely sure, but it seemed to be *sadness.* "No... my lady. We've...never met."

"Ah," she said, finally letting go of his hand. "My mistake, then."

Caliban turned to Mr. MacLeish. "I shall be...happy to show...you about the garden...such as it is...sir." He hesitated and glanced at Lily. "I believe...you were... interested in the...garden as well...ma'am? Would...you like a...tour sometime...after luncheon? Say...three of the clock?"

Lily felt suddenly breathless, but she managed to say calmly enough, "I shall look forward to it, Mr. Smith."

He nodded. "Then...if you'll all...excuse us?" He gestured with one arm, rather gracefully. "This way...if you please...Mr. MacLeish."

"Of course," said that gentleman. "Lady Phoebe, Miss Goodfellow, a positive delight to meet you both. I do hope our paths will cross again."

"As do I," Lady Phoebe replied, smiling.

Lily dipped another curtsy and murmured her farewells.

Mr. MacLeish sobered as he touched his hand to his hat. "Captain Trevillion. A pleasure."

"All mine, I assure you," the soldier drawled, so drily he might as well have been exhaling dust.

They watched the two men stride off, Caliban already explaining his plan for the garden.

Captain Trevillion pivoted back to the ladies. "If you're ready, my lady, I do seem to recall you had some 'important' shopping to accomplish this afternoon."

"Shopping is always quite important, Captain," Lady Phoebe replied in a very serious tone. "But Miss Goodfellow has been so kind as to consent to give me the secret to her jam tartlets."

"Has she." The soldier's tone was flat, with only a very small hint of disbelief.

Lady Phoebe smiled cheerily. "She has. Please be so kind as to wander a ways off so that we may consult on the matter. I'm sure the place you chose to speak with Mr. Smith was far enough away that you might not be overheard. Perhaps you can wait there."

Captain Trevillion bowed woodenly. "My lady."

He limped away and for a moment Lily felt almost sorry for the man. He was so very proud and it was obvious that Lady Phoebe used him a trifle hard sometimes.

But then the lady herself leaned close to her and whispered, "Is he far enough away?"

Lily glanced to the soldier's back, now a distance away. "I think so, my lady."

"Do be sure," Lady Phoebe muttered. "I swear the man has the hearing of a dog." She crinkled her nose. "That doesn't sound quite right. Anyway, the hearing of some animal that has very good hearing. Terribly annoying."

Lily felt her lips twitch. "Yes, my lady."

"Now tell me quickly before he comes back and sticks his long nose in: what does Mr. Smith look like?"

Lily blinked in surprise, her own voice lowering instinctively. "He's very big—over six feet, with wide shoulders and large hands. He has brown eyes and brown hair worn long. He's not handsome."

Lady Phoebe frowned thoughtfully. "Does he have any mark about him?"

"I don't think so, unless you consider an especially large nose a mark?" Lily shrugged helplessly.

"What do you know of him? His family? His friends?"

"Nothing," Lily whispered quite truthfully, dread filling her heart. "Nothing at all."

"Blast," said Lady Phoebe.

"What is it?" Lily asked, afraid of the answer. "Who do you think he is?"

"Oh, no one." Lady Phoebe waved an impatient hand. "It's just that the captain is so mysterious. I vow he does it simply to vex me. Is he still watching?"

Lily glanced up to see that the captain was indeed staring at them. "Yes, my lady."

"Of course he is," Lady Phoebe muttered. "Well, might as well wave him over. I thank you, Miss Goodfellow, for a most enjoyable morning. I hope I may call on you again someday?"

"I'd be honored," Lily replied as Captain Trevillion again joined them.

"If you're quite ready, my lady," he said.

"Oh, all right," Lady Phoebe replied, getting to her feet.

Captain Trevillion moved adroitly to place his arm just where her hand would land when she rose. "I, too, shall bid you farewell, Miss Goodfellow."

"Sir. My lady," Lily murmured.

The captain tipped his hat and she watched as they left.

But the feeling of dread stayed with her. Who had Lady Phoebe thought Caliban was? For despite her disavowal, Lily couldn't help but think the other woman had had someone particular in mind when she'd asked her questions.

Lily glanced down at the remains of their tea. The question was this: how dangerous was it for her to become involved with Caliban when she didn't know who he was?

DESPITE MAKEPEACE'S IRE, MacLeish wasn't a bad sort, Apollo thought late that afternoon—although he *was* very young to be designing and building independently. But he did seem to at least understand the concepts of architecture. The proof, Apollo supposed, would come when the architect showed them his designs for the theater and opera house and whatever else the duke wanted and was willing to pay to have built in the garden. Until then Apollo decided to give the lad the benefit of the doubt.

Now, though, he found his steps quickening as he walked to the theater. He wanted to see Lily again—without inquisitive strangers or odd architects turning up and, if at all possible, even without her scamp of a son and her disapproving maidservant. He'd forgotten, in those long years in Bedlam, through fear and grief and pain, what it was like to simply be with a pretty woman. To tease and flirt and yes, perhaps steal a kiss.

He didn't know how she felt about that kiss—or if she'd let him kiss her again, but he was certainly going to try. He had lost time to make up—much of life itself to live.

He'd spent four years in limbo, simply existing, while others found lovers and friends, even started families.

He wanted to live again.

But as he neared the theater he heard first the sound of voices raised—and then a male voice shouting.

Apollo broke into a run.

He burst from the trees to find a slight man in a purple suit and a white wig standing intimidatingly close to Lily. She wore a shawl over her red dress as if she'd been prepared for their stroll. The two stood in the clearing outside the theater.

"—*told* you I needed it," he was saying, his face thrust into hers. Apollo could see spittle flying from his mouth. "You'll never sell it on your own, so don't even try it."

"It's my work, Edwin," she replied to the lout, bravely enough, but there was a waver in her voice that made Apollo see red.

"Who are...you?" he demanded, advancing on the two of them, hands clenching and unclenching.

The man swung around and blinked at the sight of Apollo as if he hadn't heard him draw near.

"Who'm *I*? Who...who...are *you*, you great ox?" he asked, mocking Apollo's halting speech.

He didn't much mind that—he'd had far worse than verbal jeers in Bedlam—but he didn't like the way Lily's face had grown pale at the sight of him. "Caliban, please." She gripped her hands together as if to keep from wringing them. "Can you come back in a bit? Perhaps half an hour or so?"

Her voice was too low, too controlled, as if she was afraid of setting the man off. As if she'd set him off before and hadn't liked the consequences.

"You know this . . . *oaf*?" The man spat the word at her, then threw back his head in cruel laughter. "I vow, Lil, your taste in bedmates has come down. 'Fore long you'll be lifting your skirts for common *porters*, if this is the sort—"

The end of his vicious rant ended in a satisfying squawk as Apollo backhanded him. The other man staggered and fell on his arse.

"No, don't hurt him!" Lily cried, and Apollo hated to think she cared for this man.

"I won't," he assured her in a level tone. He stared at the sputtering rogue for a moment and made up his mind. "But neither will I . . . stand by while he . . . abuses you." So saying, he picked up the man and tossed him over his shoulder. "Wait here."

The man made a sort of moan and Apollo hoped he wouldn't toss his accounts down his back. He'd bathed and changed into a fairly clean shirt before coming to see Lily.

Pivoting, he marched toward the dock, the man still over his shoulder.

"Caliban!"

He ignored her calls. He didn't really care who this ass was—as long as he was nowhere near Lily or Indio.

"Put—" The knave had to gasp for breath as Apollo leaped a fallen log, jostling the man's stomach against his shoulder. When he could draw breath again he swore foully. "Do you have any idea who I am?"

"No."

"I'll have your head." The other man gulped and tried to kick.

So Apollo let the man roll off his shoulder and onto

the ground. They were far enough away from the theater anyway by this point.

The villain stared up at him, pale with rage, his wig fallen to the side. His own hair was nearly black and cropped short. "I know people—people who can and will cut off your blasted cock."

"I have no...doubt." Threats were two a penny. Apollo straddled the prone dandy and leaned down into his face, intimidating him as he'd dared to do to Lily. "Don't come...back until...you can talk...to her with a civil tongue."

He nimbly avoided the kick aimed at his groin and left the knave there on the ground. Lily, after all, hadn't sounded too pleased when he'd left.

Nor was she looking very happy when he got back. She was still in the clearing, pacing.

She whirled on him as soon as he appeared. "What did you do to him?"

He shrugged, watching her. "Dumped him...on the ground...like the rubbish...he is." His throat ached, but he ignored it.

"Oh." She seemed to deflate a bit at that, only to puff back up a second later. "Well, you shouldn't have interfered. It wasn't any of your business."

This was not how he'd hoped to spend the afternoon.

"Perhaps...I wanted it to...be my business." He approached her cautiously as he spoke.

"It's just..." She waved one hand, obviously frustrated. "You just *can't*. He's..."

Apollo cocked his head. "Indio's father?"

"What?" She turned and stared. "No! Whatever made you think that? Edwin's my brother."

"Ah." The knot that had been pulled tight in his chest ever since she'd started defending the dandy loosened. Family was another matter. One couldn't choose family. "Then he...should speak...to his sister more carefully."

She screwed up her face rather adorably. "He's not himself. He lost quite a bit of money and he's anxious about it."

He caught her hand and tugged gently as he turned down a path into the garden—away from where he'd left Edwin. "I see. And this is...your fault?"

"No, of course not." She frowned, but let herself be led, so he counted that as a contest won. "It's just that he makes money from my plays."

He raised his eyebrows. "How so?"

"Well, they're published under his name, you see," she said, peering down at her steps. She didn't seem to notice that he still had hold of her hand, and he felt no need to bring it to her attention. Her slender fingers were cool in his. "He's...well, he's better able to sell the plays than I."

"Why?"

She kicked a stone in the path. "He has better acquaintances. Better friends." She blew out a frustrated breath. "He just is better at it, is all."

He was silent, but felt confused. How did "better friends" make it easier to publish a play?

"My father was a porter," she finally muttered, sounding faintly ashamed. "A common porter. Apparently he often fetched things for the actors in the theater where my mother was appearing. Costumes and props and a cooked hen for dinner and whatever else needed moving or fetching from one place to another. Oh, you know what a porter is."

He squeezed her hand gently instead of replying.

She broke off a twig from a tree as they passed. "Edwin's father was a lord—well, a lord's son, which, compared to a porter, is much the same thing. Mama said my father couldn't even read his own name. But he was handsome, so there's that, I suppose."

"You…" His damnable throat tried to close, but he forced the words out. "You did not…know…your father?"

She shook her head, glancing at him apologetically. "Mama had a great many lovers, I'm afraid, and none ever stayed long." She inhaled and shook herself. "Anyway, Edwin's been very helpful, taking my plays and finding where to sell them. He keeps some of the money and gives all the rest to me."

"How much?"

"What?"

"You write…the plays—very good plays, I'll… warrant—and he trots off…and sells them. How…much does he…pocket for such…hard work?"

She stiffened and attempted to pull her fingers from his. He didn't let her.

She glared, her lichen-green eyes sparking. "I don't think that's any of your business."

He stopped and faced her. They were nearly at the pond, at the site where his oak had toppled. He'd found the lead branch broken from the fall and ordered a new tree, but it had not yet arrived. "How much?"

She held his gaze defiantly for a moment more and he couldn't help but admire the way the late-afternoon sun's rays made a nimbus around her face of the fine hairs escaping her coiffure.

Her eyes dropped. "Twenty-five percent."

"Twenty-five percent." His voice was flat, but inside he was horrified. "Does he know...you don't have...acting work?"

"Yes, he knows, that was partly what we argued about." She'd raised their joined hands to her chest level and was examining his fingers, probably appalled at the ingrained dirt. "I told him that I wanted him to take only twenty percent. But Edwin isn't always very practical when it comes to money, you see."

Apollo would bet his right hand that Edwin could be entirely practical when it came to his *own* money. "How do you...even know he's...giving you the proper... amount?"

She looked up, startled, from his hand. "Edwin wouldn't lie to me. You must understand." Now she was holding his hand between her own two. "He...well, Mama drank gin, you see, and by the time I was born she was no longer very much in demand, either in the theater or with men, and it was hard for her." She ducked her head, studying his fingers, spreading them against her own, comparing their lengths. His hand dwarfed hers. "Very hard. And later there was Maude, but when I was very small, all I had was Mama and Edwin. He made sure I had a place to sleep—for often we moved, from theater to theater or even from one rental room to another. He made sure I had food and clothes and taught me to read and write." She curled her fingers into the spaces between his, tightening them as if she wouldn't ever let go. "I owe him...everything, really."

"Perhaps you...do," he said softly, for he knew what it was to be beholden to someone who is unable to fully reciprocate one's devotion. "But do you...owe him Indio's life...as well?"

She looked up at him, her brows knit. "What do you mean?"

"Indio needs...food and clothes and...a place to sleep, doesn't he?"

She nodded.

"Naturally...he does," Apollo said. "And how...is he to have...all those things and...more if you let...your brother leech...from you?"

"I just..." She bit her lip. "I don't want to hurt him. I know Edwin is fickle and cruel at times, but he's my *brother*. I love him."

"How can you not?" he replied, and brought their twined hands to his lips, kissing each of her fingertips one by one.

When he raised his head she was watching him in wonder. "I don't know you at all. First I thought you a simpleton. Then you couldn't speak. And now you can, but you *won't*." She stood on tiptoe and brushed her lips along his jaw, her touch soft and searching, more intimate than any kiss on the lips. "I don't know you, but I want to. Can you let me in a little?"

He closed his eyes. This was playing with fire. "What do you wish to know?"

Chapter Ten

*The youth's name was Theseus. He and Ariadne
were escorted to the labyrinth and pushed inside.
Then Theseus turned to Ariadne. He was tall and fair
but when he saw that she had brought the spindle into
the labyrinth, he laughed in scorn. "You'll have no use
of that here. Better you follow behind me and let me kill
the beast." So saying, he took out a short sword he'd
concealed in his robes and, turning right, disappeared
into the labyrinth...*
—From *The Minotaur*

What did she wish to know? That was easy: Lily wanted
to know who Caliban truly was—a name, an identity,
something to place him in the world in relation to her.

But he couldn't answer that, she knew, so she started
with a simpler inquiry.

"You seem to know about family." The sun was beginning to set and even with the smell of burnt wood, the garden was a magical place. Birds had begun their evening
song around them in the golden rays. "Do you have family?"

He nodded. "I have...a sister."

She smiled up at him, into his muddy-brown eyes surrounded by such beautiful, lush lashes. She was relieved

that he'd answered that much—hadn't rejected her question out of hand. "Older or younger?"

A corner of his wide mouth cocked up. "The exact same...age as I."

"A twin!" She grinned in delight. "What's her name?"

He shook his head gently.

But she wasn't so easily disappointed now that he'd let her in a little. "Very well. Do you like her?"

"Very much." He paused as if searching for words. "She is...the dearest thing...to me...in the world."

"Oh," she said softly. "Oh, how sweet."

He quirked an eyebrow at her. "You make me...sound a little boy."

"I don't mean to," she said earnestly. "I think one's family, the people one keeps close to oneself, are very important. I don't think I could like a man who didn't value others."

"And...do you like me?"

She wagged her finger at him. "I'm not so easily lured as all that. Now. Were you born in London?" She turned, swinging their hands as she meandered down one of the paths.

"No."

She pouted. "In a city?"

"No."

Her eyes widened in exasperation. "In England?"

"Yes, I am...an Englishman," he said, and then relented. "I was...born in the country."

"North or south?"

"South."

"By the coast?"

"No." He slid an amused glance her way. "There were...

farmlands. And a pond…quite nearby. My…sister and I learned to…swim in it."

"And you had a mother and a father." She looked down at the charred path because most people *did* have both a mother and a father growing up—just not she, it seemed.

"Yes," he answered gently, "though…they're both dead now."

"I'm sorry," she said.

He shrugged.

"Were you close?" she asked too fast, her words running together. "Did you have a happy childhood with a father who worked and brought home money and a mother who mended your socks?"

"Not…precisely," he replied. "My childhood was happy…enough, but my mother…was often sickly and…my father…" He took a deep breath and let it out in a gusty sigh. "My father was…mad."

She stopped short—or tried to.

He tugged her hand to keep her strolling beside him. "It's not…as terrible as it…sounds. He wasn't violent…or awful to my sister…and me, or…even our mother. He was excitable. Sometimes…he would stay awake…for days on end, frantically planning…various schemes—though they all came…to naught. He'd hie away…from the house for a week…or more and we… were never sure where…he went. Just that when…he came home his pockets…would be empty and he'd…be exhausted. Then he would sleep…for a full day and perhaps spend…a fortnight abed…taking his meals there. And…then he'd…arise one day and…be off again."

He shrugged. "I thought…when I was very small… that all boys had fathers like…mine."

She was silent then, because there didn't seem much to say. They walked in companionable silence as the sun began to paint the sky in shades of scarlet and bright yellow and orange.

"Is she alive still, your sister?" she at last asked, almost lazily.

"Oh, yes."

"And you see her?" She darted a sideways glance, but he merely shook his head and smiled.

Damn. "Do you have other family, then? Aunts and uncles and, oh, cousins, I suppose? Is it a big family you're from?"

"Not big…but I have some…relations," he replied. "Though…I know none of them well. My…father's madness drove…him apart from his own…father and the rest of the…family followed…suit, I suppose." He shrugged. "I really…don't know. I certainly…never saw them as a child."

She nodded. "And now that you're a man? Have you tried to talk to them?"

He squeezed her hand and then relaxed, so swiftly she couldn't tell if the motion was in reaction to her question or not. "No."

She heaved a great sigh and tried another tack. "How did you come to know Mr. Harte?"

He laughed at that. "I met May—*Harte*…in a tavern…when we were both barely…of age."

She did stop then, and made him turn to face her. "What was that word you almost said? May? Is that his first name?"

He actually looked guilty at that. "He'll…kill me."

"What?"

"It's a . . . great secret," he warned.

"Tell me," she demanded.

She thought he wouldn't answer her. But he pulled her close and folded her hands on her breast, over her heart. "Do you promise . . . never, ever to tell?"

"Yes."

He bent, putting his mouth to her ear, so close she could feel the brush of his lips. "Harte . . . isn't his name. It's . . . Asa Makepeace."

She jerked back, mouth agape in shock. "What?"

He shrugged, looking amused. "It's true."

"But whyever did he change his name?"

"For the same . . . reason, I expect, that you"—he tapped a finger on her nose—"changed yours."

She wrinkled her forehead. "Because *Stump* sounded like a dead tree and he needed a witty name for the stage?"

"Well, perhaps not . . . *entirely* the same reason," he allowed. "I understand his family . . . doesn't approve of the theater."

"Oh, well, that makes sense," she said, because it did. "Families are very odd things, after all."

"Aren't they indeed," he breathed, and then he kissed her.

His mouth moved on hers with exquisite slowness, teasing her lips apart, sliding his tongue along the inside of her bottom lip. He caught her chin in the V between his thumb and fingers, holding her steady for his pleasure.

"Lily," he breathed as he nipped at her mouth. "Lily."

And her name, spoken in his broken voice—so sure, so tender, nonetheless—had never sounded so beautiful before.

She stood on tiptoe and twined her arms about his broad shoulders, trying to get closer, and felt a moment's frustration that she couldn't. A whimper escaped her and then he bent and simply grasped her around the waist. He lifted her easily, as if she were no more than Indio's little wooden boat, and set her high against his chest so that she might tilt her head down to continue their kiss. Such casual strength should've frightened her. Should've made her pause and think.

But all it did was arouse her further.

Her bodice was crushed against his great chest, the slopes of her upper breasts pressed with each inhalation against the coarse cloth of his waistcoat, and she wanted...wanted something.

It'd been such a very long time since she'd been with a man. The emotions, the heat between them, made her breathless, and it was her own lack of control that finally sobered her.

"Wait," she gasped, breaking away, pressing one palm to his chest. "I..."

He licked lazily at the corner of her mouth, not demanding, but seducing, which was, in this case, far more dangerous. She moaned a little and then got herself under control and pulled back.

"Put me down," she said in her most haughty voice. Had she not been so very breathless, it would've come off rather well.

"You're sure?" he drawled. There was a slash of color high on each of his craggy cheekbones and his eyes were lidded with sensuality.

Was she? "Quite," she said, much more firmly than she actually felt.

He sighed heavily and let her slide—*slowly*—down his chest.

"Erm...thank you," she said, trying and probably failing to regain some of her dignity. She brushed down her skirts, looking anywhere but at him. "We should return to the theater. I sent Maude and Indio out for meat pies for our supper and they should be back soon. You're invited, of course."

"I'm honored...to accept," he said as formally as if she were the Queen.

She nodded and began to set off before she realized that they were in a part of the garden she'd never seen before. "Where are we?"

"The heart," he said, his voice low and rasping. "The very...heart of my future garden...the center of the maze."

She shivered at his words. This place didn't look any different from anywhere else in the garden, but garden hearts, she supposed, like human hearts, could be disguised.

"I can't see it," she said.

He took a step toward her and turned her to face the same way as he, her back against his chest. "Here," he said, wrapping his arms over her shoulders to hold her hands. "There'll be a folly...of some sort right here... beneath our feet. A fountain or...waterfall or statue. Benches for lovers to sit and...kiss. The entrance will be over here"—he pointed to a space to the right—"and the maze...will wind all around us...like an embrace."

Slowly he turned with her, tracing with his outstretched hand his imaginary maze.

"You have so much faith," she whispered.

She felt him shrug behind her. "It's there already... just waiting for the right person...to find it and bring it alive," he said softly in her ear. "A maze...is eternal, you know, once discovered."

She shivered at that and pulled away, turning to give him a bright smile. "Indio will be waiting impatiently for his supper."

He nodded, but didn't return her smile. "Of course."

"I don't understand how you can see so much in what is only destruction and debris now," she commented as they turned back toward the theater. She was very careful to keep from brushing against him as they walked, for she was afraid that if they touched a spark might be lit. She felt as if a fine tension ran along her skin, making her nervously aware of his every movement.

He shrugged beside her. "I see it in my mind's eye, complete...and wonderful. It's only a matter of...planting and moving...to reveal what's already there." He glanced at her fondly. "Really, 'tisn't such a mysterious thing."

She had a certain suspicion that he was talking about something else as well.

He coughed rather harshly, and she looked at him quickly. "How is your throat?"

"Sore," he replied. "But...that is to be expected... after so long unused."

"I'm very glad you can speak again."

He smiled at her finally and then they were at the theater.

Daffodil scampered to greet them, closely followed by Indio with the news that he and Maude had brought back two large pies and they must wash at once to have them while they were still hot.

Thus instructed, Lily and Caliban washed by the old water barrel.

"Mama," Indio said as they sat, "the wherryman had only *two* teeth and he could spit *ever* so far."

And he proceeded to tell them all about the wherryman's unusual and rather disgusting skill.

Caliban expressed suitable interest in this dining conversation and Lily was content to watch the play between the two males. Even Maude unbent enough to give her opinion on long-distance spitting and the number of teeth one usually found in the average wherryman.

Lily almost forgot her nervous tension until after supper, when Maude was clearing the dishes with Indio's help.

Caliban drew Lily out the theater door, quietly closing it behind them.

"See?" he said, pointing to the North Star. "In another year...or two, you'll no longer...be able to glimpse... the stars from the garden. The lights...and fireworks will obscure them."

"So I should treasure the wildness now?" she asked whimsically.

"Perhaps," he said, drawing her close. "Or...just be glad that you...have this time, hard though...it seems at the moment. After all, most of London has not this... grand view...of the night sky. Only we two."

"As if we have a world of our own."

He smiled right before he kissed her, and she knew somehow he felt the same. They were a universe apart, Adam and Eve, in a garden that wasn't quite Eden.

And then she thought no more for many long minutes as he leisurely kissed her, mouth opened wide over hers as if he would consume her, meld with her and make them one being under the starlit night sky.

When at last he drew back she felt a little dazed, almost off-balance, as if the world had tilted a bit on its axis.

"Tomorrow," he said, walking backward into the dark. "Shall I...show you the secret island...in the pond?"

"If you must," she said, the tremble in her voice betraying her discomposure.

The last thing she heard before he disappeared into the garden was the sound of his laughter.

IT WASN'T EVEN dawn when Apollo woke the next morning, but he knew it was already too late.

He could hear people in the garden.

"In th' gallery, 'e said," a male voice called.

A disturbed bird shrilled as it flew away.

Another man swore softly.

They were close—very close.

Apollo rolled from his pallet, glad that he'd slept in his clothes, and grabbed his shoes and his pruning knife. There was no door to the alcove in the musician's gallery where he slept, only the tarp he'd hung over the corner. He slipped, barefoot, to the side, down the gallery.

Just as men appeared in the pink-gray light of morning in his garden. They were closing in on him.

Soldiers. They were soldiers. Red-coated, with bayonets fixed on their guns.

The breath caught in his throat. His right heel skidded on grit-strewn marble, and he beat back a sudden, cowardly wave of panic.

He whirled to his right only to find a soldier within

arm's distance, just a young boy beneath his tall cap, blue, blue eyes wide and frightened.

The soldier brought up his bayonet and Apollo swung his pruning knife in a vicious feint.

The boy soldier screamed, flailing as he scrambled away from the knife, his breath pluming white in the cold morning air.

"Oi!" someone shouted.

"Watch it!" cried another. "'E's a murderer thrice over!"

No. No. No.

Not again. Never again. He'd slit his own throat before returning to Bedlam.

Apollo ran.

Through the beautiful morning light, through the blackened garden he'd hoped to redeem, with demons on his heels.

Not all were corporal.

Chapter Eleven

A pounding at the theater door startled Lily awake that morning. She sat up in bed, groggily looking around as Daff barked hysterically.

Shaking her head, she found her wrap and stumbled out of the bedroom, calling, "Who is it?"

She expected perhaps Edwin's voice—although normally he never arose before noon—but it was another voice entirely that shouted back.

"Open in the name of the King!"

That made her halt abruptly, her eyes widening as she stared at her door.

The pounding came again, provoking Daffodil into a frenzy of yapping.

Lily threw a glance at Maude, who had risen as well and stood with her hand on Indio's shoulder. Indio looked excited and a little frightened.

"Catch her and hold her," Lily told Maude. "The last thing we need is Daffodil attacking soldiers."

She went to the door and opened it, putting on her most charming smile. "Yes?"

The man without was an officer. He wore a red-coated uniform with smart white facing, breeches, and waistcoat, but his face was unshaven and lined. His eyes widened at the sight of her.

"'As a man taken refuge 'ere? A big man?" he asked.

Dear God, they were after Caliban. Lily prayed that Indio wouldn't volunteer information.

"Why no," she answered, puzzled, but sweet. "We were asleep until you came a-knocking, Major."

The man actually flushed. "It's *Sergeant*, ma'am. Sergeant Green. We're searching for this man and we'll 'ave a look around your...uh...'ouse."

"It's a theater, Sergeant Green," she said, pulling the door wide, "and naturally the King's men have my permission to look to their heart's content."

He nodded curtly and three uniformed soldiers tromped in, tracking mud onto Maude's clean floor.

The maidservant's mouth's tightened, but she made no comment.

"May I offer you some tea, Sergeant?" Lily asked.

"That's right kind of you, ma'am, but I'm afeard we 'aven't the time," Sergeant Green replied. His men were already in her bedroom doing Lord knew what with her bed linen. "Is there anyone else in the, er, theater?"

"Just myself and my maid and son." She gestured to

Maude and Indio. Daffodil took the opportunity to growl at the sergeant and attempt to wriggle free from Maude's arms.

"Quite." The sergeant had narrowed his eyes at the little greyhound. "And you are . . . ?"

"Why, Miss Robin Goodfellow," she said with what she knew was becoming modesty.

One of the soldiers tripped.

The sergeant looked impressed. "The actress?"

"You've heard of me, Sergeant?" she asked, all wide-eyed amazement, her hand pressed modestly to her chest. "How flattering."

"Saw you in that play—the one in which you wore"—the sergeant blushed a deep russet and lowered his voice—"*breeches*. Awful grand, you were, ma'am. Awful grand."

"Oh, thank you," she said, feigning flustered confusion. "Can you tell me whom your men are looking for?"

"A wanted man," Sergeant Green said darkly. "Right dangerous character. Are there more rooms in the theater, ma'am?"

"Not really," she said. "Some parts of the backstage are still standing, but they've been boarded up because it's unsafe."

Naturally the sergeant ordered the door leading to the area unbarred. Two of the men went through and there was a silence as the third poked through Maude's chest. Why, Lily wasn't sure, since the chest was far too small for anyone of normal size to hide in, let alone Caliban.

Lily tried to remain calm as she fretted. Were there more soldiers searching the garden even as these messed about in the theater—or were there only these four men? Could she somehow send word to warn him?

But he must've heard the noise the soldiers were making by now, surely?

After a few minutes there was a crash and a good deal of cursing from the soldiers who had gone into the unsafe area of the theater. They returned, quite sooty, looking sheepish, and with one of them limping.

Lily smiled, trying to appear at ease and *not* as if she wanted to rid herself of the soldiers. "If that's all, Sergeant, I must be getting my son's breakfast."

"Thank you for your time, Miss Goodfellow," he replied, "and if you should see a big fellow sneaking about the garden, you must notify the authorities at once."

"Oh, you can be assured I will," she said, putting a tremor of fright into her voice. "But can you tell me what he's wanted for?"

"Why, murder, ma'am," Sergeant Green replied with grim relish. "The Viscount Kilbourne escaped nine months ago from Bedlam, where he was committed for savagely and insanely murdering three of his friends for no reason at all."

Lily stared at him, shocked into silence. She couldn't seem to even make her brain work.

Sergeant Green seemed satisfied with her reaction. "Be careful, Miss Goodfellow, you and your boy and your maid. Kilbourne is no more than a beast. He'd as soon kill you as look at you."

With that he bowed and with his men tramped out of the theater.

In the sudden silence Lily turned mutely to stare at Maude. "Oh, my God."

*   *   *

"BUT 'TIS ONLY nine of the clock," the sleepy blond wench mumbled as Asa Makepeace bundled her out his door. A blue ribbon trailed forlornly from her half-done hair. "Thought we could at least 'ave a bit of a cuddle this morn afore I 'ad to go."

"And we will, love—*next* time," Makepeace said, and then bent to whisper something no doubt salacious in her ear.

Apollo made sure to turn his back, staring at a box of marzipan sweets carelessly left open on a pile of papers. They were shaped into oranges and lemons. He wanted not only to keep from hearing whatever it was Makepeace was whispering to his paramour, but also to prevent her from seeing his face.

It'd taken him hours to get to Makepeace's door. He'd had to first escape the soldiers and then make sure he wasn't followed. After that he'd spent some time outside Makepeace's building, watching and waiting to see if the soldiers would come there next. They hadn't turned up, which could mean either that they simply hadn't arrived yet or that they didn't know his connection to Makepeace.

In either case, he couldn't stay here long.

The door closed behind the girl and Makepeace turned to him, looking unusually serious. "Damn it, when the hell did you regain your voice?"

"Only a few days ago," Apollo said impatiently.

"No one ever tells me anything," Makepeace muttered, crossing to the fireplace.

"My voice...isn't why I'm here."

"Then what is?"

"At least a dozen...soldiers in the garden." Apollo

paced as well as he could in the overcrowded room. "They knew who I was ... and they knew where I slept."

"Someone betrayed you." Makepeace stoked the fire and filled his kettle with water before hanging it from a hook he swung over the blaze. "Well, you can stay here until—"

"That's just it ... I can't." Apollo noted absently that a mechanical hen had joined Makepeace's collection. It had a key in its side to wind it. No doubt it would lay eggs or even little chicks when wound. God only knew where Makepeace had found it. "If they know ... so much about me it's only ... a matter of time before they discover ... my friendship with you and come here. I must flee the city."

And leave Lily behind. He stared blindly at the mechanical hen's glass eye. Would he ever see her again? Her inquisitive lichen-green eyes, her lush pink mouth? Damn it, would she even *want* to see him when she found out *why* the soldiers were after him? He ran his hands through his hair in frustrated despair.

"But the garden." Makepeace sat heavily on a chair, unmindful of the books that slid to the floor as a result. "Damn it, 'Pollo, no one can design that garden the way you can. It's *you* that has the vision. It'll just be another boring line of box hedges in geometric patterns without you."

Apollo winced. "I can make you notes to ... give to whomever you ... hire to take over." He slumped as well—on the only other available surface, which was the bed. The garden had been his delight. A place to make beautiful in his own design after four years of stagnation in Bedlam. This, too, he would have to abandon. And then another realization hit him. "I left my notebook. I only ... had time to ... take my shoes ... and my knife."

"Goddamn it!"

Apollo shrugged. "I have most of it...memorized anyway." He sighed, letting his head drop back. He could recreate the plans, but that notebook held all the conversations and musings he'd had since he'd been freed. He felt its loss like a tangible wound.

He closed his eyes in near-despair at another thought. "Lily's in the garden. D'you think they'll...harass her? The soldiers?"

"Lily, is it?" The other man perked up like the idiot he was.

"Makepeace," Apollo growled.

"No," Makepeace sighed. "They have no reason to think that she even knows you—do they?"

Apollo shrugged, feeling weary. "Her brother...was there yesterday. He was...quite foul to her and I...tossed him out."

"'Tossed,'" Makepeace repeated carefully.

"Not literally," Apollo snapped, then had to concede, remembering Edwin landing on his rump in the dirt. "Well, in a way. But I didn't hurt him...though he did make...several threats to me."

"And seems to've carried them out," Makepeace replied drily. He jumped up as the kettle began to steam. "No one else knew you were in the garden, did they?"

Apollo ticked them off on his fingers. "My sister...and thus His Grace the Ass...you, Montgomery, and James Trevillion."

Makepeace paused with the kettle in one hand and then swore and had to set it down when the hot handle apparently burned his fingers. "Who's this Trevillion?"

Apollo looked at him. "The man who...arrested me the morning of the...murders."

"And you didn't think to mention him until now?" Makepeace's eyes widened in outrage. "Good God, man, *that's* your betrayer right there."

Apollo was already shaking his head. "No...he'd realized he made a...mistake in arresting me. He vowed to help...discover the real murderer."

"So he told you." Makepeace furiously shook tea into a teapot from a tin without bothering to measure it. "How can you be such a fool?"

"I'm not a fool," Apollo growled.

"He was merely placating you until he could inform the King's men."

"I *saw* him just yesterday."

"And that makes my point!" Makepeace filled the teapot and banged down the kettle on the hob. A few drops of water splashed out and hit the hearth, sizzling as they evaporated. "He betrayed you, 'Pollo."

"No—"

There was a knock on the door and they both fell silent. Apollo exchanged glances with Makepeace, and then took his hooked pruning knife from the belt at his waist.

He wasn't going back.

He slid behind the door as Makepeace opened it.

"Mr. Harte?" said a familiar voice, and Apollo peered around the door. Trevillion stood in the outer hall, alone and leaning on his cane.

"Inside," Apollo muttered, gesturing him in.

"Are you insane?" Makepeace hissed as Trevillion limped in. "Who's this?"

"Trevillion, the man...I was telling you about."

Makepeace looked outraged. "This man betrayed you!"

"I didn't," Trevillion replied with stiff dignity.

"Indeed?" Makepeace thrust out his face, a sarcastic smile twisting his lips. "Then why, pray tell, are you here, only hours after 'Pollo had to flee for his life from Harte's Folly? How do you even know where I live when I'd never heard your name before this morning?"

"'Tisn't my fault you're not well informed," Trevillion replied, his upper lip curling.

Apollo nearly banged his head against the wall. *Naturally* Trevillion would rather antagonize than explain. But with Trevillion's next breath he was proven wrong.

"As for your first question," Trevillion continued, "I'm here because a man who was under my command four years ago, when I arrested Lord Kilbourne, came to me. He informed me that he'd heard there'd been a raid on Harte's Folly this morning, but that Lord Kilbourne had escaped. I arrived at your door, hoping you would know of Lord Kilbourne's whereabouts, and," he said, casting a significant glance Apollo's way, "as it turned out, you did."

"So you could arrest him anew!" Makepeace shouted.

"Had I wanted him arrested, he'd be languishing behind bars now," Trevillion replied, hard.

Apollo stiffened at how easily Trevillion talked about putting him behind bars.

The door to Makepeace's rooms opened and the Duke of Montgomery strolled in as casually as if he were entering an afternoon musicale.

"I say," the duke drawled, "am I interrupting?"

"No, but you're barging in uninvited to my rooms," Makepeace snapped.

"It's so tedious," Montgomery sighed, "to have to wait for invitations and, I find, they often don't come when you most want them to. Much easier to simply disregard formal invitations altogether. Good Lord, man," he continued in the same bored tone, "haven't you anywhere for guests to sit in this pigsty?"

"*Invited* guests are welcome to sit on the bed." Makepeace pointed. "*Un*invited guests are welcome to—"

"What are you…doing here, Your Grace?" Apollo asked hastily before Makepeace could finish his sentence—perhaps disastrously.

Montgomery slowly pivoted to him. "You've regained the use of your voice, Lord Kilbourne."

Apollo impatiently inclined his head.

"How very fascinating," Montgomery said as if Apollo were an exotic animal he'd never seen before.

"You've not answered…my question."

Montgomery spread his elegant hands wide. "I heard you were in trouble and naturally I came to help."

"You wanted to…help me," Apollo said, flat.

"You are, after all, the gardener with the grand scheme for my pleasure garden." Montgomery cocked his head whimsically.

"*My* pleasure garden," Makepeace interjected.

Montgomery cast him an amused glance, but addressed Apollo. "Helping you, I admit, helps me as well, but I see no problem with that."

"No, *you* wouldn't," Apollo muttered.

"*How* did you know about Lord Kilbourne's difficulties, may I inquire, Your Grace?" Trevillion asked quietly.

"Oh," Montgomery murmured, bending to peer at the mechanical hen, "one hears these things."

"Usually only if one has paid informants," Trevillion said, very dry.

"They *do* help." Montgomery straightened and smiled sweetly. "Now, if we're done with the pleasantries, I suggest we discuss how we're going to prove Lord Kilbourne's innocence so he can get back to work on Harte's Folly. I really must insist my garden be open for business by next spring, and this…hiccup…threatens to put the whole thing back *months*." He made a moue of discontent. "I really shan't have it."

"*My* garden," Makepeace muttered, but his heart was obviously no longer in it. He fetched the steaming teapot. "Right. Trevillion sit there"—he indicated his vacated chair—"*you*"—he pointed at the duke—"can sit on the bed or not at all. Now, who's for tea?"

And a few minutes later they all had steaming—if mismatched—cups of tea in what had to be the oddest tea party Apollo had ever attended.

"Now then." Makepeace slurped noisily at his teacup merely, Apollo suspected, to annoy the duke. He'd dumped half the contents of a rather fine gilded sugar bowl into his tea and it must have been like drinking treacle. "Let's hear it. What's your grand plan?"

Montgomery sniffed cautiously at his tea and took a very small, very delicate sip. Immediately his eyebrows shot up and he hastily set the teacup down on a pile of books. "Obviously we must find and expose the real murderer."

"Obviously," Makepeace drawled back.

The duke ignored that. "Am I to assume from Captain Trevillion's presence that you've already made some inquiries?"

Apollo exchanged a glance with Trevillion and Apollo nodded.

"Yes, Your Grace, I have done some investigation into the matter." The captain cleared his throat. "It seems Lord Kilbourne's uncle, William Greaves, is in some debt to his grandfather's, the earl's, estate."

Montgomery, who had been poking at his teacup, looked up at that. "Splendid! We have a viable candidate for a substitute murderer. Now to simply alert the authorities with a well-placed hint—"

"A hint about what, exactly?" Makepeace exploded. "We don't have a scrap of real evidence that 'Pollo's uncle did anything."

"Oh, evidence is easily manufactured, I find," the duke said carelessly as he dropped a marzipan orange into his tea. He watched it sink with interest.

There was a short, appalled silence.

The duke seemed to realize something was amiss. He glanced up, his blue eyes wide and innocent. "Problem?"

Fortunately it was Trevillion who replied. "I'm afraid we can't simply manufacture evidence, Your Grace," he said calmly but firmly. "We must discover the evidence naturally."

"How tedious!" The duke actually pouted before assuming a rather alarmingly crafty expression. "It'll take much less time my way, you comprehend."

"Oh for God's sake!" Makepeace burst out and for a moment Apollo was afraid he'd have to physically restrain him. "You're discussing falsifying evidence to *hang* a man."

"*Don't* be a hypocrite, Mr. Harte," the duke snapped. "You believe him just as guilty as I. You just want to salve your conscience by working for the evidence. The end result is the same, I assure you: an arrested man and Lord Kilbourne saved from Bedlam."

"*Nevertheless*," Trevillion said. He didn't raise his voice, but such was its command, the other two men looked to him. "We'll do it *our* way. Your Grace."

For a moment the soldier and the aristocrat glared at each other.

Then the duke suddenly knocked over his teacup, spilling the mess on a stack of papers. "Oh, very well," he said, petulant, over the squawks of Makepeace. Apparently the papers were broadsheets he'd been meaning to read. "I suppose there's no help for it. We'll have to go to William Greaves's country house outside Bath and hunt around like farmers' wives after chicken eggs."

They all stared at him.

"What *now*?"

Trevillion cleared his throat, but Makepeace, perhaps because of his sodden broadsheets, beat him to it. "How do you propose we get into Greaves's country house? Surely he'll notice four men tramping through his rooms."

"I doubt it," Montgomery purred, "since he'll be holding a country party in a little over a fortnight's time with an especial play as the centerpiece of the event. Naturally, I have been invited. I'll simply arrive with my very good friend, Mr. *Smith*"—he sent a significant glance at Apollo—"and there you are."

"There we *won't* be, because the first thing Greaves will do will be to have 'Pollo arrested," Makepeace objected.

"Actually," Apollo interjected thoughtfully, "I've never met…the man."

Makepeace swung on him, looking betrayed. "What, never?"

Apollo shrugged. "Perhaps…as a baby? I certainly

have no...memory of him or the rest of his family. He probably's never...seen me." He looked over at Trevillion calmly sipping his tea. "Can Lady Phoebe find...a way to get an invitation to...the house party?"

"No," the captain said with certainty. "Her brother does not want her to attend social events except those held by a family member. There are very few exceptions. However"—he looked considering—"I believe Wakefield has a house in Bath. It shouldn't be too hard to suggest Lady Phoebe take the waters. And, since she enjoys the theater very much, she might be able to attend a private theatrical performance for one night. I shall look into the matter."

Montgomery clapped his hands. "Then it's settled. As I see it, there's but one thing to do in the intervening two weeks."

"And what is that?" Makepeace grated.

The duke turned his bright-blue eyes on Apollo, making him exceptionally nervous. "Why, outfit Lord Kilbourne as the aristocrat he is."

Chapter Twelve

Ariadne followed the winding corridors of the labyrinth for days and nights. She ate the cheese and bread her mother had hidden in the folds of her robe and drank the dew that collected in the crevices of the stone at night. Sometimes she would hear an animal's roar or what sounded like a man's shout, but often she heard nothing at all except the scrape of her slippers on the hard earth of the labyrinth. And then, on the third day, she found the first skeleton...
—From *The Minotaur*

Two weeks later Lily looked up at the gray stone facade of William Greaves's country house and thought she should be excited.

It was the first opportunity in months and months for her to perform—and it would be in one of her own plays. By dint of nearly killing herself, she'd finished *A Wastrel Reform'd* on time and sent the manuscript by porter to Edwin, despite her misgivings. He'd already had a buyer, after all, and they both needed the money rather badly.

She hadn't been terribly surprised when the Duke of Montgomery had introduced her to the other players and she'd found out she was performing in the play she'd only just finished. William Greaves was the duke's friend who'd commissioned *A Wastrel Reform'd*, and she had the lead as Cecily Wastrel. A plum breeches role—and she should know.

All in all a lovely turn of events. Usually she'd be happy and looking forward to both the party and the work.

Instead she felt a persistent melancholy. Caliban—*Lord Kilbourne*—had to all appearances escaped the soldiers, but she had no idea where he was. Indio had spent the week she'd been frantically writing moping about the garden, bemoaning his loss and driving her half mad. Even Maude, who should've been glad all her dire warnings about the man had proven correct, was silent on the subject. The afternoon after the soldiers finally left the garden, Lily had crept into the musician's gallery and found his meager nest. He'd left a few clothes, an end of bread, and his notebook. This last she'd pocketed as some pathetic token—of what, she wasn't exactly sure.

So it was with false cheer that she entered the Greaves House hallway. It was an older manse with narrow, dark rooms. She glanced around, already worried about where they could put on the play.

"Ah, our players," Mr. William Greaves said rather pompously. He was a man in his sixties who'd probably been handsome as a youth. Now, however, he had a uniform dreary grayness about him, with a lined, sagging jawline and a puffiness around the eyes that bespoke too much drink or rich food. "I collect you must be Miss Goodfellow?"

She curtsied. "Your discernment is quite amazing, sir." She swept wide her arm to indicate the other players behind her. "May I introduce Mr. Stanford Hume." An older, florid-faced actor bowed stiffly. Poor Stanford suffered from lumbago. "Miss Moll Bennet." Moll curtsied low, drawing Mr. Greaves's eye to her lush bosom. "And Mr. John Hampstead?" John grinned and swept a lavish bow. He was tall and thin and wasn't particular as to the sex of his paramours.

They four were the principal players, though of course there were other actors to fill the remaining parts of the play.

"Welcome, welcome to Greaves House," Mr. Greaves said expansively, and then rather ruined the effect by becoming practical. "I believe my butler has your rooms ready. I do hope you'll be joining us for dinner. A most jolly company, I think. Ah, here's my son and his wife arrived. You'll excuse me?"

And they were left to the direction of the butler.

Who, naturally, looked faintly contemptuous. "Lake." He snapped his fingers and one of the footmen came forward. "Show these persons to their rooms, please."

"Ta, love," John said cheekily to the butler.

And they tramped after Lake the footman.

"Well, at least they have us inside," Moll said philosophically as they mounted the stairs. "Last house play I did would you believe they wanted us to bunk in the stables like gypsies? No, indeed, I said. Inside in a room at least as nice as the downstairs maids or back to London I go on the next stage. They grumbled, but I had my way in the end. That was *Richard II* in Cambridgeshire, d'you remember, Stanford?"

"I do indeed," Stanford intoned in his plummy voice. "Most depressing production I've ever been in."

"Don't know what they were thinking," agreed Moll. "A *history* play for a house party. Can you imagine?"

The footman, who, unlike the butler, seemed rather in awe of them, showed them to two rooms. After hearing Moll's story about being housed in the stables, Lily was a bit afraid of what they'd be given. But other than being quite at the end of the hall, their rooms seemed to be nice.

"Better'n the stables anyway," Moll said cheerfully as she poked her head in the wardrobe. "We'll be sharing the bed, looks like"—she nodded at the canopied bed—"but I don't snore, so it should be fine. Best tidy ourselves and go on downstairs. I've a feeling we're the entertainment for the night."

That was often the case, Lily reflected as they took turns at the washbasin and changed out of their dusty traveling clothes. The actors hired for a private performance were also considered professional guests by their host—there to enliven the party.

They were ready to appear in a little less than an hour. Moll was in dark brown and mauve, while Lily had on one of her favorite dresses, a scarlet affair with a deep, square neckline and white ruffles on the bodice and sleeves.

"Shall we?" Moll teased and they stepped out into the hall to find John and Stanford waiting.

"Ladies!" John swept them a ridiculously elaborate bow.

"Ass," Stanford muttered, offering Moll his arm.

That left Lily to take John's arm as they descended. She'd worked with both Moll and John before and was finding Stanford to be quietly witty beneath his role as the elder actor. In normal circumstances she'd be enjoying herself immensely: a country house, a party, genial colleagues, and the prospect of a week's worth of good food.

Tonight, though, she simply saw the party as something to endure.

On the first floor was a large salon and Lily glanced around it, mentally trying it on for size for their play. The lighting wasn't very good—it was an interior room with only two windows at the far end—but the play would be at night anyway and with several dozen candles, it might well do.

She caught Stanford's eye and when he winked, she knew he was thinking the same thing.

Then their host entered and with him the rest of the house party guests.

The first were Mr. and Mrs. George Greaves, their host's son and his wife, though, since the older man was a widower, Lily suspected his daughter-in-law had had a hand in planning the party. She was a plain woman in her thirties, quiet, but with an intelligence in her eyes when they were introduced to her. Her husband, in contrast, had a carrying voice that would've done him well had he taken to the stage. George Greaves was a big, burly man and still had the good looks age had faded from his father.

Behind them was another, somewhat younger couple. Mr. and Mrs. Phillip Warner were still newlyweds and obviously in love. They made a striking couple, as both had beautiful butter-yellow hair, and Lily couldn't help thinking they were destined to have a gorgeous brood of children.

Miss Hippolyta Royle was accompanied by her father, Sir George Royle, who had made his fortune in India and been knighted for his efforts. She was a dark beauty who obviously doted on her aging parent.

Besides Miss Royle, there were two other single ladies at the party: Mrs. Jellett, a society widow with a gossiping gleam in her eye, and Lady Herrick, the wealthy—and quite beautiful—widow of a baronet.

Lily was just thinking that the house party was weighted heavily in favor of the ladies when their host cried, "Ah, Your Grace, you've arrived!"

She turned to see the Duke of Montgomery, Malcolm MacLeish...

And Caliban.

Only he wasn't Caliban. Not anymore. He was Viscount Kilbourne, his hair tied severely back, wearing a dusky-blue suit heavily embroidered in gold and crimson, and a cream waistcoat, and looking every inch the aristocrat.

LILY WORE A crimson gown that exposed the upper slopes of her lovely breasts, white and inviting.

Apollo felt a bit as if he'd been hit square between the eyes.

"You did not tell me Miss Goodfellow would be here," he hissed in Montgomery's ear.

"Didn't I?" replied the duke. "Why? Was the information of import to you?"

Oh, the other man knew well enough that the information that Lily would be attending this same house party had been "of import." In the weeks he'd spent preparing for the house party, Apollo had endured quite a bit of time with the duke. He was frighteningly intelligent, mercurial, and selfish to the point of mania, and had the sort of impish sense of humor that found the predicaments of others funny. Rather like a little boy who enjoyed pitching battles between beetles and worms. Except the duke was much, much more powerful than a little boy.

So it was hard to tell if the duke hadn't told Apollo about Lily because he was amusing himself—or for some other more nefarious reason.

Not that Apollo gave a damn at the moment.

Over two weeks it'd been since he'd last seen her—two weeks in which he'd gone to bed every night wondering how she was and what she was doing, and waked with the image of her face behind his eyes.

Her lichen-green eyes had widened fractionally when she'd turned to see him, but she'd controlled herself all too soon, plastering on a bright social face that he was beginning to hate already.

His uncle, William Greaves, was making the introductions, but Apollo had eyes only for her.

She curtsied to him, murmuring huskily, "Mr. Smith," as she did so, for they'd settled on the silly pseudonym for the party.

He couldn't help himself. It'd been too long and he didn't know how she felt about him anymore. If she hated him or even—God forbid—believed him to be a bloody murderer.

He caught her fingers and bent over them in a bow he'd learned as a boy and relearned again just in the past weeks. "Miss Goodfellow."

One was supposed to kiss the air above a lady's hand, but he brushed his lips over her knuckles, soft, but insistent. He wouldn't let her forget what they'd had between them.

As he rose he caught the faint glimmer of irritation crossing her face and he was glad. Better he engender vexation or even outright hatred than indifference. Then they were moving past each other and away as other guests were introduced.

"Wasn't that interesting?" Montgomery chirped as he accepted a glass of wine from a footman.

"Someone's going to murder you in your sleep one of these days," Apollo returned, waving away the same footman. He wanted to keep a clear head for the coming evening.

"Oh, but only if they can get past my man-traps," the duke said absently.

He was probably jesting, but it was entirely possible Montgomery slept with an array of traps scattered about his bedroom. The man was like an Oriental potentate.

"Why did you bring me?" Malcolm MacLeish asked, suddenly and irritably.

The Scotsman's color was high and his pleasant face was twisted into a sulky scowl. For the first time Apollo realized that he might not be the only insect Montgomery was playing with tonight.

"Oh, I suppose to remind you of your obligations," Montgomery replied carelessly. "And to have fun, of course."

The question was, whose "fun" was he counting on? Apollo had an uneasy feeling it was the duke's own.

He glanced away from his sponsor and over to William Greaves, the reason he was here in the first place. His uncle was an ordinary-looking man, a bit pompous, a bit weak about the mouth, but was he capable of ordering the senseless murder of three men merely to entrap his nephew? It didn't seem possible, but if it hadn't been he, then who?

Apollo could detect no hint of a family resemblance in his uncle, but his cousin, George, had been a revelation. Like Apollo, he was a big man, well over six feet, with broad shoulders and brown hair. His facial features were rather better formed than Apollo's own, but there was enough similarity that it made seeing the man like catching his own reflection in a mirror out of the corner of his eye. It puzzled him at first, this sense of familiarity, until he realized what it was: they moved alike, he and his cousin.

Apollo frowned, thinking, only to be interrupted by Montgomery. "Try not to look too much like the tragic hero of a melodrama, if you please. We're at a *party*." And with that he sauntered over to Lady Herrick, who was not only quite a beauty but apparently wealthy as well.

Just Montgomery's type, Apollo thought sourly. Poor woman.

"He collects people, you know," the architect said. "Like a spider collects flies. Traps them, ties them up in silken threads, and keeps them until he has use of them." MacLeish turned to Apollo, his blue eyes very cynical for one so young. "Has he collected you, too?"

"No." Apollo was watching Lily again, as she threw back her head in laughter at something Mr. Phillip Warner had said. Her throat was long and white and he wanted, rather violently, to lick it until she stopped laughing at other men's jests. "He may think he has me, but he'll find he's very much mistaken."

"That's what I thought, too," MacLeish murmured, following his gaze, "but 'twas I who was mistaken in the end."

Apollo spared a glance at the other man and then

moved away without comment. Whatever was going on between Montgomery and his architect, he hadn't the time for it.

His eyes were fixed on Lily.

CALIBAN—NO, *LORD KILBOURNE*—was coming toward her and Lily wasn't entirely certain what to do. She'd been aware of him this entire time, for his eyes seemed to burn into her back no matter where she moved in the room. It really wasn't fair: it was *he* who had disappeared into thin air without so much as an explanation or word to her whether he was all right or not. And now he'd turned up at a house party of all things, still using that ridiculous name, Mr. Smith. Had he even invented an appropriate Christian name to go with Smith? A thought struck her, low and terrible. Dear God, she didn't even know his proper Christian name! She'd let him kiss her and yet didn't know the first thing about him. The realization made her bitter and a little unwise.

"What's your real name?" she demanded as he made her side, and if she had to blink back wetness from her eyes, she told herself it was tears of *anger*.

He glanced around, presumably making sure no one could overhear him. Fortunately, Mr. Phillip Warner had moved away to flirt with his own wife and no one was within earshot.

He replied in a very low voice, "Apollo Greaves, Viscount Kilbourne."

Apollo? *Apollo?* She nearly goggled.

Well, he certainly couldn't use Apollo with Smith— what an entirely inane name. Almost as bad as Caliban when one considered it. What mother looked down at an infant son and thought, *god of light*? No one could live up to a name like that. Especially since he had a twin sister...

Lily's brain stuttered to a stop and she realized simultaneously both who Apollo-the-god's twin sister was and who Apollo-the-man's twin sister must be.

"Your sister is Artemis Batten, the Duchess of Wakefield," she hissed.

"Hush," he muttered.

"Your sister's a bloody *duchess*."

"Yes?" He looked at her oddly, as if everyone had a duchess as a sister.

"Which means the duke is your brother-in-law."

"He's rather an ass, if that makes any difference."

"It *doesn't*," she said decisively. "It truly doesn't. Why are you even talking to me? I'm the blasted *help*."

"You are not and you know it," he said impatiently. "I need to talk to you. To explain—"

"I'm *paid* to be here," she said with as much dignity as possible under the circumstances. "And you're born to all this"—she waved her hand at the room, which, ill-lit though it was, still had a *gold ceiling*—"and *more*. You and I have nothing—absolutely *nothing* in common. I don't know why you're here, but I'll thank you to stay away from me."

She pasted a smile on her face and moved away from him as gracefully as she could. There was no need to cause a scene, just because her heart was breaking. Ridiculous, really. When he'd been a penniless workman in a garden, shabby and mute, he'd been well within her reach. Now that he was cleaned up and dazzling in his expensive clothes—that waistcoat alone must have cost more than she'd make in half a year—he was as high above her as the sun itself.

Apollo, indeed. Perhaps his name really *did* fit him.

If he was the god Apollo then she was merely a shepherdess or suchlike. Someone quite lowly and of the earth, not the sky. Shepherdesses might mate with gods in mythology but it always ended rather badly for the poor mortal.

And she had good cause to know that such was the case in this world as well.

The butler entered at that moment and announced supper and they went in to another dark room, this one long and narrow so as to fit an endless mahogany table. Lily found herself seated with the Duke of Montgomery on one side and the delightful Mr. Warner on the other. Directly across from her was Mr. George Greaves with Mrs. Jellett on one side and Mrs. Warner on the other.

They'd hardly begun on a rather watery beef broth when Mrs. Jellett, a lady of mature years in a frock of a startling yellow-green shade, leaned forward and said loudly, "Have you heard aught of your mad cousin, Mr. Greaves? I understand that he barely escaped capture by soldiers in the destroyed Harte's Folly pleasure garden."

Mr. William Greaves's mouth thinned into nonexistence and anyone could see that he did not like the subject—which of course hardly dissuaded his guests.

"'Tis said he killed three men with an enormous knife." Mrs. Warner shivered dramatically. "The very thought that a murderous madman is on the loose is enough to make one want to hide under the bed."

"Or *in* the bed?" the duke murmured over his glass of wine.

"Are you offering bedchamber protection, Your Grace?" Lady Herrick asked lazily.

The duke bowed from the waist. "For you, madam, I would make the sacrifice."

"Such bravery," cried Moll from the other side of the duke. "I vow 'tis enough to send a lady into a paroxysm."

That comment prompted a round of titters from the ladies.

Lily stared at her plate, trying not to feel any sympathy for Caliban—*Apollo*—but it was hard. The others talked about him as if he were a maddened beast to be shot on sight. Would she have felt that way if she'd only heard the stories and not known the man beforehand? Would she have condemned a stranger at once without benefit of trial?

Probably. Fear had a tendency to drive away the courtesy of civilization.

Mrs. Jellett was still curious about the original topic of conversation. She addressed George Greaves. "Tell me, Mr. Greaves, was your cousin always mad? Did he do anything bizarre or cruel as a boy?"

Mr. William Greaves spoke up from the head of the table, his voice grim. "I fear, madam, that that side of the family has always had strange turns. My brother, alas, was prone to overexcitement followed by melancholies from which he could hardly rouse himself. A pity"—he took a sip of his wine—"that as eldest the title naturally falls to his side."

"'Twould be better," his son joined in, "if our English great families could set aside the titles from those members who, because of some disease or defect of the brain, are rendered feeble or otherwise weaken the lineages of the aristocracy."

"If that were done," drawled the Duke of Montgomery,

"half the titles of England would go obsolete due to brain weakness. I know my own grandfather fancied himself a cowherd at times."

"Really, Your Grace?" John leaned forward to see down the table. "Not a shepherd or goatherd?"

"I'm told he was quite specific in his mania and only cows would do," His Grace replied. "Of course there were those who said his affliction was the direct result of a certain type of disease, which I won't mention in the present company as it is of an indelicate nature."

"And yet you already have," Miss Royle observed in her husky voice. "Mentioned it, that is, Your Grace."

"Touché, ma'am," the duke replied, a thread of irritation in his voice. "I hadn't thought to encounter such pedantry amongst a lighthearted gathering."

Miss Royle shrugged. "I don't find madness amusing— whether caused by disease or birth."

"My cousin doesn't even have the excuse of disease, I'm afraid," Mr. George Greaves said, abrupt and hard. "He was born with whatever ails him—and because of it, three good men are dead—his own friends, mind. I'm sorry that he was ever sent to Bedlam instead of being tried before the magistrates as he should've been."

"But a titled gentleman, sir!" his father objected. "Surely such a thing would tear apart the very fabric of our great nation?"

"Then before the House of Lords, if it came to that," his son replied. "Better a lord tried and found guilty of murder, than a madman loosed upon the countryside with the whispers that the only reason he is free is because of his rank. It sets the common people to thinking—and that is something none of us want."

"Perhaps you are correct," his father said slowly, obviously troubled by the argument.

"I know I am," Mr. George Greaves returned. "Think what ignominy he has already brought our family. What more will he bring if he murders more innocents?"

For a moment the mood at the table turned somber at this image, but then the duke spoke up. "Surely no more ignominy than my own great-uncle brought upon my own house when he attempted to have, er, marital relations with a horse."

That comment certainly lightened the conversation.

Lily glanced covertly at Apollo. He was eating his meal, his expression blank. How did he feel, hearing his father discussed so dismissively? His own history laid bare for others to titter over? This was his *family*, the one he'd said he was estranged from, and it was obvious not only that they believed him guilty of the crimes he'd been charged with, but that they would make every effort to have him imprisoned or *hanged* should they discover his ruse.

What in God's name was he doing here?

She turned and found the duke eyeing her, and she remembered that she had a role to play tonight—and the duke, for once, might not be the most dangerous person at the table.

So she threw herself into the conversation, making sure never to glance in Apollo's direction again. Whatever he was about, it was certainly no business of hers. How could it be, after all, when he was an aristocrat and she a mere actress?

When, hours later, she finally climbed the stairs to the room she shared with Moll, she was weary to the bone with trying to appear carefree and witty. Witty! There was a word she never wanted to hear again, she thought darkly as she made her way down the hallway. Wittiness was terribly exhausting.

It would be nice to let down her guard, alone with Moll.

But when she opened the door to their room she found herself very much mistaken. Moll was nowhere to be seen.

And Viscount Kilbourne lounged upon the bed.

Chapter Thirteen

*The skeleton was small and sad, lying in a heap of
frayed blue robes. Pink beads lay scattered over the
remains. The girl driven into the labyrinth the year before
had worn a necklace of pink beads. Ariadne knelt by the
skeleton's side and, saying an old prayer her mother had
taught her, sprinkled dust on the remains. Then, rising,
she continued deeper into the labyrinth…*
—From *The Minotaur*

Lily stopped dead in the doorway to her room and then
took a step back.

Apollo cocked his head. It'd been a very long day full
of trepidation mixed with tediousness and he'd used up all
his patience. "If you leave, I'll follow you out and we'll
have this discussion in the hallway where everyone can
hear."

She scowled ferociously at him, but came all the way
in the room and shut the door. "What do you want to talk
about?"

"Us."

"There's nothing to discuss."

"Yes," he said patiently, "there is."

She looked away and down for a second and then back at him. "Your voice is better."

He inclined his head. "It's been a fortnight." His voice was still rusty and his throat ached on occasion, but he no longer had to take so long to speak. "Where is Indio?"

"I left him with Maude." She wrapped her arms around her waist.

"In the garden?"

"No. They're visiting Maude's niece outside London while I'm here." She looked at him pointedly. "Why are you here?"

He stretched and folded his arms beneath his head. "You walked away when I tried to talk to you during the party. I thought since you wouldn't come to me…" He shrugged.

"Moll will be back soon."

"No. I gave her enough coin to stay away for the night."

Her eyes widened in outrage. "You can't do that! Where will she stay? She's been looking forward all day to a nice bed."

"Well, I *did* offer her mine."

"Humph." She pursed her lips, still not mollified. "It doesn't matter. You'll not be staying the night in any case. Besides," she hurried on before he could object, "you misunderstood my original question: why are you *here* at the house party?"

"To find the real murderer," he said wearily. Frankly, after two weeks of the subject, he'd grown a little tired of it. He gestured to a chair. "Why don't you sit down?"

"Because it would be quite improper," she said, and he wondered if she actually thought that or was simply making up etiquette rules out of thin air. "How are you going to find a murderer at a house party?"

"We think it's my uncle." He looked at her apprais-ingly. "You must be tired."

She lifted her chin. "We?"

"Montgomery, Trevillion, and Harte—Makepeace, that is."

She stared at him in horror, letting her arms drop. "You've trusted the Duke of Montgomery with your secret? Have you gone completely mad?"

"No, I'm just very desperate. Besides, I never told it to him—he somehow figured it out on his own." He took a breath. "Lily, I don't want to talk of this right now. I want to…" He sat up and pushed his hands through his hair. "You know what I'm charged with?"

"If I hadn't before this night, I would after that dinner," she said tartly.

He stared at her, licking his lips. "You must know that I didn't do it."

She gave him her profile. "Must I?"

"Lily…"

"You left us without word."

"They were watching the garden," he replied, his voice steady. "I couldn't get you a message without the soldiers realizing you knew me."

"I don't believe that," she said, and her face was harder than he'd ever seen it. "If you'd truly wanted to, you could have smuggled a message to Maude as she shopped or given it to one of the gardeners, or found a thousand other ways."

He simply looked at her. Perhaps she was right. Perhaps he could've gotten her word if he'd only tried hard enough. But he'd been busy with the plan, with the knowl-edge that until he could come to her a free man, he had nothing at all to offer her.

His very silence seemed to be some sort of answer to her. She lifted her chin proudly. "If we meant anything to you, you'd have gotten us word that you were *alive*."

"You mean a great deal to me," he said, low.

"Do we?" she asked, her mouth tight. "Truly? And yet you left us—*me*—without word or warning."

"Lily . . ."

"I thought we were *friends*."

He rose in one movement. "I thought we were more than friends."

Her eyes widened and she backed up a step, seemingly without conscious thought, as he advanced on her, until her bottom hit the door.

He should be gentler, should approach her with caution. Even now she might be afraid of what had been said about him. But he was weary—so very, very weary—of things being taken from him.

He wasn't going to lose her as well. Not if he could help it.

He halted inches from her. "Weren't we, Lily? More than friends?"

Her lips parted as her breath quickened, but she showed no fear of him. "You know we were."

"Then that hasn't changed."

She laughed, incredulous. "Are you insane?"

"That *was* the charge."

"Don't hide behind quips." She shook her head impatiently. "*Everything* has changed. You . . . you're an aristocrat. A viscount—someday a bloody *earl*. I'm the bastard daughter of a drunken actress and an illiterate porter."

He took her shoulders, barely refraining from shaking her. "I'm the same man I was when I labored in the garden. The same man you were so kind to when I was mute."

"No, you're not!" Her breasts were heaving now with the force of her ire. "That man was of my world. He was simple and . . . and *kind* and he wasn't a bloody *aristocrat*!"

She balled her fist and hit his chest with the last word.

"You don't know," he choked. "You don't know who I am."

"Then tell me!"

He stared into her eyes—those beautiful green eyes—and something seemed to break inside him.

Four years of torment and loss.

Four years of being told what he was and what he wasn't.

Four years of limbo. Of life suspended, lost, *abandoned* as he lay half dead in a stinking cell.

He wasn't dead and he wasn't going to lose any more of life.

"I'm everything you thought me," he whispered, his voice broken. "The gardener and the aristocrat and the madman. I endured Bedlam and it was a crucible to my soul, burning what I was before and reshaping me. I wouldn't have survived it had I not let myself be remolded."

He looked at her helplessly and she stared back, her eyes wet, her lips parted.

He laid his forehead against hers. "In truth I don't know what sort of man I am anymore, newly smelted, newly poured into some strange and original mold. I was still too hot to the touch for discovery. But I know this: whatever strange creature I have become, I am yours. Help me, Lily. Unmold me and take what form I am in your hands and blow the breath of life into me. Make me a living being again."

He had no more words to convince her, so he did what he'd wanted to do since he'd first seen her this evening: he slid his lips down to her mouth.

THE KISS WAS so sweet, so tender, that for a moment Lily couldn't think at all. All she could do was *feel*—the heat of his mouth, the puffs of his breaths on her cheek, the gentle touch of his palms on her face. He pushed his tongue into her mouth and she suckled it, wanting more.

She stood on tiptoe and thrust her fingers into his hair, pulling off the wretched tie and freeing his wild locks— freeing Caliban from Lord Kilbourne.

And then she remembered: no matter what he might call himself, she was still mad at him.

She pulled back and murmured, "I'm still mad at you."

"Are you?" His wounded voice had descended into Stygian depths. He pressed open-mouthed kisses to her jaw.

"Yes." She yanked at his hair in emphasis.

He grunted, but her grip didn't prevent him from lowering his mouth to hers again. He nipped at her lips and then licked at them, softening the sting. "I'll have to see what I can do to regain your good graces."

His hands left her arms and seized her waist instead, and before she could think, he was lifting her bodily, walking with her as if she were as light as a kitten. He pivoted and then she was falling onto the bed, with him right on top of her.

He caught himself on his elbows before his entire weight could crush her, but she was still trapped, his legs and lower body pinning her to the soft mattress.

"And how," she asked with awful dignity, "do you suppose this will help your case?"

"For one thing," he replied, trailing his fingertips over her temples, "you can't move."

She arched her brows.

His lips curved as he plucked a pin from her coiffure. "It gives me time to argue, if nothing else."

She let her hands fall beside her head in mock surrender. "I'm listening."

"Will you agree that we found an uncommon accord in the garden?" She felt the loosening of her hair as he removed another pin.

"I didn't know who you were," she objected.

"Not what I asked." He eyed her sternly. "Do you agree or not?"

She blew out a frustrated breath. "I agree that I had an uncommon accord with the man I thought you were, but—"

"Ah. Ah." He stretched over her head to set the pins on a side table, then resumed his position atop her. "We both are in agreement that we shared an uncommon accord. The problem, as I see it, is that you are under the delusion that I am somehow not the same man as I was then. I may not know exactly what I have become since Bedlam, but I know this: whatever I was in the garden I am now, new clothes or no."

"You aren't!" She parted her legs to give him more room, thinking she really oughtn't to feel as comfortable as she did.

"Am I not?" He thrust his fingertips into her hair, massaging her scalp. "In what way am I different?"

Lily had to fight to keep her eyes open. The feel of his

hands on her scalp after a day with her hair pulled tight was simply heaven. "Your name, for one."

"But what's in a name, truly?" he murmured, dipping his head to trail his lips over the sensitive skin below her ear. "You called me Caliban, but had you called me Romeo, wouldn't I still be the same man? My mother named me for a god renowned for male beauty, but does it make me any more handsome? My mirror tells me daily, no."

There was definitely something wrong with his reasoning and if she could only draw breath to *think*, she might figure it out.

"Cheat," she growled, her voice weaker than she liked.

He pulled back enough for her to see the amused quirk of his lips. "Temptress."

He bent to lay his mouth on hers, thrusting his tongue lazily past her lips until she sucked on the thick length.

"Are they any different?" he whispered against her mouth, "my kisses? Have they changed so much with my name?"

She cracked her eyelids to look at him and murmur into the humid heat between them, "I can't tell. Perhaps you should demonstrate again."

He licked at the corner of her mouth. "A scientific study, you mean?" His mouth trailed up her cheek, soft as a moth.

"Quite," she breathed.

"As you wish."

He kissed her eyelids, a mere brush of lips, before seizing her mouth again, swallowing her moan. His hands moved until he'd intertwined his fingers with hers, still at either side of her head. She opened helplessly beneath the surge of his intent, accepting his tongue, his heavy desire. His chest crushed her breasts and she wanted all the material between them gone so that she could feel his skin against hers. She arched under him, attempting to get closer, wanting to rub her naked nipples against him, but the stiff fabric of her stays prevented even the illusion of touch.

She sank back, whimpering.

He rose to his knees at the same time, eyeing her with an obnoxious twist of his lips that she'd have slapped away if she didn't want him back so much.

"The same?" he asked, and at least his voice shook just the tiniest bit. He wasn't unaffected, either.

She tilted her head against the coverlet, trying to catch her breath. "I suppose."

She'd tried to sound nonchalant, but by his sudden grin she knew she'd not been entirely successful.

"I am the same man I was in the garden," he said into the silence of the bedroom, his grin fading to something solemn, almost severe. "My limbs move as they did then, my lungs fill with air exactly the same, and my heart..." He paused as if to swallow, continuing lower, "My heart beats constant and true, and if you believe nothing else, Lily Stump, believe this: my heart has changed not at all since the garden."

She stared up at him. His words were beautiful, but she'd had nearly a lifetime's distrust of the upper classes. Such a thing wasn't vanquished in moments.

He nodded at her silence as if she'd made a rebuttal— and then he shrugged off his coat. "Did you fear Caliban?"

She shook her head slowly.

He flipped open the buttons on his beautiful waistcoat. "Caliban and Apollo are the same."

"No," she husked. "Caliban is dead."

"Do you truly believe that?" he asked nearly indulgently. "I am Caliban and I am Apollo. We are the same."

"No."

"Yes." He stripped off his waistcoat.

"There never was a Caliban to begin with." She felt sad, as if she truly mourned for that gentle giant, that enigmatic mute man she'd apparently made up from whole cloth.

He actually laughed, the cad. "Do you think I pretended to dig holes and hack down trees? I am Caliban and I am Apollo and I am Smith." He pulled his shirt over his head, laying his chest bare. "Is this not the same body you saw emerge from the pond?"

She couldn't help it. She did now what she hadn't been able to do then—she touched his chest, running her fingertips lightly over his shoulders, down into the wedge of short hairs between his nipples.

He took her hand and moved it so her palm lay over his left nipple. "My heart beats here," he said, pressing until she could feel the steady thump. "The same heart, the same beat as in the garden."

He lifted his hand, but she kept her palm there, feeling the pulse beneath his warm skin. Slowly she curled her fingers until she could trace lightly around his nipple. It puckered beneath her touch, a tiny brown bead, and she felt a sudden urge to feel it beneath her tongue. Instead she raised her other hand and circled the corresponding nipple as well, fascinated by how his flesh responded. It wasn't until she heard the sharp inhalation that she looked up and realized what she was doing to him.

His head was thrown back, his throat rippling as he

swallowed again and again, and his mighty shoulders, so strong, so broad, actually trembled at her simple touch.

Her being lit with awe that she'd moved such a powerful man. That he literally shuddered beneath her fingertips.

"Caliban," she whispered. "Can I call you that?"

He tilted his head down to look at her, his brown eyes half-lidded. "Caliban, Apollo, Smith, even Romeo, it matters not. I am the man that I am and always will be."

She nodded at that, for with this she could at least agree: what she called him had never been the problem.

He arched away from her suddenly, and she was forced to let her hands fall. "Let me show you." He stood and stripped out of shoes, stockings, breeches, and small-clothes, until he was entirely nude. He spread wide his arms, and turned before her. "I am as God made me, no more, no less. Take me as I am."

He completed his turn, standing proud before her, and she couldn't help but like what she saw. He was tall and well-made, with a narrow waist and muscular thighs. The hair on his chest was repeated in a knot around his navel and traveled down in a thin line into the tangle about his groin where his cock had half-risen, thick and straight and bold.

He was masculine, not beautiful. Compelling. But more importantly, with the stripping of his clothes he'd discarded all that she disliked and become merely the man she'd met in the garden.

She held out her hand. "Caliban, Apollo, Smith, Romeo, *you*. Come to me, *you* that you are."

He took her hand, but instead of climbing back on the bed, he drew her up instead. "I have an urge," he murmured in her ear as he drew her against his nude body, "to make you as I am. Then, truly, shall we be equals."

So he patiently unlaced, untied, and unclothed her, his fingers working deftly on delicate material and tight cords. Reverently he drew off her bodice, her skirt, her petticoats, her stays, her chemise, her slippers, and laid them neatly aside until he knelt at her feet to unroll her stockings. She placed her palm on his shoulder as he set her foot on his knee and untied her garter. Her stockings were her best, but even so they'd a mended hole at the heel. He unrolled them as carefully as if they'd been lace, pausing to kiss her instep as he pulled them off. Then he set that foot down and picked up her other, drawing her so close that his bent head nearly brushed her bare mons.

She swallowed, watching as those wild locks came perilously close to her maiden hair. She felt his fingertips trailing behind her knee and then he bent and pressed an open-mouthed kiss to the same place.

Her hand moved from his shoulder to his head, threading through his hair, clutching as he moved up her thigh, licking, sucking, the stocking entirely abandoned, until she felt the whisper of his breath against her damp flesh.

She nearly toppled, her knees going weak. He grasped her hips and turned with her until she could rest against the bed, and then he took her leg and flung it over his shoulder and kissed her.

There. Open-mouthed, licking across delicate flesh.

She gasped and could not breathe out again. He'd seized her lungs, made her forget everything but that place between her legs as he lapped at her, thoroughly debauching her.

Helplessly she grasped at his head, holding on for

dear life as he found her nub and fitted his lips around it, licking delicately, relentlessly until she suddenly felt the gentle scrape of his *teeth* and that was it.

She shoved her fist into her mouth and only just in time as she arched into him, her leg tightening on his broad shoulders convulsively. She shook, wailing behind her fist, black spots in her vision as warmth flooded her. And all the while he licked and licked and licked until she had to weakly push against his shoulders to make him stop.

He raised his head and wiped his chin and mouth with his hand before prowling up her body, stopping to lave her navel. He pulled her all the way on top of the bed and then pushed her thighs farther apart. He settled between them, his belly at her center and his head just on a level with her breasts.

"So pretty," he crooned, and for an amused moment she wondered if he was talking directly to her breasts.

Then he dipped his head and licked around one nipple.

She whimpered and he opened his mouth over her nipple, suckling gently but urgently. With his fingers he tapped the other nipple, making it peak. She ached with want, almost painful so soon after her orgasm. Surely he was hard by now? Surely he was ready to join with her?

But he seemed in no hurry, lifting his head only to move to the nipple he'd fingered. When he pinched the one he'd left she nearly screamed at the feel against her wet flesh.

"Please," she moaned, grasping his head, trying to pull him up. "Please, please, *please*."

He looked up at her, lazily licking her breast. "Who am I now?"

She shook her head, restless, on edge, and so very, very wet for him. "It doesn't matter."

He smirked then and rose over her.

She looked down, watching as he grasped his penis, fully engorged now, an angry red pillar rising from his pubic hair. He brought it between her legs, rubbing it up and down, wetting the head with her moisture.

She lifted her legs, wrapping them over his hips loosely. "Now, now, now."

He glanced up at her and his smile had left his face. He bit down on his bottom lip as he notched himself, the skin white beneath his teeth. He flexed his hips and nudged inside.

Big. He was a big man.

She gasped, holding her legs wider, higher, trying to give him more room.

His eyes were closed, his upper lip hitched in a snarl, almost as if he were in pain.

Or great pleasure.

He thrust again, *hard*, and the entire length of his erection filled her.

She made a sound, restless, wanting.

He opened his eyes, looking down at her with concern. "Are you all right?"

She was stretched and so delightfully full of him. She twined her arms over his shoulders, digging her nails into his back. "Yes. *Move*."

And he did.

He pulled nearly out and then pressed in again, over and over, each time a little faster, a little harder, until he was pounding into her.

His back was slick with sweat and her hands slid

against him as her fingers moved restlessly over him. She trailed her nails down, scoring him, probably hurting him, and she no longer cared. She reached his buttocks, muscled and rounded, and grasped him, pulling him tightly into her.

He propped himself on his elbows and screwed his hips into hers, his cock deep in her. And as he did so, he watched her, a bead of sweat slipping down the side of his dear face. He pushed a lock of her hair off her face and brought his mouth crashing down on hers, open and wet and not entirely in control.

But his hips kept moving, plundering her, owning her, making her climb those heights again.

She groaned into his mouth, animal and wild, and felt the slip of his hard chest against her nipples.

This man.

Whatever his name.

This man.

She broke, shuddering nearly violently, throwing back her head, wailing her release as he slammed into her one more time and withdrew, suddenly and awfully.

She stared up at him, shocked, as cold air caressed her entrance and hot semen spilled on her belly.

He shook with his release, moaning as if in pain, and another splash hit her thigh. He slumped against her, a heavy weight, but she couldn't push him away.

Instead she stroked his cooling back, staring at the ceiling and wondering what she'd just done.

APOLLO WOKE TO the feel of soft flesh under his palm. He stroked upward, cupping a silky breast in his hand, and smiled without opening his eyes.

This, this must be paradise.

"Thank you," she murmured, and he realized for the first time that she was awake as well.

He opened his eyes. It was a small room that she and the other actress had been given, with only one bed that apparently they had been expected to share. A candle still guttered on the bedside table, throwing a flickering yellow light across her face.

He couldn't read it. "I think it's I who should be thanking you."

"Not for that." She turned her face to his suddenly, her mouth curled wryly. "Thank you for not spilling inside of me."

A delicate tint colored her cheekbones.

He remembered Indio. Obviously some man had once *not* bothered to pull out at the crucial moment.

Apollo bent to kiss her shoulder and then took a corner of the sheet to tenderly wipe his seed off her belly and thighs. "May I stay?"

She sighed. "Yes, unless Moll returns before morning. I'd"—she licked her lips—"I'd like for you to stay."

He smiled against her shoulder, ridiculously pleased.

Her hand reached up and he felt her fingers in his hair. "So they're your family?"

He wasn't sure he wanted to delve into the matter now—his blue blood seemed to dismay her. "Yes."

She moved as if she were looking at him. "Are they all you have left?"

His head was on her shoulder and he concentrated on tracing around one rose-tinted nipple. "Besides my sister, yes."

"She knew you were in the garden?"

"Artemis?" He finally cocked his head back so he could see her expression. She had a tiny frown between her brows. "Yes. She brought me food and clothes and other things when she could. It's how Trevillion found me."

"*Found* you?"

He sighed, abandoning the nipple with regret. "Trevillion was looking for me. He knew Artemis was my sister and he followed her until she led him to me one day. The day you saw us fight."

"But..." The frown had grown deeper. "Why was he looking for you in the first place?"

His jaw clenched as a sudden shiver shook his frame. The fire had died down in the grate and the room was drafty. He got up, padding to the fireplace.

"Apollo?"

He closed his eyes. She'd stopped calling him Caliban and he didn't want that. Didn't want his past to rise up between them again.

He glanced over his shoulder to see that she'd sat up and pulled the coverlet over her breasts like a barrier between them. There was no help for it, then—it always came back to that wretched night. The night his life had been destroyed.

"Trevillion was the soldier who arrested me for the murders."

Chapter Fourteen

*From that day forth Ariadne found more and more
skeletons, and for each one she stopped and respectfully
prayed and scattered dust. As she neared the center
of the labyrinth, she wondered what horrors awaited
her there. But when, on the seventh day, the tall stone
walls revealed their heart, she discovered something
entirely unexpected...*
—From *The Minotaur*

Lily watched Apollo. He squatted unselfconsciously nude
at the hearth, stirring the fire. He was silhouetted in the
firelight, powerful shoulders black and almost monstrous,
narrowing to muscled hips and thighs. No wonder they'd
thought him a murderer. No wonder they'd taken one look
at such a big man and been afraid.

But was that entirely what had happened? He'd told
her little, and what else she'd heard was from snippets
of gossip and newssheets. Trevillion was the soldier who
had arrested him, but now that same man was working to
prove him innocent. There were gaps in her knowledge
and she was tired of secondhand information.

She cleared her throat, the sound loud in the silence.
"Can you tell me what happened that night?"

He'd been about to lay a scoop of coal on the fire, and at her words, he paused for a fraction of a second before continuing. He rose, dusting his hands, broad back hunched, the flames reflecting off the sheen of his skin. He turned his head so that she could see his profile, large nose, prominent forehead, craggy lips and chin.

"You have to understand," he said quietly. "I was young. Four and twenty. That might not seem so very young to you, but I'd spent most of my life in schooling. First at Harrow, where my grandfather paid for my education, and then Oxford. When I came to London I had a very small stipend from the earl, delivered through his lawyers. I spent it drinking and wenching, mostly."

He turned at last, though she still couldn't see his features.

"That's what men of my rank do. They spend money and drink. They don't labor—even if their family might be starving."

"Was your family starving?" she asked sharply.

He shook his head immediately. "No. But neither did they have very much to live on. My father had gone through nearly all the money he'd had and the earl refused to give him more. My sister and mother lived very simply in the country because of it. Artemis never had a season, nor a dowry." He began walking toward the bed. "But I grew weary of the aimless days, the expectation of *nothing*. I was supposed to live my life waiting for the old earl to die."

She couldn't imagine him—so physically and mentally active—consigned to waiting on another's death.

He'd reached the bed now and he climbed in, sitting up against the headboard and pulling her back to lie on his chest.

She laid her head on his shoulder, listening.

"I'd met some fellows at Oxford who had new theories on gardening. Grand schemes that broke from the medieval idea of straight little lines and ordered plantings. They were thinking in terms of vistas. Of beautiful sights that would last for generations. Of natural lines and shapes—made better. I began corresponding with them while I was in London, exchanging ideas and plans. Then I was hired to help on an estate outside Oxford itself."

He wrapped his arms around her, and she leaned forward to kiss his hand, silently urging him on.

"It was a great opportunity," he said, but his voice was sorrowful. "It was practical work when before all I'd done was dabble in theory. That garden took a season to build and after that I was recommended to another estate. And then my grandfather found out what I was about."

She frowned. "Why would that matter?"

"Because," he whispered, leaning his cheek against her temple, "remember what I already said? Aristocrats don't labor. When my grandfather found out, he cut me off. He considered my desire to learn the art of garden planning on a grand scale to be an early sign of the same disease that had driven my father mad. He thought our entire line tainted."

"Oh, Apollo." She hadn't much family herself, but to be so harshly judged simply because one had found an interest in life? It seemed ridiculous.

He nuzzled her hair. "That day I was in London. I met up with three friends. We resolved to spend the night together—two were from school and I'd not seen them in some years. We reserved the back room of a tavern in Whitechapel and ordered wine and food."

She stirred. "Why such an awful part of London?"

"We hadn't much money, I'm afraid. The tavern was cheap."

He stopped speaking, but she could feel his uneven breaths.

"What happened?"

He inhaled. "I don't know. We shared a bottle—and after that all is blackness. I woke the next morning with my head pounding as if it would split. As soon as I moved I vomited. And then I saw my hands."

"Apollo?" She tried to twist her face to see him, but he tightened his hold on her.

"I'd been drunk before," he rasped. "But this was nothing like that. It was as if I were dreaming and couldn't wake. My hands were covered in blood, I held a knife in my right hand, and there was screaming. I couldn't stand—when I tried, I fell. And my friends..."

She squeezed his hands. She already knew what had happened to his friends. The scene of the murder had been recounted in countless newssheets—and whether the details had been correct hardly mattered at this moment. They'd been murdered.

Horribly slaughtered.

"I'm sorry," she whispered, "so sorry."

"The soldiers came," he murmured, his voice flat now. Had he even heard her? "They took me away in chains—on my ankles, wrists, and neck, for they were afraid of me. I was taken to Newgate to await trial. I vomited again and again and was half out of my mind for several days. I don't remember much of Newgate. But I remember Bedlam."

She raised his hand, pressing her lips to his palm to

keep from blurting that he didn't have to tell her. For she was very much afraid that he *did* have to tell her—not for her, but for himself.

"It…" He panted for a second, then burst. "The *smell*. Like a stable, only the manure is from *humans*, not horses. They chained me there as well, for I raged, in fear and desperation, for the first days. Until I was too weakened by lack of food and water."

She sobbed, turning swiftly. She could not bear to hear of this—such a strong, good man brought low. Chained like a beast by petty people who didn't understand him. She knelt on the bed, wrapping her arms around his head, bringing it to her breast, and only then did she feel the wet trails of tears on his face.

He kissed her between her breasts, a sweet brush of his mouth. "Artemis came when she could. She brought me food and gave all her coin to my attendants—more jailers, in truth—to make sure they wouldn't beat me to death while she wasn't there. My father died a year before the murders and our mother passed away in the first month I was in Bedlam. No doubt my incarceration hastened her death. My sister, my brave, proud sister, was forced to become a companion to our cousin."

His voice broke.

She smoothed her palms over his great head, running her fingers through his hair, trying to comfort though she knew she must be failing.

He turned his face, laying his cheek against her chest. "At least Artemis had a roof over her head and food aplenty. I lay awake for nights after I received word of our mother's death, fearful that Artemis would be tossed into the streets. I could do nothing. Nothing. She was—is—my sister. I should've been able to protect her, to care for her and make sure she never had to worry, and yet I was helpless. Hardly a man at all."

"Shh," Lily murmured, pressing kisses against his hair. She could taste her own tears on her lips now. It wasn't fair. It wasn't fair that Apollo—her Apollo—should've had to endure such inhumanity.

"The things they did there..." His voice was hoarse, broken. "There was a woman," he whispered. "A poor mad thing, but she sang in such a lovely voice. One night the keepers came to do her harm and I called to them, mocking them, and they came to me instead."

She stiffened, her throat clenching in fear. Oh, her brave Apollo! How noble and how foolish to draw the ire of his jailers.

"They beat me until I passed out," he said. "That was when I lost my voice. Afterwards—after I was rescued by the Duke of Wakefield, after, when I lay abed, regaining my strength, though not my voice, I thought of her. I went back one night, but she was already gone. Some fever had taken her. Perhaps it was for the best."

She looked down and saw that he'd closed his eyes, though his brow was knit fiercely.

"But I made sure that guard—the one who'd meant to harm her, the one who'd led my beating—could harm no one ever again. I dragged him from that place and gave him to a press-gang. Wherever he is now, he's not around women. I never would've done that before. Bedlam changed me."

They had taken away something very important from him when he'd been made helpless. It should've broken him, being forced into chains. Yet it hadn't.

Even in her grief she was amazed.

She framed his face with her hands, tilting it up so she could look in his eyes. "You survived. You endured and survived."

His lips curved bitterly. "I had no choice."

She shook her head. "There's always a choice. You could've given up, let them take your soul and mind, but you didn't. You persevered. I think you are the bravest man I have ever met."

"I think, then, that you've not met many men," he whispered. His voice was light, but his face still held the years of tragedy.

"Hush."

She kissed him, not as a lover, but almost platonically, to acknowledge all that he was. Her lips brushed his forehead, both cheeks, and finally his mouth. Softly. A benediction.

"Let us sleep," she said, and helped him to lie down on the bed.

She arranged the covers over both of them and then laid her head upon his chest, listening to the beat of his heart: *ba-thump ba-thump ba-thump*.

And that was how she fell asleep.

APOLLO WOKE TO the realization that he'd overslept. When he'd worked in the garden, he'd awoken as the birds had heralded the rising sun. But here inside, in a soft bed with a softer, warm woman against his side, he found it harder to brush away the tendrils of sleep.

"What?" Lily mumbled as he gently removed her arm from his belly.

He'd like to linger longer. To kiss her awake and make

love to her again, but it was only a matter of time before the servants descended on the room. Besides, the sooner he left, the less likely that he'd run into other guests.

So he dressed quickly as she sighed and rolled to burrow into the warm spot he'd left.

Apollo gathered his coat and gave a last glance around the room before bending to kiss her again on the lips.

Her brow wrinkled ferociously and she cracked her eyelids to mutter, "Is it?"

He smiled. Evidently she wasn't an alert waker. "I'll see you later."

Her only reply was an unfeminine grunt as she pulled a pillow over her head.

The smile still lingered as he crept into the hall and gently shut the door behind him.

He caught a movement out of the corner of his eye and turned to look to his right. Had someone just disappeared around the corner at the end of the corridor? Or had the movement been imagined?

Apollo narrowed his eyes, thinking, but in the end decided that even if he'd seen someone, most likely it had been a servant at this time of the morning.

He turned in the other direction—only to find the Duke of Montgomery watching him.

He prevented himself from starting only by sheer willpower. "I hadn't thought you an early riser, Your Grace."

Montgomery cocked his head. "What makes you think I've slept?"

Apollo examined the other man. He was perfectly groomed in a bloodred suit, pumps, and clocked hose. His golden hair had been swept back into an elegant tail, the ends curled. Or perhaps his hair curled naturally. In any case, Apollo felt like a rat next to a sleek greyhound.

Not that he cared in particular.

"Have you?" he asked curiously, approaching the other man. "Slept?"

A secret smile curled the duke's lips. "I find sleep a bore—especially when I might spend the nocturnal hours in more...pleasurable pursuits."

"I see." Apollo fell into step with the other man. He had no idea where the duke was headed, but he himself was bent on the breakfast room in search of strong coffee.

God, he hoped his uncle provided coffee for his guests.

"Morning is the best time to discover the inhabitants of a house sneaking out of bedrooms not their own." The duke gave him an entirely too-innocent look. "As you were doing just now from Miss Goodfellow's room. I now understand your ire yesterday at the unexpected sight of her."

Apollo glared. "I'll thank you not to spread my connection to her about."

"Why would I do that?" Montgomery looked honestly puzzled and Apollo repressed an urge to punch the man in the nose. "What good is knowledge if one shares it with everyone?"

Anything he answered would only provide fuel for Montgomery's scheming, so Apollo changed the subject. "Have you discovered anything of interest in your sneaking about, Your Grace?"

"*Sneaking* sounds so very...*bad*." Montgomery sniffed as they descended the stairs.

Apollo looked at him.

"Very well!" The duke threw up his hands. "Don't lose your temper, I don't know if I could withstand your hamlike fists. I've discovered that Mrs. Jellett has a rather handsome, rather *young* footman she brings everywhere, that Mr. William Greaves has a valet who spent most of his youth in Newgate, that Mr. and Mrs. Warner, despite their newly wedded bliss, keep separate bedrooms—although I'd suspected that already"—the smile he gave was rather nasty—"and that Lady Herrick has a birthmark in the shape of a butterfly on her left buttock. Oh, and that said birthmark turns an interesting shade of lavender when slapped."

Apollo stopped in the hallway outside the breakfast room and simply stared at his companion.

"What?" Montgomery looked irritated. "I defy any man to not take the opportunity when presented to slap a lovely arse."

Apollo sighed and continued walking. "Anything else?"

The duke frowned for a moment before supplying, "Miss Royle dislikes me exceedingly."

Apollo arched an eyebrow. "I'd think any number of young ladies dislike you."

"Yes, they do," the duke replied carelessly. "That's not the interesting part. The interesting part is that I seem to care one way or the other. It's rather fascinating, truth be told."

Apollo rolled his eyes at the man's vanity. "You've collected a quantity of knowledge, Your Grace, and none of it is in any way helpful to my case."

"Ah, but one never knows," the duke replied. "Knowledge has a strange way of becoming applicable at the oddest moments. It's why I take care to gather any and all information, no matter how trivial it may seem at first. But never fear: we've only been at the house party for less than a day and I anticipate more discoveries today."

Apollo's eyes narrowed. "Why today?"

"Didn't you know?" Montgomery had that look of amusement that Apollo was beginning to loathe. "Additional guests arrived late last night."

And he threw open the door to the breakfast room, revealing Edwin Stump, his mouth full of toast.

But it wasn't Edwin that Apollo stared at. There were two other people in the room—a rather plain but gentle-faced lady and, beside her, a big man with an olive complexion, a scowl twisting his features. He had one green eye and one blue.

Beside him Montgomery went very still before whispering, in a tone of delight, like a little boy offered a huge bag of sweets, "Oh, how utterly wonderful!"

LILY WATCHED FROM a chair later that morning as Stanford struck a pose and declaimed, " 'An' if ever I see my daughter in such a position again, mark me well, gentlemen, I shall' … er …"

He sneaked a glance at Lily, who didn't have to refer to the pages in her hand. After all, she'd written *A Wastrel Reform'd.* " 'Disembowel the deceiver,' " she said, supplying the rest of the line.

" '*Dis*embowel the deceiver.' 'Dis*em*bowel the deceiver,' " Stanford muttered to himself before nodding and resuming his pose. " 'I shall disembowel the deceiver so that ne'er again may he so deceive again.' "

Lily winced. It wasn't exactly her best line, but then

she'd written the second half of the play in only one week. Her first play had taken a year to write.

Of course, she'd burned it after that.

"Darlings!"

She turned at the voice and stared, hardly believing her eyes. Edwin stood in the doorway, arms thrown wide, in a new sky-blue satin suit, apparently expecting his usual welcome.

Well, and she supposed he had cause to. Moll and the other actresses rushed to him, Moll cooing over him. Stanford and John approached more slowly, but they were equally admiring in their own way.

Ridiculous to pout. No one but her and her brother knew that *she* was the real playwright.

"Robin, sweetheart," Edwin called, strutting toward her.

Lily repressed the urge to roll her eyes at him. He was always careful to call her by her stage name in the company of others, even when all the other actors knew quite well what her real name was.

She submitted to a buss on her cheek and then smiled sweetly at him. "Might I have a moment of your time, brother dear?"

"Naturally." He glanced about to let the other actors know what a doting older brother he was.

"Alone."

The first inkling that something might not be right seemed to seep into his eyes. "Erm...certainly."

She rose, set down the pages, and led him into the small antechamber, closing the door quite firmly behind them.

"What—?" he began, but she cut him off quite satisfyingly with a slap across his face.

"Lily!" His eyes were wide and hurt, his hand to the side of his face.

She set her hands on her hips. "Don't you 'Lily' me, Edwin Stump!"

"I don't understand," he tried.

So she slapped him again. "You set the soldiers on Apollo. They might've taken him to Bedlam—or hanged him. All because you were miffed that he'd thrown you out of the theater."

"I wasn't *miffed*," he said, drawing himself up and straightening his white wig, which had become rather askew. "I was worried about your safety."

"*My* safety?" She knew her mouth was agape, but she just couldn't help it. Edwin could be such a prize ass sometimes—and what was worse, he seemed to be under the delusion that she was a simpleton. "Are you insane?"

"No, but he is." Edwin backed up a step. "A deranged killer! Everyone has heard."

"He is not a deranged killer," she said very, very softly as she crowded Edwin into a corner of the room. "And you know it quite well. You're being spiteful—and you're hurting me."

He'd already opened his mouth for a retort, but his eyebrows drew together at that. "What? Hurting you?"

"Yes, hurting me, Edwin," she said patiently. "I like Lord Kilbourne, and I find your cruelty toward him—and me—quite unforgivable. He's here, at this house party."

"I noticed him just now in the breakfast room," Edwin said sulkily. "He's taken the ridiculous name Mr. Smith."

"He's here to look for the real murderer. I don't want you to even think about turning him in again, do you hear?"

"I..." He gulped. "But Lily..."

"Not even *accidentally*, Edwin."

He dipped his chin, looking a bit shocked. "Yes, very well."

"Good." She turned to go because anything else she said at this point would not be conducive to a good future relationship with her brother, but Edwin caught her arm.

"Lily..." He cleared his throat nervously. "I think I ought to warn you."

She looked at him and saw his forehead was shining with sweat. A feeling of sick dread settled low in her belly. Had he already told someone about Apollo? "What is it?"

He swallowed. "Richard Perry, Baron Ross is here."

Chapter Fifteen

*For at the heart of the labyrinth was a wild and
beautiful garden. Vines climbed over tumbled stones,
so worn they might've fallen millennia ago. Gnarled
trees twisted between the stones, branches thrust upward
and covered in emerald leaves. At the center of the
clearing lay a still, blue pool with small white and
yellow flowers scattered along its mossy bank. But
the monster lay there as well, sprawled half in the pool,
his blood dyeing the waters red...*
—From *The Minotaur*

Apollo strode into the drawing room where the actors had
decided to put on their play. They were gathered there,
Moll Bennet at one end with her arms raised as she spoke
her lines. She glanced at him as he entered, winked, and
jerked her head in the direction of a small door to the side
of the room.

He nodded as he changed his course for the door. He
and Moll had become friends the night before when he'd
talked her into abandoning the room she shared with Lily.

He could hear voices as he drew near. Lily saying,
"...Indio..." and Edwin hissing in reply.

Apollo pulled the door open sharply and Edwin Stump

nearly fell into his arms. He pushed the man back inside, stepped in, and shut the door behind him.

Lily was in the corner, looking rather pale, but he kept his gaze on Edwin. "Say one word about me or my past and you'll—"

Edwin held up his hands defensively. "No need, my sister has already made all the threats."

"Has she?" Apollo stepped closer because he didn't like how Lily looked. What had her weasel of a brother said to her? "I'm sure she was most thorough, but I still wish to make myself clear. Whatever she might've threatened you with, know this: I don't like you. Hurt her or me and you'll regret it to the end of your days."

Edwin's Adam's apple bobbled in his throat. "Quite. Yes...erm...that's very clear, I think." He darted a glance at Lily and for the first time Apollo saw a trace of regret in the man's face. "But you must know I'd never do anything to hurt my sister."

"Do I?"

Edwin glanced down. "Perhaps...there's something you should know."

Apollo narrowed his eyes, not trusting the other man a whit.

"Lily told me that you're looking for the man who might've murdered your friends. That is, I suppose, if you didn't do it yourself."

"I didn't," Apollo bit out.

Edwin blinked rapidly, backing into the wall. "Yes, of course, we all know that, don't we, Lily?"

She sighed, speaking for the first time. "He *didn't*, Edwin."

His brows knit as if her calm assurance confused him.

"All right, all right. It's just that I saw you come into the breakfast room with the Duke of Montgomery."

"So?" Apollo said. "His Grace is helping me."

Edwin shrugged, looking shifty. "But is he, though?"

"What do you mean?" Lily frowned. "Do speak plainly, Edwin, please."

"I'm trying to!" Oddly he looked wounded by his sister's words. "The duke likes to collect information—things other people would rather keep hidden."

"You're saying he's a blackmailer," Apollo said.

Edwin grimaced. "Nothing that unrefined. More of a manipulator, perhaps. But it doesn't do to let one's secrets fall into his hands."

"You think I don't know that?" Apollo replied drily.

"I think you haven't realized you're already in his hands," Edwin shot back. "He knows you're an escaped murderer—" He held up his hands as Lily sputtered a protest. "Yes, all right, an *accused* escaped murderer. What reason does he have to help you when he has such a hold over you?"

"I have no money," Apollo replied. "He had nothing to gain from me."

"Don't think that you have only monetary things to lose," Edwin said. "Some things of value have no price."

Apollo felt a bead of sweat run down his spine. Without taking his eyes from the other man, he instinctively held out his hand to Lily.

Lily clasped his fingers and stared at her brother, her face shuttered.

"I'm trying to warn you," Edwin huffed and actually turned to Apollo for help.

Apollo raised one eyebrow at him.

"Very well." Edwin drew himself up with martyred pride. "If you're *quite* done with me?"

Apollo waved at the door, but made no move to step aside, making Edwin brush nervously against him as he went for it.

Edwin turned with his hand on the doorknob. "Lily, I..."

She waited, but when he said no more, she simply sighed. "Just go, Edwin."

He nodded and opened the door.

The moment it was shut again, with only the two of them inside the little room, Apollo turned to Lily and looked at her with concern. "Who," he asked softly, "is Lord Ross?"

THE THING WAS, Lily had never had to make this choice before. Indio had always—*naturally*—come first. Before Edwin, even before Maude, it was Indio she looked after, Indio she cared for. Because he was a child—*her* child—and therefore the most vulnerable.

But was that true anymore?

She tilted her head back, staring at Apollo. He wore the same suit as yesterday, but at some point this morning, he'd taken time to club his hair back.

Frankly, she preferred it the way it'd been last night—wild and about his shoulders.

He meant something to her. She couldn't hide from that fact. She'd slept with Apollo—the first man she'd taken as a lover since before she'd become Indio's mother. Even now, as he challenged her with soft words and sympathetic eyes, she was aware of his body. Of the breadth of his shoulders, the scent of his skin, so close in the little room. It wasn't fair. She'd been so careful, so very wary, and he'd broken through her barriers without even trying—or so it seemed.

She folded her arms in front of her breasts, trying to keep some space between them. If she didn't take care, he'd surround and overtake her, make her forget what mattered most and what was at stake.

Indio.

Indio was vulnerable. She must protect him.

And like that the decision was made.

She looked at him. "Richard Perry, Lord Ross is a wealthy gentleman—an aristocrat like you."

He opened his mouth as if he wanted to refute the comparison, but he couldn't, really, could he?

Apollo was an aristocrat. Richard was an aristocrat. These two things were facts, simple and true.

She drew strength from that. "He's married with children, I believe. Two sons? I don't know. I haven't seen him in years." And for that she was very glad.

He took a step closer and despite her folded arms, she could no longer keep herself entirely apart from him. His body heat invaded her skin—her very bones. He said, "He has one green eye and one blue one. Like Indio."

She took a careful breath. "Yes. He's Indio's father."

His eyebrows drew together—not in condemnation but in puzzlement. "Lily, I—"

"Ross doesn't know," she said bluntly.

He looked at her in question.

"I never told him." She stared at him, trying to convey this one truth. "It's *important*, very important, that he not know about Indio."

"But..."

She couldn't hold herself together anymore. The danger was too close. She grabbed his arm with both hands. "Apollo, please, *please* promise me you'll not mention Indio, or…or *any* suggestion that I have a child, to Richard."

He nodded slowly. "Of course." He frowned down at her hands and slowly took them in his own. "Did he hurt you? Because if he hurt you, I—"

"No." She almost laughed—though not in amusement. "You have no need to play my protector. In fact, I wouldn't be happy if you said anything at all to Richard about me."

"He was your lover."

She tried to pull her hands away, but he wouldn't let her. "Is that what all this is about? Jealousy? God, I can't believe—"

He did an odd thing then, something that startled her into silence: he laughed, a bitter, tormented sound.

"Jealousy," he grated, pulling her close, pulling her into his arms, though she struggled to get away. "I would that it were something as easy, as simple, as mere jealousy." He bent and murmured against her mouth, his lips caressing her with each word. "This is far more awful than jealousy."

And then he was devouring her mouth, his breath hot and tasting of the coffee he must've drunk when he'd broken his fast. She wished, suddenly, that she might've been there when he had. That she could've watched those strong, unlovely lips sip at a cup, that she could've seen his throat move as he swallowed toast or eggs or gammon or whatever he'd consumed at that meal. She wanted to be there with him whenever he ate, whenever he rose, whenever he went to bed. She wanted to watch as he let himself go, as he succumbed to slumber and dreams. She wanted to see him shave. To find out if he raised his chin and stroked upward with the razor as she'd once seen Edwin do when she was very little.

She wanted…oh, dear God! She wanted everything. She wanted *him*.

And in that moment she forgot resolve and carefully plotted plans and all else. Her vision, her mouth, her very being were filled, simply and completely, with Apollo Greaves.

She opened her lips, desperate for him as if she hadn't seen him for years, when he'd risen from her bed only hours before. She bit at him, whimpering.

He caressed her face, murmuring, "Shhh."

There were others nearby, she knew that somewhere in a part of her brain that still worked, but it really didn't matter to her. She clutched at his shoulders, his hair, wanting him naked with her. Wanting him to be Caliban, not Apollo.

He lifted her suddenly, setting her on a table nearby, which wobbled under her weight.

He cursed softly and tossed her skirts up, thrusting his hand underneath. He gave her no warning, no gentle persuasion. His fingers were at her mound, blunt and unhesitating. He traced through her folds, spreading and exploring, as if he had every right. Claiming her sex as he'd claimed her mouth.

She groaned and he broke away to admonish, "Hush!" against her cheek.

Then his thumb found her clitoris and he was pressing against her, moving in small, devastating circles.

She bit into his shoulder.

He bent and licked her throat.

"Shit," he breathed. "I can't—"

And then he took away his hand and she *growled* at him.

He laughed, low and sensuously, and flipped open his falls. He shoved between her thighs, making the table shake, spreading her thighs even wider to give himself room.

"Stop," she hissed. "The table will break."

He simply looked at her, grinned, and *thrust*.

She grabbed his upper arms as he entered her, rough, sudden, searingly hot—and so good she had to bite his shoulder again.

"Someday," he panted as he thrust again, his cock stretching her, filling her, "I'm going to take you in a place where you don't have to be quiet. Where I can hear all your moans and little squeaks. Where I can make you scream."

And he seated himself fully, his pelvis pressed to hers, her skirts in a wadded mess between them.

He started to withdraw slowly and she pounded on his back with both fists. "Move!"

He braced one hand on her hip and one on the wall and thrust in again, making the table knock against the wall.

Her eyes widened, and she gasped. He was hitting her just there, and it was marvelous, but at the same time the table's knocking would bring someone soon. She groaned. She didn't want to end this but there was *no lock on the door*.

"Put your legs around me," he huffed in her ear, humid and hot.

"They'll hear us."

"Lily," he groaned, "please do it, love."

The endearment jolted through her, going straight to where he still shoved into her.

She wrapped her legs around him, as high as she could, and as she did, he grasped her bottom in both his hands and lifted her. She clung to him, impaled on his penis, the position so obscene she should've fainted from just the thought.

Instead she nearly came.

He leaned his shoulders back against the wall and moved his big hands to her waist. She watched as his eyes shuttered, his face going slack with sensuous want as he lifted and lowered her on his cock, using her as a tool to pleasure himself.

Each pull upward was a draw against her most sensitive flesh. Each jolt down a powerful slam of pleasure.

He was driving her insane, driving her with need, and she wasn't sure she could keep from screaming.

He must've known her peril, for his eyes opened, his pupils large and black, and he looked at her. "Kiss me."

He couldn't do it himself, she realized. He was using all his strength to keep them both upright against the wall.

She leaned forward, feeling like a doll in his strong arms, and placed her closed lips against his, a chaste, gentle kiss, even as his flesh plundered hers below. She was swollen and wet, so heated with want that she wasn't sure it could ever end. Maybe she didn't want it to end. Maybe she wanted him to fill her forever, to just keep ramming her with that long, thick, perfect cock until she became insensible. He could thrust into her all night long and when she woke he'd still be screwing her, his body hard and everlasting, hers wet and wanting.

But it couldn't last forever, that was a fevered fantasy born of heat and his smell, and when he began losing his rhythm, she reached between them, pinching her clitoris with two fingers.

He watched her, his lips curled. "You . . . you're . . ."

She leaned close and whispered against his sweaty neck. "I'm touching myself. Pleasuring myself as you fuck me."

He gritted his teeth and the tendon in his neck stood out in stark relief.

She felt his come flooding her, seeping out around his penis.

And when she climaxed herself, she bit down on that tendon, tasting salt. Tasting life.

Greaves House was a dreary mansion.

Trevillion looked up at the darkened edifice as he helped Lady Phoebe and her elderly cousin, Miss Bathilda Picklewood, from their carriage. Only one lantern was lit at the door—either from miserliness or because their host wasn't particularly welcoming.

"Oof," Miss Picklewood muttered as she made the gravel drive. "Well, 'tisn't a lovely place, but I expect the play shall be quite good."

"It was very nice of Mr. Greaves to invite us," Lady Phoebe chided. "He doesn't even know us and I'm sure it was merely a courtesy to Hippolyta. Actually, it's a lovely coincidence that he even found out we were staying in Bath."

Miss Picklewood darted an arch glance at Trevillion as she took Lady Phoebe's arm. "Yes, *quite* a coincidence."

He didn't bother replying as he followed the ladies.

Miss Picklewood was a disconcertingly perceptive lady for her age and he'd had the feeling for quite some time now that she'd be formidable should the need arise.

The door was opened by a fawning butler who took the ladies' wraps before showing them into a first-floor drawing room. This room at least was brightly lit—dozens of candles fluttered at their entrance, mounted on chandeliers, and candelabra were set here and there on tables. One end of the room had been cleared to serve as a stage, with a trio of musicians in the corner. Several rows of chairs faced the area. A dozen or so guests were already seated in the chairs, chattering as they waited for the play to begin.

A man some sixty years of age approached them. "Ah, Lady Phoebe, I presume?"

His voice was very loud and he was looking at Miss Picklewood.

Lady Phoebe's smile was a bit strained. "Yes, I am she. Mr. William Greaves?"

"Indeed, my lady," he replied, still loud.

"May I present my dear cousin, Miss Bathilda Picklewood? And this is Captain Trevillion."

Trevillion noted with amusement that Lady Phoebe didn't bother explaining his presence. Their host bowed to Miss Picklewood and turned to him, his eyes widening when he saw the pistols Trevillion wore upon his chest. "Oh…er…most welcome."

"Thank you, sir," Trevillion replied.

"There'll be a ball after the play—a sort of midnight festivity. I hope you'll be able to attend, Lady Phoebe?"

"Lady Phoebe will be returning to her home after the play," Trevillion replied for her, earning himself a glare from his charge. It couldn't be helped, however. A seated performance was one thing. A dance at a stranger's house was another. Wakefield wouldn't like it—and Wakefield paid his wages.

"Yes, well, let me show you to your seats," Greaves said, indicating two empty chairs at the front row. "Miss Royle said that she was friends with you, my lady."

"Yes, indeed." Lady Phoebe smiled.

A dark-haired lady next to the empty chairs turned and waved at their approach.

"I wasn't aware, however...that is, I'll have a footman fetch another chair," Greaves mumbled.

"No need," Trevillion said briskly. "Let the ladies sit amongst friends. I'm quite happy to find my own seat."

Greaves nodded gratefully and led the ladies to their places.

Which left Trevillion free to slip into place in the empty chair beside Kilbourne at the back.

"I see you found a way to attend," Kilbourne said, low.

"Indeed." Trevillion watched as Greaves fussed over Lady Phoebe's seat. "Lady Phoebe enjoys the theater in whatever form."

"And had she not?"

Trevillion glanced at the viscount. "Had she not, I would've found another way to meet with you. I wouldn't force her to attend an event she didn't like."

"I meant no offense," Kilbourne said.

Trevillion inclined his head, his mouth thinned. "Have you discovered anything yet?"

Kilbourne hesitated, but shook his head. "Not as of yet. I'd hoped to search my uncle's rooms, but haven't found the right moment."

"More guests mean more servants about," Trevillion replied. "Yet you hesitated before you spoke, my lord?"

Kilbourne grimaced. "It's nothing. The duke mentioned this morning that my uncle has a valet who spent time in Newgate—an odd origin for a manservant, you must admit."

Trevillion shrugged. That was the thing about London: a man could completely remake himself.

"And then," Kilbourne continued, "Miss Goodfellow's brother took care to warn me that we couldn't trust Montgomery."

Trevillion snorted softly. "That's nothing new, my lord."

"No, yet now I wonder if the man is actively working against us."

"For what purpose?"

Kilbourne gave him a sardonic glance. "For what purpose does he work *for* us?"

"He said so that you may finish his garden," Trevillion replied, "but I take your point."

Kilbourne glanced at him. "Have you found out anything about my cousin? Could he be the one behind the murders, not my uncle?"

"Nothing," Trevillion stated. "He lives rather frugally, in fact. It's only his father who is in debt."

Kilbourne shook his head. "Should I trust Miss Goodfellow's brother? Or Montgomery? Or neither?"

"Hmm. Point the brother out to me."

Kilbourne looked around. "There. He's just come in the door with Montgomery."

Trevillion turned discreetly and saw a wiry man in a white wig a step behind the duke. On the other side was the Scots architect they'd met in the garden—MacLeish. "Strange that he should warn you against the duke and then keep his company."

"Mmm," Kilbourne murmured in assent. "I've been trying to think what Montgomery gets out of all this."

"You don't believe that he wants you for his garden?"

"Possibly." Kilbourne shrugged. "But I'm hardly the only gardener he could hire. There has to be another reason."

"He probably doesn't do anything but for a minimum of at least two things to his advantage." Trevillion stiffened as he watched Montgomery approach Lady Phoebe. "Damn."

"What?"

He'd forgotten the obvious: rank. Lady Phoebe, as the daughter and sister of a duke, was most likely the highest-ranking lady in the room. And since Montgomery was a duke and thus the highest-ranking *gentleman*, naturally he'd be seated next to her.

Trevillion nearly growled. "I don't like him near my charge."

"He'll hardly do anything in a crowded room," Kilbourne said. "Besides, she has her chaperone. That one looks a Tartar."

Trevillion grunted, not liking having to leave Lady Phoebe's protection to an old woman, no matter how sharp.

The musicians began a tune, prompting the audience to quiet. After a moment an actor strode in with Miss Goodfellow and began an argument—something about a maid he wanted to woo. The male actor was apparently her twin brother.

A farce. Not to his taste—theater seldom was. Trevillion fixed his eyes on his charge instead, surprised to see that Montgomery had switched chairs with his architect friend. The younger man now sat next to Lady Phoebe, his red head close to hers.

Trevillion frowned and turned to Kilbourne, but one look showed that was a lost cause.

The viscount's gaze was riveted on Miss Goodfellow.

Chapter Sixteen

*Ariadne thought at first to flee, but the monster
made neither move nor sound. At last, gathering her
courage, she ventured near. He lay facedown and nude,
his massive arms outstretched among the innocent flowers,
his lower limbs in the water. Blood flowed from numerous
cuts to his legs and torso. His bull's head was turned to the
side, and as she stared, he opened his eye…*
—From *The Minotaur*

He'd made love to her, but he'd never truly *see* her, Apollo
realized as he watched Lily on stage. She'd changed the
dress she'd initially appeared in to breeches and a coat,
her dark hair hidden under a man's white wig. Anyone
with half a brain could see she was a woman disguised as
a man, but the point wasn't to fool the audience, but rather
to entice it.

And entice she did.

Lily was…he stared in wonder. He didn't have the words
to describe the spell she cast over the room. It was as if she'd
caught and channeled light, a prism of delight. She was
quick and bright and he found himself leaning forward, to
catch a little of her illumination. He wanted her to speak to
him, only him. To hold her attention as she held his.

The damnable thing was, he knew he wasn't the only one. Everyone in the audience wanted a small part of Robin Goodfellow for their very own. As a friend to confide in. As a lover to shower with affection. He was half hard simply watching her swirl about the stage, flinging quips at the male actor who was supposed to be her rival. How was it possible that he'd been *inside* her only that morning and now he felt as if he knew her not at all?

He watched as she leaned a little closer to the actor, flirting with her mischievous green eyes, and he was half admiring, half outraged that she would look at any other man that way.

Every man in the room must have an erection.

Apollo swallowed, trying to lean back, trying to break from her spell, only to find that he couldn't.

He wasn't the only one.

He watched as his elderly uncle blushed when she bit her lip and glanced over her shoulder at the audience.

Dear God, but she was dangerous.

He was a great ugly lump, he knew this. He'd always been, ever since the day when he'd been but fifteen and he'd topped his own father's height. How could such a mercurial fairylike creature want anything to do with him? And yet she had. She'd let him touch her intimately. Had let him claim her.

In that moment Apollo resolved that no matter how ridiculous their mating might be, he wasn't going to let her change her mind. She was his now—and if he had any say in the matter, she'd be his always.

THE PLAY HAD gone well, Lily thought later as she sat before a looking glass and washed the paint from her face. True, Stanford had managed to forget an entire speech in the third act, and the boy playing the overly handsome valet was much too prone to trying to upstage the other actors playing with him, but Moll had delivered her lines with graceful humor touched with ribaldry and John had been so handsome and chivalrous she'd nearly fallen in love with him herself. Yes, overall a great success.

"About done, dear?" Moll called, turning in front of her own little looking glass to try to see her hair from behind. "I've a mind to dance with that pretty duke tonight—and have a glass or two of Mr. Greaves's wine. I hope it's good." She winked at Lily. "Not that it'll stop me if it's not."

Lily laughed. "Go ahead. I still have to re-pin my hair."

Moll twirled one last time and left.

Lily smiled into her mirror. It made no sense, but she wanted to look her best for Apollo. He'd never seen her perform before and she was a bit nervous about his reaction. Had he liked the play? Had he recognized the lines that she'd written in the garden with his help?

She wrinkled her nose at herself. Silly. If she didn't hurry, she'd miss the ball and then her primping would have been for naught.

In the silence of the little chamber off the drawing room she heard footsteps approaching. Hurriedly she pushed a last pin into her coiffure and stood, smiling as the door opened.

Her smile froze on her face when she saw who entered.

Lord Ross hadn't changed much in seven and a half years. He still had a stiff, nearly military bearing. He still wore a properly curled and powdered white wig. He still had a flat stomach and big shoulders. And he still had one blue eye and one green.

But the lines around his mouth and eyes had deepened and multiplied and his mouth seemed permanently turned down now.

Perhaps cruelty could stamp itself upon a man's face.

"Lily Stump," he drawled, his voice smooth and light. Apollo's voice would never sound like that, she knew. His voice would always grate, no matter how much his throat healed.

And she was glad.

"Richard," she replied evenly.

"Lord Ross, if you please," he snapped, and although his voice didn't rise, her gaze darted to his hands.

They had half-fisted.

She nodded. "My lord, then. How may I help you?"

"You," he said, prowling into the room, "can help me by staying out of my way and *remaining* quiet."

She pivoted so that he wouldn't back her into the corner. The little room held only two tiny tables and a single chair, her box of paints, and the costumes. But there was the looking glass. If she had to, she could break it. The edges would be sharp.

"Very well," she said quietly.

"Swear it," he said, advancing.

She ducked and darted around him. There was a pull and a tearing sound and then she was out of his grasp and out the door, running with her skirts bunched in her fists.

"Lily Stump!" he roared behind her, but she'd be a fool to stop.

And she was no fool.

She skidded around a corner, nearly barreling into a wide-eyed footman.

"Miss?" he asked, clearly surprised.

"I do beg your pardon," she gasped, smoothing her skirts. One wasn't supposed to apologize to servants, she knew, but to hell with that. She smiled at the man—really just a very tall boy. "Where is the ball being held?"

He pointed to the stairs. "Ground floor, ma'am. Shall I show you?"

She beamed at him. "That would be lovely."

Lily followed the strapping footman down the staircase, never looking back, and now that she was no longer running with her heart beating in her ears, she could hear the music playing.

He bowed at the entrance of the ballroom and she gave him a quick grin in thanks before entering.

The room was lit with dozens of beeswax candles. They, together with the vases of hothouse roses placed around the room, perfumed the air with a sweet stink that was nearly unbearable. It was terribly hot and she wished she had a fan. A glance around showed that Mr. Greaves must have invited quite a few of his neighbors as well as the house party guests, for the ballroom was crowded. She'd hardly taken a step before Mr. Warner appeared before her, asking for a dance.

She was put out—she'd hoped to find Apollo—but she made sure not to let that show on her face. This was part of her job, after all, to entertain the guests.

So she danced a country dance with Mr. Warner, and then another with Mr. MacLeish. By that time she had caught a glimpse of Richard, glowering by the ballroom doors, and decided to head in the opposite direction—

toward the wall of French doors that led out to the garden. She was glancing over her shoulder to make sure Richard wasn't following her when she felt a hand on her wrist.

She was hauled rather unceremoniously onto the slate steps that ran along the back of the house and led into the darkened garden itself.

Lily squeaked and looked up.

Into Apollo's shadowed face.

"Oh" was, unfortunately, all she could think of to say.

"You look frightened," he murmured. "Why?"

She smoothed her skirts. "You did just yank me out of the ballroom. Practically a kidnap."

In the light from the ballroom she thought she saw his lips twitch. "If I'd wanted to kidnap you, I'd've thrown you over my shoulder."

She drew herself up. "What makes you think I'd let you?"

He moved his fingers to her hand and clasped it. "Oh, you would."

"You're quite sure of yourself." She sniffed.

"Mmm." He pulled gently, leading her down the steps. "I liked your play."

"Oh." She could feel herself blushing like a green girl. "Thank you."

She caught the flash of his teeth as he grinned back at her.

Although the French doors had been open, the party wasn't meant to spill into the garden, so there were no lanterns. There was a moment beyond the light coming from the windows of the house, in the dark of the garden itself, when she felt quite blind.

"Where are we going?"

"I discovered something this afternoon." His voice floated back to her on the night breeze. "I wanted to show you."

It was rather cool and if she hadn't just been running and then dancing, it might've been too cold, but as it was, the night chill was rather nice on her overheated skin.

"Careful," he whispered as her slippered feet trod on grass. "We've left the pavement behind."

She closed her eyes a moment and when she opened them again, she looked up. "Oh, the stars."

She could see him now—or at least his silhouette.

He tilted his head back. "They're rather nice tonight."

They walked in silence for a bit, the music wafting behind them, and then a sort of wall seemed to loom ahead.

"What is it?" she asked.

He paused for a moment and she knew—she wasn't sure how, but she knew—he was smiling. "A maze."

PERHAPS APOLLO WAS mad to bring a girl to see a maze at night, but somehow it'd seemed exactly the right thing to do.

"Come on," he said to her, pulling her hand.

Lily followed easily enough, but her voice was uncertain as they made the first turn. "We'll get lost."

"No," he said easily. "I found it this afternoon and explored it then. It's simple enough."

"Even in the dark."

"Even in the dark," he assured her. "But it's not quite dark, is it?" He pointed up at the stars and the crescent moon.

"Humph." She didn't sound entirely reassured, but she followed him nonetheless, and that made him glad.

The maze was an old one with a fully matured hedge over eight feet tall. In places the hedge threatened to grow into the path and he had to lead her single file, but she never protested. He could hear the rustle of her skirts, the sound of her breathing right behind him, and once in a while her scent came to him, orange and clove, tantalizing and sweet.

He tightened his grip on her hand.

By the time he turned the final corner he was heavy and hard.

"Where are we?" she whispered, as if she knew the import of this place. Of where he'd brought her and why.

Before them was a shallow stone pool, rimmed with stone benches, a statue standing at the center. It had probably once been a fountain, but time and neglect had stopped it running, and now it was dry save for a few rotting leaves blown against the edges.

"We're at the heart," he replied, his throat thick.

She tugged his hand as she stepped closer to the stone pool. She stared at the statue and then back at him. "The heart of the maze?"

He looked into her eyes, reflecting the starlight, the entire universe, really, and nodded. "The heart."

She stood still a moment, watching him, and he had no idea at all what she was thinking.

Finally she laughed quietly, gesturing with her free hand at the marble figure. "It's a minotaur. I suppose that's appropriate."

He looked at the figure, all horns and massive shoulders. "The monster in the maze?"

"Yes." She turned in the dark to face him, and all he could see was the limned starlight on her cheek, the glimmer of the reflected moon in her eyes. "Indio thought you were a monster at first. Did I ever tell you?"

He shook his head slowly. "Am I still a monster to you?"

"No." She reached up to trace his eyebrow. "You're not...that. You never were, really."

And she pulled his head down to meet her mouth. She kissed him with a woman's passion, a woman's want, frank and sweet. He fought to keep from grasping, from holding too tight, lest the very harshness of his grip drive her from him.

He let her lead, opening his mouth when her tender tongue ran across his lips. Let her explore and seek. She thrust her hands into his hair, pulling the tie out, framing his face with his coarse locks.

"Apollo," she breathed against him, her hands restless on his waistcoat. "Apollo, make love to me."

It was all he was waiting for. He pressed her against him, angling his head to deepen the kiss. He placed his palm over her upper chest, feeling the delicate collarbone beneath his fingers, the gentle swell of her breast. Even this little amount of flesh was like wine in the desert. He traced the edge of her bodice, dipping his little finger into the hot, shadowed recess between her breasts. It was moist there and suddenly he had to taste. He bent her back, ducking his head to slide his tongue between her sweet breasts and taste her salt.

"Apollo," she moaned, grasping his hair. "Please."

He licked up over her breasts, finding the rise of her shoulder and biting there.

Her fingers moved in a shaking flurry between them and he realized she was scrabbling at his falls, but before he could help her, she had them open.

Had them open and had him in her hand.

He froze, groaning, trembling at her touch. Her cool fingers circled him confidently, stroking up once before caressing his head, exploring where he wept liquid tears.

She pulled one hand away and he saw, in the moonlight, as she drew a single wet finger to her lips and sucked.

That was too much.

He had her turned before she could make another move. He ripped off his coat and threw it down before one of the benches edging the pool.

"Kneel," he said, and his voice was a guttural rasp that made him wince.

She obeyed, though, as if sacrificing herself to some ancient monster. "Like this?" And the look she gave him over her shoulder was enough to make him swallow hard.

"Exactly like that," he said, kneeling behind her. He pulled up her skirts reverently, as though he unveiled a work of art, seeing first the gleam of her white stockings in the moonlight, then the silver of her thighs.

Then the rounded mounds of her arse. Her delightfully carnal arse, curved and sweet, that secret darkness between. If he died right now, he'd dream for all eternity of Lily's arse and be happy.

He laid her skirts over her back and ran his fingertips over her buttocks, watching as she shivered.

"Spread your legs for me," he ordered.

She shifted, revealing more of herself, though the darkness kept her tantalizingly modest.

He ran his finger down the dip between her cheeks, slowly, until he encountered her moisture.

"Apollo," she whispered, wiggling just a little.

"Do you like that?" His words were nearly slurred as if he were drunk on her feminine scent.

"You know I do," she said, bending farther. She put her head in her arms on the stone bench, jutting out her hips farther, as if she were presenting herself, a mare to be mounted.

God, he wanted her.

He took his cock in hand and crawled closer, close enough that he could run his cockhead through her weeping slit.

She moaned and arched her back, forcing herself against him.

He couldn't think. Could only feel—and want. He shoved his prick into position, placing his palm on the small of her back to hold her still. He didn't want to hurt her—and if he moved too fast he was liable to spill.

He eased into her tight, hot passage, throwing his head back, staring blindly at the starlit cosmos. She was so wet for him, so slick and beautiful, that tears gathered at the corners of his eyes even as he thrust and thrust again. He pushed into that sweet tunnel, uniting them, making them one, until his flesh and her flesh merged.

And then he separated them again, drawing entirely out, just so he could feel again the wonderful pleasure of joining.

She whimpered, her face against her arms, and he bent over her, his woman, his Lily, surrounding, protecting, claiming her as his. "What do you want, love?"

"Th...that."

He licked the bared nape of her neck. "Tell me."

"I want you," she whispered. "I want your cock in me. I want you to fill me and stuff me full until I can't talk or remember my own name."

He lost all control at her words. He reared, withdrawing and slamming back into her, the man entirely subsumed in the animal. All he was, all he could feel was his cock conquering her pussy, making her his mate for now, forever.

He bowed over her and bit into the back of her neck, holding her hips still so that he could plow into her over and over again until he felt her shudder under him, contracting around him. She moaned, low and lost, as she came, and he knelt up then, never stopping, never slowing, pounding as she trembled beneath him until he threw back his head and roared his own release into the night.

The stars whirled above them as he slowly sank back over her, panting, wondering if he'd ever again regain his humanity.

Or if he'd lost it forever to this woman.

Chapter Seventeen

*Now, though a bull's visage may be wild and beastly,
its eyes are quite beautiful. Ariadne saw a soft brown
eye, large and liquid, surrounded by thick lashes and
filled with pain. In that moment she forgot fear of
the monster and felt only pity. Instead of fleeing, she
knelt by his side and began to bind his wounds, and
as she did, she wondered what had become of Theseus,
for surely it was he who had hurt the monster...*
—From *The Minotaur*

Lily woke late the next morning with a feeling of both elation and dread. Elation because she would see Apollo again. She knew now that their liaison would by necessity be short. Soon she'd have to go back to her own life and he to his—wherever that was. Aristocrats and average persons could not permanently join—at least not happily. Their worlds were too different, the imbalance of power between highborn and low simply too great. Even if he cared for her in some way, Apollo would have to wed a lady of his own rank one day. Lily hadn't the heart to be a mistress. But knowing that their time together was finite made it all the sweeter. She vowed to enjoy every minute left to her.

But her anticipation at seeing Apollo again was tempered by a feeling of dread. At a house party there was no way she could avoid Richard forever.

She pushed the second thought aside, however, and made sure to walk down to luncheon with Moll.

All the guests were gathered there, it seemed, for it was quite late—nearly one of the clock—and well past the time a working person might break his fast. Of course working people didn't stay awake dancing past dawn, either.

Three large tables had been set up to accommodate so many at once and footmen were moving swiftly, bringing coffeepots and plates of cold meats, coddled eggs, and rolls. Lily saw Apollo almost at once and shared a secret smile with him. Then she glanced around and found Richard, sitting next to a pleasant-looking woman who had to be his wife.

Lily felt nothing but pity for her.

She ducked her head and marched determinedly with Moll toward a table holding John, the Warners, and, unfortunately, her brother. But it was on the opposite side of the room from Richard and that, at least, made it the best choice. When she glanced up again, Apollo was frowning thoughtfully at him.

Damn. The man was much too perceptive.

"Miss Bennet," lovely Mr. Warner exclaimed as they approached. He rose at once, followed more slowly by Edwin and John. "And Miss Goodfellow. What a splendid accomplishment your production was last night. Mrs. Warner and I enjoyed ourselves enormously. And you must be very proud of your brother, for I understand he is the playwright." He turned and beamed at Edwin, who, for once, seemed a bit taken aback by the approbation.

"Indeed," John said. "Mr. Stump is well known in the theater community for the intelligence and wit of his plays. I've acted in two myself."

"How wonderful," exclaimed little Mrs. Warner. "You are very talented, Mr. Stump. I vow I would not be able to write a single line, let alone five entire acts."

Lily met her brother's eyes and saw a shadow of guilt there. She really ought to be used to seeing him lauded for her own work. Still, it hurt, just the tiniest bit, like a pinched heart.

An odd look came over Edwin's narrow face and suddenly he threw wide his arms. "Gentlepeople! Might I have your ears!"

The other guests turned, faces startled or expectant according to their personalities.

Edwin was in his element with an audience. He bowed and strutted to the middle of the room. "I have received many accolades for the play you enjoyed last night, but now I must reveal to you the real talent, the real playwright of *A Wastrel Reform'd*." Edwin paused for a pregnant second and then turned and bowed to Lily. "My own sister, Miss Robin Goodfellow!"

Even knowing what he might say, Lily was caught by surprise. For a moment she simply stared, wide-eyed, at her brother. Then, grinning, he took her hand and drew her to the center of the room.

The guests rose, clapping, and she could do nothing but curtsy and curtsy again. In the back of the room a footman tapped on Mr. William Greaves's shoulder and leaned close to whisper something in his ear before Mr. Greaves turned and left the room.

Amid the uproar, Lily looked at her brother. "Why?"

He shrugged, his look rueful. She wondered if he'd already begun to regret his decision to reveal the authorship of her plays. "It was time," he murmured, close to her ear because the applause was continuing. "And, no matter my own self-interest and pettiness, I do love you, Sister."

Tears sparkled in her eyes and she threw her arms around her brother. Over his shoulder she could see Apollo, standing and clapping with the other guests, his eyes full of pride.

APOLLO WATCHED LILY blush and smile as she was finally acknowledged for the words she'd written. He wanted to go to her and take her in his arms, to congratulate her himself, but they hadn't progressed to a point where he could claim her in public—yet. So instead he used the distraction to slip from the room.

Outside the breakfast room, footmen scurried back and forth, paying him no mind. He strode down the hall and ducked around the corner. His uncle's study was at the back of the house on this floor, in an area normally reserved for the family.

He was nearly at the door when he was hailed from behind.

"Mr. Smith."

He turned to find his uncle staring at him in puzzlement. "Might I help you, Mr. Smith? I fear there is nothing of interest down this way, merely my own study."

"I apologize," Apollo said easily. "I must've gotten turned around."

"Quite." The older man's gaze sharpened on him and he cocked his head. "I've been meaning to ask you, Mr. Smith. Have we perchance met before?"

"I don't think so, sir," Apollo replied, holding his uncle's gaze. It was the truth, after all: he had no memory of his father's family's ever visiting when he was young, save for the one time his grandfather had come to announce Apollo's enrollment in Harrow.

"Strange," the older man murmured as they turned back toward the front of the house and the rest of the party. "But I find that something about you is reminiscent of..." He trailed away, shaking his head. "I feel that I've seen you before."

He slowed as they came to the end of the corridor, and although Apollo wanted to rush away, he made himself slow as well.

"My father," the older man said suddenly, "the earl, is a big man. I used to be quite afeard of him as boy. Broad shoulders like a bull, huge hands." He seemed lost in a not entirely happy memory. "My brother and I did not inherit his frame—much to my father's chagrin—but I'm told my nephew is at least as large as my father. And, of course, my son George bears him some resemblance."

He looked at Apollo and there was a sort of frightened question in his eyes.

"Mr. Greaves."

Both men looked up at the low voice. A servant stood at the other end of the hall, backlit by the window there.

"Ah, Vance," the older man said. "There you are." He turned back to Apollo. "If you'll excuse me, Mr. Smith?"

"Of course," Apollo murmured. He watched as his uncle walked to the manservant.

"I hope you have the matter well in hand?" William Greaves asked.

"Just as you ordered, sir, but if I may..." Vance leaned

toward his master, murmuring something in his ear. As he did so, he turned his head just enough for his face to be revealed. Vance had a port-wine stain over much of his left cheek and chin.

Apollo stepped back, merging into the shadows of the corridor, his heart beating fast. He'd seen that face.

Four years ago in a tavern in Whitechapel.

He waited as the two men disappeared into Greaves's study before slipping back to the breakfast room. It was simply too much of a coincidence for his uncle to have in his employ a man who'd been in the tavern that night. Was he an assassin? Had his uncle sent Vance that night to do such ugly work?

When he reentered the breakfast room, the guests were still dining. Quietly he slipped back into his seat beside the Duke of Montgomery.

"Did you learn anything?" His Grace asked casually as he buttered a piece of toast.

"In the necessary?" Apollo knit his brows as if confused.

"Come now," the duke said. "Don't prevaricate with a master like myself."

He crunched into his toast.

Apollo sighed. He didn't trust Montgomery, but at the moment the man was his only ally. "William Greaves's valet was there at the tavern—the night before the murders."

Montgomery paused mid-crunch. "You're sure?"

Apollo gave him a look. "The man has a conspicuous port-wine stain on his face."

"Ah." The duke swallowed. "Then it seems to me that we ought to find out how long the man has been in William Greaves's employ."

"How—?"

But before Apollo could finish his question the duke had leaned forward over the table. "I say, George, how long has your father had that valet of his?"

"Three years," George Greaves replied slowly, looking between the duke and Apollo.

Apollo swore to himself and hunched over his plate of eggs.

The duke, naturally, wasn't perturbed at all. "Strange. Saw a man with a birthmark just like his in Cyprus two years ago."

Cyprus? Apollo glanced up casually to see if George Greaves had bought this ridiculous story.

Judging by his suspicious look, he had not.

Apollo sighed as the other guests chattered around them. "What the hell was that?" he hissed at Montgomery.

"A question." The duke reached for another piece of toast.

"Did you mean to alert him to our investigation on purpose?" Apollo growled.

"Yes and no." Montgomery shrugged. "I'm bored. Nothing's happening. Sometimes it's best to send the fox into the chicken house to see if a snake slithers out."

Apollo glared. "You know nothing at all about chickens."

"Don't I?" Montgomery smiled winsomely as he slathered butter on his new piece of toast. "If you think that, then perhaps you really ought not to be taking my advice on poultry, hmm?"

Well, and that was the question, wasn't it? Apollo thought as he took a bitter sip of coffee. Should he be trusting the duke with anything at all?

He glanced again at his cousin, blithely drinking his tea. George had said that Vance hadn't been in William's employ four years ago. But that didn't mean William couldn't have known Vance at the time of the murders. And, of course, George might've simply lied. Perhaps father and son had acted together. After all, it was to George's benefit as well should Apollo be hanged.

Apollo shook his head, taking a bite of coddled eggs. If only he had concrete evidence against his uncle.

That decided him.

He had to take another chance at his uncle's study— tonight.

APOLLO WAS IN her rooms again when Lily returned that night. She should have been outraged at his presumption, but all she felt was happiness tinged with sadness.

She doubted that they'd last much beyond this house party. He'd find the murderer and justice and return to his life, she was sure of it. Apollo had a sort of calm resolve that she'd seen before in men who got what they wanted. He was born to be an earl and he would be someday.

An actress had no place in such a life.

As the days of the party passed, so too did their time together.

"You look pensive," he said quietly, holding his hand out from where he lay on the bed. He wore only his shirt and breeches.

She went to him without protest. Why pretend when they really had so little time left together?

He gathered her against him, her back to his front, and began plucking the pins from her coiffure. "Have I told you how much I admire your hair?"

"It's just plain brown," she murmured.

"Plain, lovely brown," he replied, raising a lock he'd freed to his face.

"Are you smelling my hair?" she asked in amusement.

"Yes."

"Silly man," she said lightly.

"Smitten man," he corrected, spreading her hair over her shoulders. "I've been watching you today."

"In between escorting Miss Royle about the garden?" she asked, glancing over her shoulder at him.

"Yes. I'd rather it'd been you, but that wouldn't've been prudent." He frowned down at the strands of her hair caught between his fingers. "Or, perhaps, safe."

She stilled. "What do you mean?"

"My uncle commented that I looked like my grandfather today, and then later Montgomery said some rather unwise words to my cousin."

She turned all the way so she could see his face clearly. There was a small dent between his brows. "They've discovered who you are?"

"Maybe." He shrugged. "Maybe not. My uncle suspects, I think, but only that. As for my cousin…" He trailed away, shaking his head. "That I simply don't know."

"You need to be careful," she said, placing her hand on his chest. "Your uncle killed before to prevent you gaining your title. There's nothing to stop him doing so again."

"I can take care of myself," he said, smiling indulgently down at her.

"Don't be a fool," she whispered urgently. "No man can withstand a bullet."

His smile slipped from his face. "You're right." He kissed her forehead. "Now tell me why Ross is troubling you."

She blinked at the sudden assault. "There's nothing. I—"

"Lily." He trailed his fingers along her hairline. "I care for you. I would protect you if I can. Please tell me."

She opened her mouth and then shut it again. In a little while they would part and probably never see each other again. Did she really owe him anything when such was the situation?

But in this time—this stolen time *before* all that would come next—they were close. If things had been otherwise, she might've made this man her husband. Might've borne his children, kept his home, slept beside him night after night until they both had white hair.

Perhaps in this in-between time she did owe him the truth.

So she laid her head on his chest and listened to his reassuring heartbeat as she spoke.

"When I was little, living in various theaters with my mother, there was another girl my age. Her name was Kitty and she was my friend. Both her mother and her father were actors and I suppose we grew up together. Kitty had flaming red hair and blue eyes and when she laughed, her nose scrunched up so adorably. Once she was old enough she always played the heroine. She was funny and kind and I loved her. She was very fond of seedcake, I remember. Maude would sometimes smuggle a small cake in for us especial and we would have a tea party behind the stage as my mother and her parents worked in whatever play they were in at the time."

Apollo stroked her hair, not commenting. She wondered if he had any idea what it was like to have a friend when one was as alone in the midst of many people as she'd been growing up. How very attached one could become to that person.

"When we were both seventeen," Lily continued, "Kitty met a man—a man outside the theater and far from our world. An aristocrat." She fingered one of the buttons on Apollo's shirt, remembering. "He was handsome and rich, but most importantly, it seemed to us, was that he was so terribly taken with her. We were girls, of course, and even though we'd grown up in the theater, we knew very little of life. It never even occurred to me to be worried. I remember Maude making a comment once—that blue blood and common red blood don't easily mix—but we disregarded her. It was so *romantic*, you understand. He would come and stand by the backstage door, once even in the rain. He said he loved her and we believed him. How could we not? Isn't love standing in the rain and showering a girl with flowers and jewels?"

His arms came up to wrap around her as if she were a small child.

"Once..." She swallowed, steadying her voice. "Once I saw a greenish bruise upon her cheek before she covered it with paint and I thought it rather odd—it was such a strange place to be bruised. But Kitty said she bumped into the corner of a door in the dark and I *believed* her. Believed her without question. I never even thought to question that silly lie."

Her voice had risen and he brushed her hair back from her face, laying his lips on her temple, still saying nothing.

"She married him, after more than a year of courting,

for he was that much infatuated—he actually *married* an actress despite his family's opposition and his own lineage."

Apollo stirred at her words as if to make comment, but she continued before he could.

"I didn't see her then for nearly a year. She sent letters, writing about how happy she was and how her new husband didn't like to share her, even with old friends, and I missed her dreadfully, but I was glad that she'd found her true love. She visited after many months and though she walked with a limp I thought nothing of it when she said she'd fallen in the street and twisted her ankle. But her accidents became more common as her visits grew less and less. When I met her, in the second year of her marriage, at a tea shop and saw, despite the paint she'd used, that her eye had actually been blackened…"

He kissed her, high on her temple, and whispered, "What happened?"

"I pleaded with her to leave him, of course. She had friends, many friends, in the theater. I told her we could hide her if need be, find work for her."

"Did she?"

"No. She wouldn't hear of leaving him. The maddening thing was despite his monstrous treatment of her, she still loved him. Kitty felt that he'd made a sacrifice for her by marrying her against his family's wishes, and if he had a horrendous temper, then that was the price she must pay."

His hand stilled on her hair and he said, very carefully and calmly, "There is never any excuse for a man to hit a woman—*any* woman—let alone one he professes to love."

She was quiet a moment, just basking in his gentle strength.

Then she took a breath and continued. "The next time I saw her, she was expecting a child and she was so happy, Apollo. I began to think I'd been wrong. That her husband had realized how sweet Kitty was and had vowed to never hurt her again. That was what she told me, at least, and I wanted—*truly*—to believe her."

He'd stiffened when she'd spoken of Kitty's pregnancy and he made a sound like an exclamation hastily cut off.

"I was so naïve," she whispered.

"You..." He stopped, his voice shaking. "You weren't to blame, no matter what happened."

She just shook her head. If she'd argued more strongly, appealed to Kitty's instinctive motherly feelings...but she hadn't.

She hadn't.

Lily took his hand, squeezing it. "Kitty came to us one night, very late. She woke us—Edwin, Maude, and me— by pounding at the door. Mother had passed by this point, and Edwin was only staying with us in rather cramped rooms because he'd lost all his money at cards. Maude was the one who opened the door. When I heard her scream, I leaped from my bed. Kitty..." She bit her lip, breathing harshly, trying to fight down sobs.

"You don't have to tell me," he said, low. "You don't have to tell me."

She shook her head violently and gasped, "You won't understand completely otherwise. She...she was all over blood. I don't know how she'd managed to come to us, but she loved her baby very much." She inhaled, choking on a sob. "Very much."

"God," he groaned, holding her, rocking her now. "Oh, my darling girl."

"He'd beaten her quite badly. One eye was closed completely, the other swollen so much..." She caught her breath. "Even had she lived it would've scarred her. I'm not sure she ever would've been able to see again from the closed eye. Something was wrong with her cheek and her nose was flattened into her face. She had to breathe through her mouth, and Apollo, oh, Apollo, some of the blood came from inside her. She was bleeding. Her baby was coming."

He pressed her face to his cheek and she realized it was damp. He was weeping for a woman he'd never known. Weeping for her pain.

"There wasn't time to call a midwife. Maude...Maude was a wonder. She got Kitty on my bed and put clothes beneath her and she scolded Edwin until he pulled himself together enough to help. He shouldn't've been there, of course, but I don't think Kitty knew at the last. She fainted and Maude said...said..."

She covered her face with her hands then, the old, old grief and shock overcoming her. Kitty, poor Kitty. She'd been so pretty, so vivacious, and now all Lily could remember of her was a bloody, beaten face. It wasn't fair. It simply wasn't fair.

"Hush, my love, my love, hush," Apollo murmured into her hair, rocking her like a babe.

"I'm sorry," she said, wiping her face with the heels of her hands. Her nose was running and her eyes were red, she knew. This wasn't what he'd come for tonight, an ugly, weeping woman.

"Don't," he said sharply and she jerked and looked at

him for the first time in minutes. His eyes were bloodshot. "Don't," he said more gently. "Don't apologize for what that monster did and how it hurt you."

She nodded, catching her breath. "He was born only an hour or so after she arrived, just before dawn. So wrinkled and red and Kitty never saw him, she wasn't breathing by the time he came into the world. I thought he wouldn't last either, he was so small, but Maude knew what to do. She sent Edwin to find a wet nurse and bundled the baby with a hot brick on either side of him to warm him." She smiled then, despite the painful memories, because he'd been her baby boy right from the first. "He never cried, do you know? He simply blinked and looked around with big dark-blue eyes. Of course later one eye changed to green, but when he was first born, they were both blue like the night sky, nearly black, and he had a little tuft of black curls on the top of his head, so adorable. Edwin said we should call him George, but I told him that was too common. I named him Indio."

She looked up at him.

He stared back, steady and true. "Who was Kitty's husband, Lily?"

"Lord Ross," she replied, as easily as telling him the time of day, though she'd never told another soul the truth. "We knew at once that if he thought the baby had lived he would hurt it, for he'd told Kitty as he'd beaten her to death that he wanted a new wife. One who would give him heirs of a proper pedigree. So I left the city for a little while, playing in smaller towns, traveling about the country with Maude and the baby and a very young wet nurse. When I came back to London I simply said Indio was my own."

"Ross doesn't know."

"He doesn't know," Lily agreed. "And he must never know. He has a new wife, two small boys, one of them his heir. I shudder to think what he'd do if he knew he already had an heir—one born of an actress with no family."

Apollo slowly clenched his fists. "But for him to've beaten a woman to death—his *wife*—and face no punishment at all…" His face twisted. "It's not *right*."

She scrambled to her knees to face him, for she had to make him understand. "You mustn't go after him, Apollo, and you mustn't tell anyone. As long as he thinks the baby died with Kitty, he's no real danger."

His eyes snapped to hers, darkening. "Then why has he been watching you this entire party?"

She shook her head. "I saw Kitty at the last. He must realize whom she went to. I know what he did to her."

"Then he sees you as a threat to his freedom."

"I'm an actress—no one of consequence in his circles."

"Did you not see the entire room stand to applaud you this morning?" He caught her hands, bringing them to his chest. "You might not think yourself important—and perhaps in strictly titled circles you are not—but in society as a whole? Before we knew you were a great playwright, you were lauded as a fine actress. Lily, he has good reason to fear you."

"Even if you're right, I don't…" She closed her eyes, trying to gather the words. "I don't want you telling anyone, Apollo. Indio has to be kept safe. He *has* to."

"Hush," he murmured, framing her face with his big hands. "I'll not put you or Indio in any more danger, I promise."

"Thank you." She leaned forward to kiss him on the jaw, feeling the rasp of stubble beneath her lips. "Thank you."

"I'm sorry it ever happened to you," he whispered, catching her chin and lifting her face to his. "No one should have to bear witness to the worst that men can do, and especially not you."

Her lips curved in amusement. "Especially me? Why should I be sheltered in particular?"

"Because," he said, pulling her into his lap, "you are my light and my laughter, and if you would let me, I would spend the rest of my life protecting you from everything that is ugly."

"That can't be done," she whispered. "To live is to see both the beauty and the ugliness of life."

"Perhaps not," he said stubbornly, "but that wouldn't stop me from trying. Every day I want to see your eyes alight with happiness."

"Thank you," she said, oddly touched by something that would never—*could* never—happen.

She kissed the corner of his mouth, and when he moved to more fully engage hers, she opened her lips beneath his, accepting his tongue in a long, languorous kiss.

"Help me," she whispered, rising on her knees above him. She unhooked her bodice as he untied the tapes of her skirt, then together they unlaced her stays until he could draw them up over her head.

Another tug and her chemise followed.

She knelt, straddling his thighs, in only her stockings, gartered just above her knees. She placed her palms on his shoulders, looking down at him as he ran his rough fingertips up her legs to her hips.

"You're lovely," he said, his voice hoarse. "I thought that the first time I ever saw you in the garden, when you were clothed, but here, naked..." He swallowed, his eyes darkening as he watched his thumb trace a circle near her maiden hair. "You're everything I never dared to dream of when I was in Bedlam."

"Apollo," she breathed, oddly touched. She stroked his hair, unable to keep from pulling the tie from it.

He smiled as if it were an old habit—a gesture between lovers who had known each other years instead of days.

Tears pricked at her eyes and she bent forward to hide them from him, cradling his face to her breasts.

He turned his head, mouthing at her nipple, and she arched her head back, trying to quell her sudden melancholy. Not now, not here. She didn't want to ruin this by bringing the future in too soon.

But he must've sensed her mood. He lifted his head, trying to see her. "Lily?"

She scooted back, pushing him firmly against the pillows so that she might have access to his lap.

He wouldn't be dissuaded, though, stubborn man. "Lily?"

"It's nothing," she muttered, working at the buttons on his falls. "I...I just want to forget." She flicked her eyes to him, letting him see the mess she must've made of her face earlier. "Can you help me forget?"

She should've felt guilt for her prevarication, but she didn't. She had the right to this little bit of joy, even if it only lasted hours.

So she pulled apart his breeches and reached in to untie his smallclothes. His penis rose, ruddy and proud, from a thatch of coarse hair. She stroked both hands through that hair, scratching, watching smugly as his cock bobbed in reaction.

"Take it off," she ordered him imperiously, tapping at his shirt.

He lifted to do so, pulling the shirt over his head, and then he lay sprawled against the mound of pillows, all naked chest. She sat back on his legs to look her fill, and if she did so to store the image in a corner of her mind, she tried not to think about it too much. His head was cocked back, his shaggy brown hair falling in tangled waves to his shoulders and, oh, his shoulders! If she had the money, she'd commission a sculpture of him nude and never regret the expenditure. His shoulders were mounded with muscle, wide and strong, with upper arms she doubted she could span with both hands. His dark nipples were peaked in a chest the color of sunlight, the dark hairs between making a lovely masculine contrast. Why painters never showed male hair she could not fathom. Wasn't that part of what made a man? Hair upon the body? In any case she loved his.

She stroked a single finger through his chest hairs and when he made to move shook her head firmly. "Don't. I'm not finished."

His eyes narrowed, but he only said, "As you will."

She bit her bottom lip to keep from smiling and traced through the divided muscles of his belly to his navel. She circled that lightly, watching as his belly contracted in reaction. Farther down she followed the trail of dark hair that led to his groin. His penis lay slightly to the side, pulsing. His foreskin had pulled back, revealing his glistening head. She stared frankly, for if he found her lovely, she found him devastating.

She ducked and took him into her mouth, warm and bitter, without waiting to think or ask if it was permissible. She wanted him—all of him.

He jackknifed at her sudden movement, and she saw, out of the corners of her eyes, his hands hovering, fingers spread, on either side of her head, as if he didn't know quite what to do.

Well, neither did she—she'd never done this before—but she wasn't going to let inexperience keep her from this moment.

She sucked lightly at the head, tasting bitter salt, holding him to her mouth with both hands. She ran her tongue slowly around the silky head and then along the edge of his taut foreskin.

He moaned above, though she doubted this was helping him much. After all, it was nothing like the motion he made inside her.

That led to another thought and she gave him an openmouthed kiss before looking up. "What do you do when you're alone?"

He blinked sleepily, eyes widening. "What?"

He must know exactly what she meant. A corner of her mouth kicked up. Had she shocked him? "Show me, please."

She sat back, releasing her hold on him. She watched as he grasped himself with his right hand, pausing.

She bent and kissed him again, the moisture at the tip slipping over her lips. She looked up into his eyes from her position and whispered, "Please?"

His nostrils flared and he nodded, stroking his closed fist up, and then palming the head to spread the seeping moisture around. He stroked down, much faster and stronger than she would've done herself, and she watched in absolute fascination. How often did he do this? And what did he think about when he did?

She looked up to see that he'd flung his arm across his eyes like a debauched faun, the muscle of his upper arm bunched, the tufts of underarm hair strangely erotic. She leaned forward, licking his chest as his fist bumped against her belly and he started.

"Don't stop," she husked, scooting closer, and closer still until his hand was rubbing against her with every stroke, his knuckles brushing through her lips. She ground her pelvis down on his hand as she drew aside the arm covering his eyes and took his face in her hands, kissing him deeply.

He placed his hand on her bottom, urging her closer as he aimed himself, and with one thrust entered her. She leaned forward so that the angle pressed the apex of her slit against his pelvic bone. Then she began to ride him, fast and hard, grinding against him with every downstroke, using him to pleasure herself. She was trembling, her body melting with the heat and desire they made between them, and she watched him as she rode his cock. He swallowed, his eyes on her, his upper lip curled.

Until she saw stars and she had to close her own eyes. She swiveled against him, finding that spot—that perfect spot of friction and heat—and sobbed aloud as she came, her body liquid with melting desire.

He took her hips and thrust forcefully up into her as she curled down into him, holding on as he slammed repeatedly into her, finding his own release. Finding his own point of desire.

And afterward, as she lay exhausted against him, tracing a finger through his sweat-dampened hair, she wondered if there was a way back to her old life after this.

Or if he'd led her into a maze in which she'd be lost forever.

Chapter Eighteen

*The monster watched Ariadne with his beautiful
eyes as she tended to him. When she was finished he
made to stand, but stumbled, swaying. Impulsively she
wrapped her arms about his muscled waist to steady
him. He looked down at her curiously, then led her to
a bower, where he offered her berries and clean water.
And although he did not speak, she thought there was
intelligence in his soft brown gaze…*
—From *The Minotaur*

Apollo crept down the corridor toward his uncle's study.

Well. As much as a man his size *could* creep.

It was past midnight and as far as he could tell all
the guests were asleep, including Lily. He'd had to leave
her sweet warmth to go investigating, and he hoped it
wouldn't take long.

He wanted to return to her.

The door to his uncle's study was unlocked, thank
God, and he ducked inside as quietly as he could. It wasn't
a very big room. A single bookshelf appeared to hold led-
gers, with a table and chair in front of it, while a desk and
chair stood at one end near a fireplace.

Apollo crossed to the desk and set the candle he'd

brought on a corner. The top of the desk held only a jar of quills and an inkpot on a blotter. He went around the desk and sat in the chair to try the middle of the three drawers that ran across the front of the desk. It was unlocked and he drew it easily open to find a thin pile of papers, a pencil, and a penknife. Nothing else.

Frowning, he tried the left-hand drawer and found it entirely empty. Obviously his uncle wasn't much of a man of business—which might be the reason he was so deeply in debt. The right-hand drawer, unlike the other two, was locked.

Apollo had his head bent, examining the lock as well as he could in the dim light, when a voice interrupted.

"What are you doing at my desk, sirrah?"

Apollo nearly hit his head on the desk. He looked up and found his uncle frowning at him. He opened his mouth to lie...and found he was simply too tired to do so.

He sat back in his uncle's chair, making it squeak with his weight. "I'm looking for evidence that you murdered three men in order to steal my inheritance and title."

The older man's mouth dropped open. "You...what?"

Apollo sighed. "I'm your nephew, Apollo Greaves, Viscount Kilbourne." He bowed mockingly. "At your service, naturally."

"Kilbourne..." William Greaves backed up, nearly dropping his candle. "You're mad."

"No," Apollo said patiently, if a little grimly, "I'm really not, and you of all people should know it."

"Why're you here?" William asked, apparently not following the conversation at all.

Apollo started to rise, but the other man gave a little

shriek and held out both hands. "Stay where you are! Don't come near!"

"Uncle," Apollo said quietly.

"No!" The other man dashed from the room, moving quite swiftly considering his age.

Apollo's brows rose.

"Help! Help! Murder!" screamed his uncle, his voice diminishing as he ran away.

Well, that settled that.

Apollo picked up the candle and strode out of the room. He met a single footman as he made his way to Lily's room, but he simply nodded and kept walking. Below, he could hear the household rousing as his uncle called the alarm.

Miraculously, she was still sleeping when he entered her bedroom.

He sighed, taking one last look at her peacefully slumbering form, and then reached down and shook her shoulder hard. "Lily."

"What?" she asked sleepily. She sat up as she heard the commotion. "Apollo!"

"Shh." He sat on the side of the bed. "I love you."

Her eyes went wide. "I . . ."

"There isn't time," he said calmly. "My uncle has discovered me and will come with all his footmen to detain me soon. I have to flee."

She blinked and took a deep breath. "Of course."

"Meet me tomorrow night," he said, looking into her eyes to make sure she didn't mistake him. "In the garden by the pond where you saw me bathing. Do you remember?"

"I . . . yes." Even now he was charmed by the blush that pinkened her cheeks.

"About six of the clock, I think. If there's any trouble, send word to Makepeace," he said, rising. There were footsteps approaching. He turned and kissed her fast and hard. "I love you. Never forget that."

Then he rushed the door.

There were two footmen plus the middle-aged butler. Apollo shoved the butler out of his way, and would've done the same to the footmen had not one swung at him. Apollo knocked aside the man's blow and drove the point of his elbow into the man's belly, doubling him over. The remaining footman backed up a step, obviously torn between duty and the desire to keep his ribs intact. Apollo feinted with his right and when the man flinched back, gave him an additional push to make him fall. Then he was running down the hall past half-dressed ladies and gentlemen who didn't do very much to stop him.

Wheeling around the corner, he half slid down the main staircase, past a startled Mr. Warner, obviously returning from a room *not* his own—most interesting— and then he was out the front doors and running.

Running into the black night.

He could hear the shouts behind him, and then hoof-beats gaining on him fast. He whirled at the last minute, hands up, ready to dodge the horse.

Only to find the Duke of Montgomery pulling a great black beast to a half-rearing halt.

"Well, what are you waiting for?" the duke snapped, for once discomposed. He thrust out a hand. "Get on!"

HE'D SAID THAT he loved her.

Lily stared at the doorway, not sure she should believe what had just happened.

He loved her.

What did that mean to him? Was he going to offer to keep her? Or was it something he said to every woman he bedded?

But no. As soon as the thought crossed her mind, she disregarded it. Apollo was a good man. If he said he loved her—loved *her*—then he did.

She sat in the bed, entirely nude, the coverlet pulled over her breasts, and felt a strange, tenuous feeling: happiness. Ridiculous. She didn't even know if he'd escaped—and she had more than enough proof from Richard and Kitty's marriage that aristocracy and actresses couldn't mix. But...

He would escape. He was strong and determined and he was Apollo. He'd battled past the footmen and butler and the other gentlemen guests were certainly no match for him. He'd escape and she'd meet him in the garden tomorrow, and...

And what?

Perhaps they could find a way. He wasn't the usual aristocrat, after all, and... and she loved him.

She shivered, thinking about it, such a risk, not only for herself, but also for Indio and Maude. Could she risk their happiness as well?

"He has good taste at least."

She started at the strange voice and saw George Greaves stroll into the room as if he were entering an afternoon tea party.

She stiffened. "I beg your pardon?"

"As well you should, you little whore," he said without any heat at all. He closed the door behind him.

Lily fisted her hands, prepared to jump out of the bed and run—nude, if she had to. "Get out of my room."

"*My* room, actually—or my father's, which amounts to the same thing," George said, taking a chair and placing it so he faced the bed. "You, Miss Goodfellow, have abused my father's hospitality."

"In what way?"

He crossed his legs and she noticed that he was completely dressed in breeches, waistcoat, coat, and immaculately tied neckcloth. What had he been doing as his guests slept? "You've been conspiring with my cousin, it seems, against my family."

"Not conspiring," she said, hoping against hope that this might be explained away. "He didn't murder those men. He just wants to prove it."

"Do you really expect me to believe that?" he asked with clear contempt. "As I said, *conspiring* with my cousin, *Lord* Kilbourne, perhaps to kill us all in our beds."

"*What?*" She stared at the man. Did George Greaves truly believe that Apollo had come here to murder everyone in their beds? He must realize how ridiculous that sounded.

"He's a madman—everyone knows it and I'm tired of him dragging down the family name." He looked at her with a reddened face, his eyes bulging.

Oh, dear. Perhaps George was the real madman in the family. Lily put on her most fluffy-headed female face. "I'm afraid I don't understand all these matters and it's not quite nice for you to be in here when I haven't even my chemise on. If you'll just go—"

"My *father* should've been the viscount, not my mad uncle or his bloodthirsty son," George said, and Lily wondered if he'd even heard her. "Ridiculous that the family line has sunk into the mire of insanity and mental disease. I'm going to put a stop to this outrage once and for all."

Lily blinked and then shook her head, taking a deep breath. Fluffy-headedness hadn't worked. Perhaps bluntness would. "Why are you telling me this?"

"Because," George said precisely, "your connection to my cousin has provided me with an opportunity to end all this. You're going to help me right the wrong. Kilbourne has escaped into the night, I have no idea where, but I'm sure *you* do."

"I don't," she said immediately. "I'm sorry, but I don't. He's probably decided to flee England."

His smile wasn't amused at all. "No, I doubt that very much. And it would be a very great pity if you don't know where he's headed, because if you don't then I have no further use for you—or your supposed son."

"What . . ." She swallowed, her throat thickening. "What do you mean?"

"I believe you call him Indio? A boy of about seven with one blue eye and one green."

"How do you know about Indio?" she breathed, bewildered.

For a moment George's eyes flickered to the side before he glared at her. "Eyes just like my good friend Lord Ross."

She simply stared at him. She ought to get up, dress, and leave the room. Walk out of here and forget everything he'd insinuated. But there was Indio.

Indio.

"Have you met his wife?" he asked softly. "Daughter of a rather wealthy marquis. Ross was ecstatic to've caught such a wife. Mind, a large portion of her dowry is tied to her eldest son's inheriting his name. He won't be very pleased to find that his perfect little lordling has been displaced by a child got on an *actress*. God only knows what Ross would do if he found that his eldest son still lives. Really, I wouldn't give tuppence for the boy's life."

She sat in silence, her world crashing down around her ears, because there wasn't any choice, any hope for her and Apollo. Probably there never had been any hope. It'd been the dream of a silly girl, easily burned away with the rising of the sun.

He'd said he loved her. Something in her clenched, sharp and painful, as if she'd been cut deep inside and the blood were slowly leaking out where no one could see.

But that didn't matter anymore.

She was a mother and Indio was her son.

She lifted her chin and looked George Greaves dead in the eye, and she was oddly proud that there was no tremor in her voice when she said, "What do you want me to do?"

Chapter Nineteen

Ariadne stayed by the monster's side for days as he recovered from his injuries, and despite his fearsome aspect she found him gentle and kind. Around them the garden was lovely, but terribly silent. One day Theseus burst from the maze, dirtied and smeared with dried blood. "Get thee away from the beast!" he cried to Ariadne, brandishing his sword. "For I shall not be routed this time. I shall not rest until I have severed this terrible monster's head from its body."…
—From *The Minotaur*

It was near six of the clock the next evening when Lily cautiously approached the pond in Harte's Folly. The sky was just beginning to take on a mauve cast as the sun floated low in the sky, and the birds had started their evening chorus. It was almost lovely, and for the first time she saw how the garden would look one day. Most of the dead trees and hedges had been cleared and in the few days she'd been away the remaining plants had burst into the light green of spring.

Of life.

Except she wasn't walking to life. She marched to death with a gun at her back.

Behind her, George Greaves's tread was heavy and ominous. He was probably stamping on the new grass she took care to avoid.

In the last day and a half he'd not left her side except when she'd had to relieve herself, and even then he'd stood close outside the shut door. If she'd disliked him before— and she had—she'd grown to loathe him in the last thirty-six hours. He was a truly disgusting man without, as far as she could see, any redeeming quality. He'd even refused to pay the wherryman a fair price when they'd made the garden docks.

A nasty, petty, small-minded man, but sadly a dangerous one as well.

She was going to betray her love to this man.

"Make no sound, now," he murmured in a voice she'd come to despise. "We'll wait for your lover and then you'll be free to go."

She doubted that, but she didn't have much choice, either, so she kept walking until she saw the glint of blue water.

Lily stopped. "Here. This is where I agreed to meet him."

"Truly?" George glanced around, his lips twisted in a sneer. "Well, I suppose mud must seem romantic to the insane—and their common lovers."

She rolled her eyes, not bothering anymore to protest Apollo's innocence. She'd begun to suspect that George knew full well that Apollo hadn't killed his friends.

"Just stand where you are," he instructed, backing behind some obscuring bushes. "And don't turn to look at me. You give any hint that I'm here and I'll shoot first him and then you, do you understand?"

She folded her arms. "Quite."

There was a small silence in which she thought she heard the call of seagulls by the Thames.

"Where is your son?" he asked with horrible casualness. "You left him with a nursemaid, didn't you?"

She didn't bother replying. All this would be for naught if she simply gave away Indio's location.

He chuckled softly at her silence. "We'll discuss it later, you and I, never fear."

Something seemed to move behind them and she turned her head to look.

All was quiet.

"A dog or some such," George said, which was ridiculous. She would've known had a stray dog been living in the garden.

Then came the sure tread of a man who knew his way about the garden.

Lily straightened.

He was nearing.

Damn it, he was *early*.

George cocked his gun.

She swallowed, though she didn't look at him. "I thought you meant to arrest him."

"He's a dangerous murderer," he whispered back. "Better to be safe than sorry. Don't worry. I'm a good shot. You won't be hurt."

Not externally, anyway, she thought, and took a step backward, toward him.

"What are you doing?" he hissed. "Stay where you are."

She took another step closer to George, just as Apollo came into sight. He wore a plain brown suit and black tricorn and he looked like a man of middling means, perhaps a doctor or the owner of a shop or a head gardener. Someone from her own station in life.

Someone she could love and live with until she and he grew old.

He looked up and smiled at her in that moment and she whirled and caught George's pistol, pulling it down, away from her lover, her love, her life.

Pulling it toward her own breast.

The shot, when it came, was deafening.

APOLLO SAW LILY turn and wrestle with George Greaves.

Saw the spark and the plume of black smoke.

Saw her stagger back and fall, dead.

Dead.

Strangely, he didn't hear a thing.

George turned and saw him and raised the pistol, but he'd already used the one shot to kill Lily, his beloved Lily, so Apollo batted it aside. The pistol went spinning into the underbrush as Apollo raised his hand and plowed it into George's face.

He didn't hear that, either. Or feel it.

Just as well.

George went down and Apollo followed, beating into that face, because it was the last thing Lily had seen—the face of her killer—and he meant to destroy it.

Blood spattered and George opened his mouth, his teeth scarlet-stained. He might've been saying something, might've been begging, but since Apollo couldn't hear, it didn't matter.

Something crunched beneath his knuckles, and Apollo realized he was grinning, his lips pulled back from his bared teeth, turned into the monster Lily had first thought him.

It didn't matter.

Nothing mattered anymore.

George spat blood and a bit of broken white that might've been a tooth and Apollo split his ear.

But the eyes were still there—the eyes that had looked on Lily's death—and he aimed his fist toward them.

"Apollo." The voice was Lily's, but that couldn't be, because... because...

Her hands, white and soft, wrapped about his bloodied knuckles and gently stopped him.

Sound suddenly rushed back in.

George was breathing with a harsh rasp, Apollo was making a noise like a sob, and Lily...

Dear God, Lily was saying his name.

He looked up and saw her face, blackened on one side with flecks of blood high on one cheek.

He let the front of George's shirt go and his head thudded against the ground.

Apollo turned on his knees and cupped her sweet face with his unclean hands. "How?" he choked. "I saw you die. I saw you fall dead to the ground."

"The pistol fired over my shoulder," she whispered. "Apollo, what have you done to your poor hands?"

"God!" he cried, pulling her face down to his, kissing her nose and cheeks and eyelids, making sure she still lived and breathed. "Dear God, Lily, never do that to me again."

"I won't, love." Tears were making muddy streaks through the gunpowder on her cheek. "Ow, that stings."

Richard Perry, Baron Ross stepped out from the bushes. "Get away from her."

"Sod off," Apollo retorted, possibly because he was too tired to be surprised.

"Get away from her or I'll shoot her." Ross, of course, had not one but two pistols.

Reluctantly Apollo stood and took a step away from Lily. "We really must talk, darling, about the sort of riff-raff you bring to secret meetings."

"I didn't know he was there," Lily said grumpily.

"Did you really think my good friend George wouldn't tell me about my son?" Ross said. "Jesus, he said this would be easy—capture you, Kilbourne, and get my son. Look at this mess now. Have you killed George?"

"Sadly, no," Apollo replied without glancing at the man on the ground. He could hear his cousin's harsh breathing. "Put the damned gun down." He was becoming tired of people pointing guns at his Lily.

Ross ignored him, his gaze worryingly focused on Lily. "Where is he? Where is Indio?"

And before Apollo could think of what to do, Lily opened her mouth.

Chapter Twenty

*Then the monster rose, his massive shoulders
bunched, his hands fisted, his bull's head lowered, the
two curved horns pointed menacingly at Theseus.
The lad didn't hesitate. With a warlike cry he ran at
the monster, his sword raised. The monster did not
move until the last moment, and then with a brutally
swift toss of his head he impaled the youth upon
his horns...*
—From *The Minotaur*

"Are you insane?" Lily asked Ross pleasantly. "Do you really think I'd tell you where he is after you beat his mother, my dearest friend, to death?"

"Tell me or I'll shoot you," he replied, not very originally, but it still put a thrill of fear into Apollo's heart.

"Lily," Apollo said gently.

Lily crossed her arms. "Go ahead, then. I'll not give my son up to a rat like you."

"Don't you mean *my* son?" he snapped back, stupid and irate.

Apollo lost what little patience he still had. "Damn it, Montgomery, aren't you *ever* going to act?"

"Oh, fine," the duke replied sulkily from behind him and shot Richard in the leg.

Richard fell to the ground, moaning.

Lily blinked. "What—?"

The duke glanced at his pistol and frowned. "Pulls a bit to the right. I was aiming for his groin." He toed Ross's pistols away from the writhing man and turned to Apollo. "I'll have you know this entire business has been a loss to me—a dead loss."

Lily blinked again and looked uncertainly at Apollo. "How—?"

Apollo pulled her into his arms. He was still quite shaken from having nearly lost her, and the warmth of her body was a balm. "Shh. There's no point in trying to get him to make sense. Best to just let him ramble. I learned that on the carriage ride to London."

"He was such a lovely pigeon," Montgomery said mournfully, watching Richard writhe on the ground. "A secret marriage, a hidden heir. I could've milked him for years."

"You were going to blackmail him for money?" Lily asked.

"Money?" The duke looked affronted. "Nothing so crass. Information, knowledge, leverage. That's the sort of stuff I adore. But"—Montgomery sighed gustily, folding his arms with his pistol dangling from one hand—"my sentimental heart got the better of me. That, and I really do want this garden finished. Kilbourne is the most imaginative gardener I've ever encountered."

Lily's eyes widened and she turned to Apollo as if only just now realizing something. "You brought him with you to meet me?"

He shrugged. "It seemed like a good precaution. After all, I intended to flee with you from England and I wasn't sure if you'd be followed here."

"But I thought you didn't trust him," she complained.

"I don't, mostly." He grimaced. "But he did help me get away from my uncle's house."

"And I shot Ross just now, too," the duke said brightly. "Shall I shoot Greaves as well? No doubt he deserves it and I've another pistol in my pocket."

At which point Edwin Stump burst from the shrubbery, followed closely by the Duke of Wakefield and Captain Trevillion. All three were holding pistols and breathing rather hard.

Apollo blinked.

"Are we late?" Edwin asked, panting.

"Yes," Lily replied from Apollo's arms. She sounded rather querulous.

"Good Lord, His Grace the Ass hiding in the bushes," Apollo muttered. "Whatever are you doing here?"

"Ah, Kilbourne, you've regained your voice," Wakefield drawled. "Pity, but I presume my wife is thrilled. And you are?" He looked pointedly at Montgomery.

Montgomery bowed mockingly, still holding his pistol. "Montgomery. And you're Wakefield, yes?"

One of Wakefield's eyebrows rose. "Quite." He turned to Apollo. "I was told that we were here to save you. I see that I've been sadly misinformed."

"You *would've* saved him had my brother been *on time*," Lily said, glaring at Edwin.

"I've been shot," Ross moaned from the ground.

George merely groaned.

Wakefield turned very slowly to Ross and said gently,

"Lord Ross, I believe? Your son from your first marriage is playing with my wife at the moment. She seems to have grown quite fond of him in a very short time. Felicitations on finding him alive and well. It's not every day that one discovers one's heir."

Ross's lip curled and Apollo wished that Montgomery's aim had been better. "Then I'll take him. He's *my* son, after all."

"I think not," Wakefield murmured. "I've heard a rather distressing tale from two upstanding citizens regarding his mother's death. If you would rather I not investigate the matter further—and I really think you *would*—I suggest you never attempt to see your heir again."

For a moment it looked as if Ross would cry, and Apollo really couldn't find it in himself to care.

"Thank God," Edwin Stump said, and sat abruptly on a charred log. "That's over, then. I don't mind telling you, Lily, that I near had an apoplexy when I got that message from you."

Apollo frowned. "What message?"

"The message I had to slip to one of the footmen as I left Greaves House with George. I just hoped that Edwin would know what to do." Lily looked at him in wonder. "And he did—even if he was a bit late."

Edwin Stump actually looked bashful.

"I don't understand." Apollo frowned. "George caught you at the house party after I left?"

She nodded. "And kept a pistol on me practically all the way to London."

He felt his heart stop. Fool. He should've realized he would put her in a position of danger when he fled. "I'm sorry, love. I should've never left you there."

She shook her head. "You weren't to know he would do that—and had you stayed you'd be in Bedlam right now. You had to run, Apollo."

He grimaced, still not ready to absolve himself of blame. Things could've turned out far, far worse. "So you slipped your brother a message to go to Trevillion?"

"And to go to your sister," Lily said. "After all, she's a duchess. I thought that might help."

Trevillion cleared his throat. "I decided His Grace might, in this case, be more useful."

"Then why in God's name did you grab for George's pistol when you knew help was coming?" Apollo asked.

"They weren't here yet and he was going to shoot you," she said, placing her palms on his chest. "I couldn't let him."

His throat closed and he couldn't reply. All he could do was pull her into his arms and hold her close.

Someone cleared their voice.

He didn't care in the slightest.

Edwin toed George Greaves, who was still moaning very quietly. "What are we going to do with him?" He glanced at Ross and winced. "*Them?*"

Wakefield drew himself up. "As it's quite clear that Montgomery shot Ross to save Miss Goodfellow's life, I shall make a full report to the courts and deal with the matter myself. Sadly, as he's titled, he'll probably serve no time in prison. *However*, the scandal of trying to murder one of London's most famous actresses might make a sojourn abroad seem quite a nice prospect. As for Greaves..."

"He murdered those men," Lily said from Apollo's arms. "I'm quite sure of it. I just have no way of proving it."

"No, I didn't!" George gasped rather unconvincingly from the ground.

"As to that." Trevillion cleared his throat. "I took the liberty of having the valet, Vance, detained after you left the house party. Montgomery told me that you recognized him, Lord Kilbourne. It seems Vance was in George Greaves's service before he went to William Greaves's employ. When I informed Vance that he'd been seen on the night of the murders at the tavern he became quite talkative."

"What?" George screamed.

"You really ought to employ more intelligent assassins, Mr. Greaves." Trevillion smiled coldly. "He seemed to think I had all the evidence needed to hang him and confessed embarrassingly fast. And since you apparently never paid him well, he's quite vindictive. He told me in front of witnesses that you hired him to kill Lord Kilbourne's friends in an attempt to paint Kilbourne a murderer."

"It's not true," George whispered.

"I'm afraid your father heard the confession and was stricken with the shock," Trevillion said softly.

"My uncle never knew?" Apollo asked.

Trevillion shook his head. "I think not. When I left Greaves House he'd taken to his bed and a doctor had been sent for. They're not sure he'll recover."

George swore foully, red-tinged spittle flecking his lips. He glared at Apollo. "You should never have been the heir—your line is tainted. Had Brightmore not intervened you would've hanged for sure instead of being sent to Bedlam. Everyone knows you're insane—everyone! I should've killed you myself instead of sending Vance."

"Now we have your confession," Trevillion murmured gently. "And in the presence of two dukes."

Trevillion bent to haul George to his feet, which put an end to his cursing. The captain looked quietly satisfied.

Wakefield nodded grimly. "Excellent." He turned to Apollo. "I think we'll be able to clear your name within days. Artemis will be very pleased—and I won't have to worry anymore about her sneaking off with baskets of provisions for you."

"So glad to put your mind at rest," Apollo said drily. He looked at Lily. "Shall we go see how Indio and Daff are faring with my sister's dogs?"

She nodded, and he took her hand, leading her from his garden.

IT WAS VERY late—well past midnight—before Lily retired to bed. There had been the reunion with Indio, made even more chaotic by the duke's four dogs—two greyhounds, a silly spaniel, and an elderly white lapdog—all of whom Daffodil seemed to regard as very large play toys. There had been the rather nerve-racking introduction to Apollo's sister, who, no matter how nice she seemed, was after all a *duchess*. There had been a positively decadent bath followed by a very good late-night supper of roast duck and baby carrots.

So it was understandable that Lily didn't at first notice the very large man in her bed when she entered the room assigned to her.

When she did, she stopped dead and hissed, "You can't be in here!"

The covers were pulled to his waist, but he appeared to be quite naked underneath.

"Why not?" Apollo asked, apparently having forgotten all the social niceties that *someone* must've taught him as a small child.

"Because this is your sister's house."

He cocked his head. "Actually it's His Grace the Ass's house, but I do see your meaning. You know she's a floor above us?"

"Why do you even call him that?" she asked as she began removing her bodice. "He seems a perfectly nice man, if a bit stiff, and as I understand it, he actually rescued you from Bedlam."

Apollo frowned ferociously. "He seduced my sister before they were married."

She looked at him, eyebrow raised.

"*And* he's an ass. But mostly it's my sister."

"So if Edwin chose to call you out over your very thorough debauchment of me...?"

"He'd be well within his rights," he assured her. "In fact, he really ought to."

She couldn't tell if he was joking or not, and honestly she rather thought he *wasn't*.

"Gentlemen have very odd minds," she commented as she slipped out of her skirt.

"We do," he replied lazily. "For instance, I'd rather like you to become my wife."

She was silent, frowning as she unlaced her stays.

After a moment he cleared his throat. "This is where many a gentleman might think that it's ladies who have odd minds."

"Richard—"

"Please don't do me the insult of comparing me to that worm," he said, quietly and seriously.

"I'm sorry," she said at once, because she was. Apollo was nothing like Richard and she more than anyone else knew that. "But you must understand: even without his violence, I don't think their marriage would've been a happy one."

He rolled to his side and propped himself up on his arm. "You're still comparing," he said gently. "I don't give a damn about bloodlines. I think today's events more than prove that only madmen do, really."

She swallowed, pulling off her stays gingerly. "Your family won't like an actress for your wife."

"My family consists of Artemis and, I suppose by default, His Grace the Ass. Did you find either of them unwelcoming?"

"No, but—"

"And they won't be." He rose, gloriously nude, and walked to her, taking her hands. "Lily, my light, my love. What are you afraid of?"

"I . . ." she began and then couldn't answer because she didn't know what it was she feared. She looked up at him helplessly.

He smiled his gentle smile and brought her hand to his lips, tenderly kissing each fingertip. "I love you and you love me. I might've been in a little doubt before this afternoon, but when you flung yourself in front of a pistol, it did rather clarify things. And, since you love me and I love you, it is right and meet and wonderful that you and I become man and wife and spend the rest of our lives sleeping together and rising together and having masses of children together and living joyfully."

"Masses?" she muttered a bit doubtfully, but fortunately he ignored her.

Apollo sank onto one knee there before her, with her only in her chemise and him in...nothing at all.

"Lily Stump," he said, his voice rasping a little as it always would, "will you take me as husband and be my wife? Will you be my sun and light all the days of my life and never make me regret bathing in a muddy pond?"

And she laughed as she drew him up to kiss.

"Yes," she said against his lips. "Yes."

Epilogue

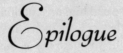

A cry broke from Ariadne's lips at the gruesome
sight. The monster shook his head and Theseus's body
fell to the ground, bloodied. She ran to kneel by the
man, but saw at once that the wound was too deep and
too terrible. Theseus looked up at her, his eyes wide in
surprise, and gasped with his last breath, "I am the hero.
It is the monster who should die, not me."
And then his spirit left his body.
Ariadne bowed her head and said a prayer. When she
raised it she saw the monster wading in the pool, washing
the gore from his chest and head. She stood, but he did not
look at her. In fact, he turned his back.
"Monster!" she called, but the moment the word left
her lips, she knew it was wrong. "I'm sorry," she
said, softer. "You aren't a monster, no matter what
others say."
At that he raised his bull head and finally turned to
look at her.
There were tears in his beautiful brown eyes.
"I do not know your name," she said. "Perhaps
you've never had one—not a proper one, at least. So
I'll call you Asterion—ruler of the stars—if that meets
with your approval?"
Gravely, Asterion bowed his head.
Ariadne held out her hand. "Will you come with me out of
the labyrinth? It is beautiful here in your garden, but no
birds sing and I think it rather lonely."

So Asterion took Ariadne's hand and she, following the red thread from the spindle the queen had given her, retraced her steps out of the labyrinth. Of course it took many days, for even with the thread to follow, the labyrinth's corridors were long and winding. But Ariadne passed the time telling Asterion about the island outside the labyrinth, and the people who lived there.

When at last they reached the entrance of the labyrinth and Ariadne heard birds singing in the trees, she turned to Asterion with a joyful smile upon her face.

But what a surprise met her when she gazed upon her companion! For while Asterion still retained his coal-black hue, his massive shoulders, the horns of a bull, and the tail as well, his visage had changed to that of a man.

And with a man's lips and tongue came the power of speech. Asterion fell to his knees before Ariadne. "Gentle maiden, I owe you my life," he said, his voice hoarse and halting. "For years others have entered into my labyrinth bent on killing me. Only you saw me as a thinking being. A man with a soul. In this way you have broken my curse."

"And I am glad of it," she said.

Ariadne and Asterion went to the golden castle. But how it had changed since she'd last seen it! The great halls were empty, the courtiers and soldiers disappeared. Together Ariadne and Asterion wandered for many hours before they at last found the mad queen.

What tears the queen wept when she saw her son! For the first time in years she put down her spinning, and she opened wide her arms to receive him. As for the king? Why, he was quite dead. One morning he'd grown irritated at the singing of sparrows on his balcony, and when in a fit of ire he'd chased them, the balcony wall had given way, and the king had fallen to his death.

*But the island was in chaos with no one to rule. The people
crowded the streets, confused and fearful. So Asterion went
to the king's balcony and raised his hands.*

*"My people," he shouted, and immediately all turned their
heads to stare in wonder. "My people, I was born a beast,
but by the kindness of Ariadne, I have become a man. I
know violence, but I prefer peace. If you will accept me as
your leader, I will try to rule more justly than my father
and I will keep Ariadne by my side as my wife so that I
never forget the importance of kindness."*

*And as the people cheered, Asterion turned to Ariadne
and smiled with his new-formed human lips. "Will you, my
sweet maid? Will you be my wife and queen and tutor me in
gentleness? Will you be my love forevermore?"*

*Ariadne placed her palms on his dark cheeks and smiled
up at him. "I think you have no need of my tutoring, my
lord, but if you will have me as wife, I will gladly wed you
and be your love forevermore."*

And so she did.

—From *The Minotaur*

THREE MONTHS LATER...

Apollo stood with his adopted son and looked with pride
at the newly planted oak. The tree stood beside the pond,
gently waving dark-green leaves reflected in the clear
water's surface. A sublime sight indeed.

Indio had slightly more down-to-earth thoughts about
the new planting. "Can I climb it?"

"No," Apollo said firmly, for he'd found that simple,
blunt statements were least likely to be wriggled out of by
a crafty seven-year-old boy. "And Daff can't, either."

The little dog barked and spun in a circle at her name, nearly landing in the pond.

"Awww!" Indio moaned in disappointment and then almost immediately perked up at another thought. "Can I start our picnic now?

"Yes."

"And eat the leftover wedding cake first?"

"If you can get Maude's permission," Apollo replied, because he was certainly no fool.

"Huzzah!" Indio whooped. "Come on, Daff!"

And he and the dog raced off in the direction of the ruined theater. Apollo followed more slowly, inspecting the progress of his garden as he went. He and his gardeners had successfully planted more than a score of trees as well as flowering shrubs. Many of the trees and shrubs would take years to mature, so to fill in he'd planted faster-growing vegetation such as evergreens, both to provide background and to give shelter to the tender hardwoods. Along the paths he'd also planted annual flowers, which made bright pools of color.

"There you are."

He turned at the sound of his wife's voice. Lily was wearing scarlet, his favorite color on her, and she stood out like a bright poppy in his garden.

He smiled into her green eyes and held out his hand. "I'm afraid Indio has rushed off to ravage the rest of the wedding cake."

"Well, someone has to eat it," she replied, taking his hand. "Maude baked far too much. There's plenty more at home."

They'd married only three days ago, in a small private ceremony marked mostly by the abundance of Maude's seed cake. They'd been eating it ever since, often on the picnics Lily, Indio, and Maude brought for his luncheon at the garden.

"And how have you spent your morning?" he teased Lily, for he knew very well what she'd been doing.

Artemis had given them a small town house not far from the garden. She had insisted it was a wedding present, but Apollo expected to repay her the cost of the house when he came into his inheritance. From the reports, it wouldn't be too long.

"Have you any idea how hard it is to paint a room?" Lily asked. "I thought peach for my writing room, but then it turned the most ghastly shade of orange on the wall. The painters are going over it now in yellow, although with my luck it'll turn some terrible shade of brown."

"Mmm," he murmured, listening more to the sound of her voice than to her words.

"Next I'm considering painting your study lavender," she continued, "perhaps with pink stripes."

He looked at her. "I *am* paying attention."

"Good." She took a deep breath, suddenly serious. "I've something for you."

He stopped, turning to face her. "What is it?"

She fumbled in the pocket of her dress. "I found it this morning while I was unpacking the chest I had at the theater, and I thought..."

She held out his notebook.

He took it wonderingly as she continued to talk, her words coming more and more rapidly.

"I found it after the soldiers came and I kept it. I don't know why because at that point I wasn't sure I'd ever see you again. But then when I uncovered it this morning, I knew...that is..."

She reached out and flipped the pages of the notebook until the last page lay open in his hands. She'd written something there. He bent and read.

I love you, Beast.
I love you, Caliban.
I love you, Apollo.
I love you, Romeo.
I love you, Smith.
I love you, Gardener.
I love you, Aristocrat.
I love you, Lover.
I love you, Husband.
I love you, Friend.
I love you, You.

He inhaled and looked up.

She was twisting her hands together. "For a writer, I'm awfully ineloquent. I don't know—"

He dropped the notebook and pulled her into his arms, kissing her passionately. He held her sweet face between his palms and caressed her temples with his thumbs as he opened his mouth over hers, inhaling her gasp.

When at last he drew back, he whispered against her lips, "Do you know where we are?"

"Yes," she murmured, her eyes closed. "At the heart of the maze." And when she opened her lichen-green eyes he saw all the love he'd ever hoped for shining in her eyes just for him. "At your heart—and mine."

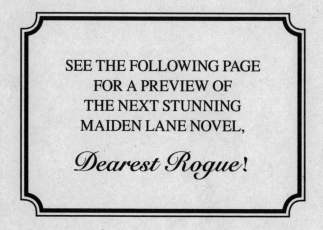

SEE THE FOLLOWING PAGE
FOR A PREVIEW OF
THE NEXT STUNNING
MAIDEN LANE NOVEL,

Dearest Rogue!

Chapter One

JULY 1741
LONDON, ENGLAND

Captain James Trevillion, formerly of the 4th Dragoons, had been in many dangerous places, but until now he wouldn't've thought Bond Street in the middle of a sunny Wednesday afternoon was one of them.

"Do you have the package from Furtleby's?" inquired his charge, Lady Phoebe Batten.

The sister of the Duke of Wakefield, Lady Phoebe was plump, pretty, and quite pleasant to nearly everyone excepting himself. She was also blind, which was both why she had her hand on Trevillion's left forearm and why Trevillion was here at all: he was her bodyguard.

"No," he answered absently as he watched one—no, three—big brutes coming toward them, moving against the brightly dressed, fashionable crowd. They looked ominously out of place. He leaned heavily on the cane in his right hand and pivoted to look behind them. Lovely. A fourth man.

"Because the lace was especially fine," she said, "and

also at a special price which I'm quite sure I won't be able to find again for quite some time."

"Was it?"

The nearest brute had a nasty scar on his cheek and was holding something down by his side—a knife? A pistol? Trevillion transferred the cane to his left hand and gripped his own pistol, one of two holstered in black leather belts crisscrossed over his chest. His right leg protested the sudden loss of support.

Two shots, four men. The odds were not particularly good.

"Yes," Lady Phoebe replied. "And Furtleby made sure to tell me that the lace was made by grasshoppers weaving butterfly wings on the Isle of Man. Very exclusive."

"I *am* listening to you," Trevillion said as the first brute shoved aside an elderly dandy wearing a full-bottomed white wig.

"Are you?" she asked sweetly, "because—"

The brute's hand came up with a pistol and Trevillion shot him in the chest.

Lady Phoebe gripped his arm tighter. "What—?"

The other three men started running. *Toward* them.

"Don't let go of me," Trevillion barked, glancing quickly around. He couldn't fight three men with only one shot remaining. "*Left.* Now."

He shoved her in that direction, his right leg giving him hell. The bloody thing better not collapse on him—not now. He holstered the first pistol and drew the second.

"Did you just shoot someone?" Lady Phoebe panted as a screaming matron brushed roughly against her. The panicked crowd was surging around them, making their progress harder.

"Yes."

There. A couple of paces away a small boy was holding the reins of a bay gelding in the street. The horse's eyes showed white, its nostrils flared, but it hadn't bolted at the shot, which was a good sign.

"Why?"

"It seemed a good idea," Trevillion said grimly. He looked behind them. Two of their attackers had been detained behind a gaggle of screeching society ladies. The other, though, was determinedly elbowing through the crowd in their direction.

"Did you kill him?" Lady Phoebe asked with interest.

"Maybe." They made the horse and boy. "Up now."

"Up where?"

"Horse," Trevillion grunted, slapping her hand on the horse's saddle.

"Oi!" shouted the boy.

Lady Phoebe was a clever girl. She felt down to the stirrup and placed her foot in it. Trevillion put his hand frankly on her bottom and pushed her up hard onto the beast.

She gave a little squeak.

"Thanks," Trevillion muttered at the boy, now wide-eyed at the sight of the pistol.

He dropped his cane, grabbed the reins, and scrambled inelegantly into the saddle behind Lady Phoebe, still holding the pistol in one hand.

The third brute made the horse and grabbed for the bridle, his lips twisted in an ugly grimace.

Trevillion shot him full in the face.

The horse half-reared, but Trevillion sternly kneed it into a canter even as he holstered the spent pistol.

He might be a cripple on land, but by God, in the saddle he was a demon.

"Did you kill *that* one?" Lady Phoebe shouted as they swerved around a cart.

"Yes."

"Oh, good." She threw back her head and laughed breathlessly as he grasped her around the waist.

He leaned forward, inhaling the scent of roses in her hair, and kicked the horse into a full gallop.

Right through the heart of London.

Fall in Love with Forever Romance

UNLEASHED
by Rachel Lacey

Cara has one rule: Don't get attached. It's served her well with the dogs she's fostered and the children she's nannied. But one smile from her sexy neighbor has her thinking some rules are made to be broken. Fans of Jill Shalvis will fall in love with this sassy, sexy debut!

MADE FOR YOU
by Lauren Layne

She's met her match... she just doesn't know it yet. Fans of Jennifer Probst and Rachel Van Dyken will fall head over heels for the second book in the Best Mistake series.

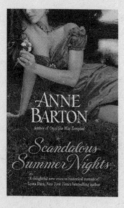
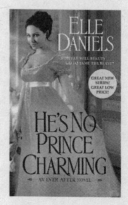

Fall in Love with Forever Romance

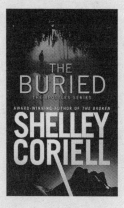

THE BURIED
by Shelley Coriell

"It's cold. And dark. I can't breathe."

Grace and "Hatch" thought they'd buried the past, but a killer on a grisly crime spree is about to unearth their deepest fears. Don't miss the next gripping thriller in the Apostles series.

SHOOTING SCARS
by Karina Halle

Ellie Watt has been kidnapped by her thuggish ex-boyfriend, leaving her current lover, Camden McQueen, to save the day. And there's nothing he won't do to rescue Ellie from this criminal and his entourage of killers in this fast-paced, sexy *USA Today* bestseller!

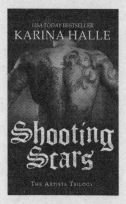

JON DESSEN, ILLINI STUDIO

The author of the *New York Times* bestselling Maiden Lane series and the Legend of Four Soldiers series as well as the Prince Trilogy, Elizabeth Hoyt writes "mesmerizing" (*Publishers Weekly*) historical romances. She also pens deliciously fun contemporary romances under the name Julia Harper. Elizabeth lives in central Illinois with three untrained dogs, two angelic but bickering children, and one long-suffering husband. Central Illinois can be less than exciting, and Elizabeth is always more than happy to receive missives from her readers. You can write to her at: PO Box 17134, Urbana, IL 61873.

You can learn more at:
ElizabethHoyt.com
Twitter @elizabethhoyt
Facebook.com/ElizabethHoytBooks

ISBN 978-1-4555-8630-1

A MAN CONDEMNED...

Falsely accused of murder and mute from a near-fatal beating, Apollo Greaves, Viscount Kilbourne, has escaped from Bedlam. With the Crown's soldiers at his heels, he finds refuge in the ruins of a pleasure garden, toiling as a simple gardener. But when a vivacious young woman moves in, he's quickly driven to distraction...

A DESPERATE WOMAN...

London's premier actress, Lily Stump, is down on her luck when she's forced to move into a scorched theater with her maid and small son. But she and her tiny family aren't the only inhabitants—a silent, hulking beast of a man also calls the charred ruins home. Yet when she catches him reading her plays, Lily realizes there's more to this man than meets the eye.

OUT OF ASH, DESIRE FLARES

Though scorching passion draws them together, Apollo knows that Lily is keeping secrets. When his past catches up with him, he's forced to make a choice: his love for Lily...or the explosive truth that will set him free.

$8.00 US / $9.00 CAN.

ISBN 978-1-4555-8630-1

EAN

5 0 8 0 0

9 781455 586301